# A.K.A. DANNY BOY

A NOVEL

JOHN MARRON

First Edition

PAGE PUBLISHING, INC.
Conneaut Lake, PA

First originally published by Page Publishing 2020

ISBN 978-1-64628-509-9 (pbk)
ISBN 978-1-64628-510-5 (digital)

Printed in the United States of America

*Boston, Massachusetts—Present Day*

"So, John. How was your vacation?" Neville inquired.

"Oh, nice and quiet. Paris is beautiful, found a great jazz club there." I continued to tell him some of the highlights. "Look, I know you're busy," I said, changing to the subject of my call. "The loan will be a personal one to her, on a couple of conditions. It will be secured by twenty percent of the company stock. The other condition is a right of first refusal on the sale or transfer of any stock. That is to say, if for any reason she should wish to dispose of any of her shares, even give them to family members, the option to purchase those shares could be exercised."

"This would only be for the period of the loan, correct?" Neville asked. "When she has paid the loan off, she would have no further obligation regarding the transfer of stock." I hadn't thought about that. "John, are you there?"

"Yes, I'm here. Let me ask you to hold a second—better still, I'll call you back." I hung up the phone and reconsidered my plan.

Several minutes passed as I sat in remorseful contemplation. She hardly made a sound as she entered the room silently and sat opposite.

We stared appreciatively at one another for a long time. She had recovered her composure, but she would always look different to me now.

I called Neville again.

"Sorry that took so long."

"Yes," he said, "I understand."

"Well, the answer is no. The note will read, 'The right of first refusal on the transfer of any shares,' or there is no deal. You can tell her, however, that on the transfer of stock to any children, there would be no problem. The same right would transfer to their stock. Should the children wish to dispose of the shares, the same option could be exercised. That only really guarantees that she or her children would get the best price for the shares."

"What about the terms of the loan?" Neville queried without comment. "We never did discuss interest and length."

"One quarter of a percent over whatever the rate of the savings certificates are paying at Shawmut Bank or First Bank of Boston. Use whichever you wish. Interest only payments to be made quarterly. The principal may be paid in full or in part whenever she wants. Frankly, I feel that is fair, don't you?" I didn't want any interest, but it would be outrageous to say that. It had to appear as though it was a business loan.

"Fair? I think it's marvelous. She couldn't have got that kind of deal anywhere. I have some land on the Cape that we could develop into a holiday camp for wayward girls."

"Good. Paul Lehman is the attorney. You will be hearing from him within the next day or so," I said, ignoring his levity.

"Great, well, the only thing she might squawk about might be the stock option. But I think I can persuade her that it is a form of protection for her.

I replaced the receiver and looked again at her.

"What are you going to do about…," she asked.

"I don't know."

"You're going to kill the bastard, aren't you?"

"Probably."

"How?"

"I don't know."

"You won't be able to just follow him home."

"I know."

"You'll have to find out about his movements. Plan the thing properly."

"I know all that."

"No, you don't, you horse ass. You made one screw up after another."

She had raised her voice not to a shout but to a level of intensity that hurt my ears. My mouth gaped in protest as she recounted the tragic comedy of errors; suddenly I felt scared. They say when your life is in jeopardy, two things happen: you crave for the safety of your mother's arms, and you acknowledge God. There are no atheists in foxholes.

"Introibo ad altare Dei," I whispered to myself. "I will go to the altar of God."

# *Chapter 1*

# Introibo Ad Altare Dei

Mam leaned over from the waist as she said the opening prayers to the start of the mass. I knelt there beside her, squinting up, making sure she was doing it the same way we had done it dozens of times before.

At seven years old, I had set my first goal—to be an altar boy. I glanced quickly up at the sideboard that served as our altar. The candles were set properly, and the book was on the right side. The crucifix in the center of the wall was a permanent fixture. Above it was the picture of the Sacred Heart.

| | |
|---|---|
| "*Introibo ad altare Dei.*" | I will go to the altar of God. |
| "*Ad Deum qui laitificat juventutem meam.*" | To God who gives the joy to my youth. |
| "*Adjutorium nostrum in nomine Domine.*" | Our help is in the name of the Lord. |
| "*Qui fecit caelum et terram.*" | Who made heaven and earth. |

The Latin quickly lost its meaning. From now I only knew the words by heart. We had spent hours repeating it over and over again. Now we were learning the movements of the server or altar boy.

I was kneeling on the cold, cracked, brittle linoleum floor. My knees were already becoming numb. Mam had explained it was only a little sacrifice of pain compared with what Jesus had gone through on the cross. To be an altar boy, I had to be tough enough to be able to kneel for hours on the marble altar floor at church.

We quickly got through the Confiteor and the Kyrie. Mam was moving to the right-hand side of the "altar" to read the Epistle. She had told me to watch carefully. When she came to the pause for the response, she would bow slightly toward the crucifix and touch her hand on the sideboard, I mean altar. That would be my signal to stand, move to the center, then genuflect and walk round to the side of the altar to be ready to transfer the book over to the left side for the gospel.

Just then one of the twins started to cry. I couldn't believe it; they hadn't been in bed two minutes. I had waited all day for these wonderful moments with Mam.

"I'm sorry, love. But I'll 'ave t' go an' see to 'em. Whichever it is, they'll waken t'other one."

She started up the steps, and I held back my tears of fury. My eyes followed her. I couldn't help thinking how splendid she looked in the red cape she was wearing for the priest's robes. I had spotted it at the jumble sale last Saturday and pointed it out to her. I don't think she really wanted to buy it. She only had a couple of shillings, and she had to get a couple of heavy coats to make a blanket for my bed.

But she bought it even though that posh Mrs. Blackburn had said that it cost six pounds new and was only eight months old. Mam had haggled her down from ten shillings to two shillings. She also got me this ladies' black slip for a cassock and a lovely white silk blouse for my surplice.

I was so proud when I became an altar boy. Granddad came to mass every day. He didn't work anymore. He was getting very old. Sometimes, if I was scheduled for the late mass, we would walk together through the park. I would have to leave him to run ahead to get ready before mass started.

Granddad rarely spoke he had a hard time breathing. He was a huge man, over six feet, and very heavy around the waist. He walked with a stick. Flossie, his dog, would trot at the side of us, dutifully obeying his motions. If I ran, sometimes she could follow and play. Other times she mustn't follow and stay with Granddad.

One day, without any warning, Granddad asked, "And when are y'goin t' join the choir?"

The choir wasn't as important as the servers on the altar. The servers actually assisted the priest. The choir only sang at the eleven o'clock mass on Sunday mornings and at Benediction Sunday evening. They sang at holy days and weddings sometimes, but they weren't as important as the servers.

"I'm not a very good singer, Granddad," I said, hoping he wouldn't pursue it.

"Aye, ye be right," he said. "Not now, you're not, but there's no doubt about it—you sure 'ave the makins. I'll be willing to bet that a fine Irish tenor is inside the young body of yours. Sure, it'll be a soprano now. But later, when you're all grown up, you'll have a fine voice, just like your Uncle Sean. Sure, you're the spittin' image of your uncle Sean, y'know."

Uncle Sean was Granddad's younger brother. I had only seen him once that I could remember, but he was a legend throughout Ireland. He'd moved from Galway to Belfast some years ago. He was the one, if anybody, who could bring about a united Ireland, they said. A singer, poet, and politician, he didn't believe in killing the Proddies. Granddad had said, "Sean Donavan could reason with the devil himself…and he might have to one of these days."

I wished that Uncle Sean, Auntie Kath, and my cousins, Sean, Bridget, and Aileen, lived near us. I had lots of other relatives here in, Galway but they were just the same as us. Uncle Sean's family were exciting. We always got Christmas cards and birthday cards from him. Sometimes they were from different cities, even from England. He always wrote a special poem for me in the cards he sent. He wasn't really my uncle; he was my great uncle. But with the dozens of aunts and uncles that I had, it got very confusing to qualify how far removed they were. So they were all referred to as aunts, uncles, and cousins.

"One of my dreams it to 'early' singing *Adeste Fidelis* at midnight mass. And singing 'Danny Boy' at the Saint Patrick's concert before I die. You're the only one that can do it for me."

It was two years later when I fulfilled that dream. I had sung my heart out at the audition, and when I announced that I would sing the solo at midnight mass, I couldn't control my excitement.

I dashed home to tell Mom and Dad. Dad was down at the King's Head, so I ran across the street and proudly stepped into Grandma's kitchen. Granddad was sitting with his back to me, in front of the fire. Grandma was making a new tab rug, and Flossie was jumping at me as though seeing the excitement.

"Guess what? Guess what? Granddad."

"You're going to sing the solo at midnight mass."

I had only been told twenty minutes earlier. How did he know? It was supposed to be one of the most closely guarded secrets in the parish.

He could see the amazement in my face.

"You said you would, and I knew you would. John, mi boyo, whatever your mind says you can do, you can do. You're gifted, boyo. You're like your uncle Sean. Someday he'll be the prime minister of a united Ireland. Sure, there's nothing you can't do if you really want to."

"I wish Uncle Sean could come to hear me. Do you think he would?"

"I'll ask him. It might be difficult but…if it's the Lord's will, it's the Lord's will. But now you're the man of the hour. Let's be hearing a song for your grandma now," he commanded.

"Alma, Alma, A-a-a-alma, redemtoris mater, quia pervia ceali…"

I was still singing when Uncle Bartley came in slightly tipsy as usual.

"You got the solo," he said, smiling. "Laurie Muldoone announced to the whole Home Rule Club." Laurie Muldoone was a great tenor in the choir. He was an older man with a mustache; he must have been twenty-five or six. He also had his own trio of piano, bass, and drums that played in the local pubs. "Laurie sez, 'Pat Donavan's grandson's going to sing the solo at midnight mass.'

They all drank to your good health, Da." He turned to Granddad. "Pat will not have to buy a drink in this house for the rest of the year," he said, "Da." Turning to me, he continued, "You'd better be off. It's after ten, and your da was there too. He'll be wanting to tell you how proud of you he is."

I panicked. Surely, he won't be mad at me, not tonight. Not when I have brought honor to him and Granddad.

"Good night and God bless all in this house," I shrieked back over my shoulder as I dashed out the door. I could see Dad framed in our doorway at the opposite side of the street.

"Sorry I'm late, Dad. Granddad had me singing for Grandma, and I didn't know what time it was."

"I seem to remember your grandma has a clock right in the middle of the mantelpiece," he glowered. "Off to bed right now."

"Good night and God bless," I bid them both and scooted upstairs.

"Oh Jim, why couldn't you tell him how thrilled you were?" I heard Mam say quietly as I rounded the top of the stairs. "He's so excited he probably won't be able to sleep for a week."

Dad's response was lost in the flurry of getting undressed. I wasn't going to let him spoil my night of glory. I'd done it. I'd done it. Just as Granddad had said I would, and Mam had said I would. Nobody was going to spoil this night.

I dreamt that I was singing in church. I didn't see the congregation, but I knew that they were enthralled. I sang every solo for every holy day celebration that I could recall.

The next few weeks were some of the happiest moments I had in my life. Uncle Sean came to hear me sing at midnight mass. He'd come alone though; Aunty Kath wouldn't travel with the three little ones, he said. I sat on his knee in granddads kitchen and listened to him recite his poetry. It was a rare privilege for Dad to let me stay up all night like this. I was feeling tired when he announced, "Come along, John. Time for bed."

"Give your uncle Sean a hug then." Uncle Sean smiled. "I'll be away at first light. God only knows when we'll see each other again."

I hugged him and whispered in his ear, "Just sing one song for me."

Sean's handsome face exploded with laughter. His curly black hair streaked with silver bounced as he threw his head back and lifted me high in the air.

"I'll sing one chorus with you. Then you need your beauty sleep."

Sean stood in front of the crackling fire and held my hand. I started to sing with him but only a couple of bars. I wanted to hear that voice that everyone talked about. It was marvelous. The clear enunciation of the words that somehow had a deeper feeling when sung in Gaelic.

| | |
|---|---|
| *Sinne Fianna fall* | Soldiers are we |
| *A la fa seal as Eirinn* | Whose lives are pledged to Ireland |
| *Buibean dar sluag* | Some have come from |
| *Car ruin bo raims cuzainn* | A land beyond the wave |
| *Famoib bere saor* | Sworn to be free |
| *Seantir ar sinn sear feasla* | No more our ancient sireland |
| *Fasfar tioranna fantrail* | Shall shelter the despot or the slave |
| *A nocht a teigean sa bearna baogail* | Tonight we man the coming fight |
| *Le sean are gaebil cum bais no saogail* | In Erins cause the morning light |
| *Le zun a szreac fa la macna pilear* | Mid cannons roar and rifle peal |
| *Seolib canaid Amran na bflann* | We'll chant the Soldier's song. |

That night's sleep was the happiest night of my whole life. I remembered the poems he had told of lads and lasses dancing and running in the meadows, of beautiful mountains and majestic lakes, of birds and fawns and peace throughout the land. I dreamed of the faces that sat in rapture as he wove his spell. The life that had come to the faces of the men and women who usually looked so old.

A week later, they brought Uncle Sean's body home in a casket. He'd been killed in a terrible accident. The menfolk huddled with one another, and I had to mind the kids. When I asked questions, they just rubbed my head and sniffled or grunted a reply that made no sense at all. When I could get close to Granddad, he just hugged me, and the conversation died.

Aunty Kath stayed with her mother in Spiddal. It was only a few miles up the road. I'd walked it many times, nearly always getting a lift from someone. I couldn't go; again I had to mind the twins. I didn't get to see my cousins except at the graveside.

Uncle Sean was buried in the center of the graveyard with his feet toward Galway Bay. I watched Granddad as he stayed behind after everyone drifted away. His gigantic frame stood out in black against a sky that threatened rain. The broad shoulders heaved as the grief inside him seemed to scream to be released. Wiping a nonexistent tear from his cheek, he dropped the single flower and walked toward me. The marble and granite headstones of the other families all seemed to join him in his mourning of a great loss for Ireland.

# Chapter 2

It was just one month later that Dad announced we were leaving for America. He explained to Mam that Uncle Sean had taken out insurance policies on himself and had made Granddad the beneficiary. Granddad wanted us to go to Boston with him and Grandma. There was enough money to buy fares for all of the family who wanted to go. They had the choice of staying and keeping the money or caning with us.

Uncle Bartley wasn't married, so he came with us first and got a job immediately. His brothers and sisters and their families all followed within a few months. John and Florrie came next, and when they had jobs, Harold and Kathleen came and stayed with them until they got jobs, and so it went. The Donavans soon built a reputation for good, honest work and everyone prospered.

Boston was frightening at first. Almost everyone in our neighborhood claimed to be Irish, but none of them spoke Gaelic. They didn't even speak English the way we did. The tenement building we lived in was different to anything I'd seen in Galway. Eight and ten families in the same building, all on top of one another. On Sundays sometimes Granddad, and other times Uncle Bartley, would walk with me down to the water, and we'd look out at the sea. Sometimes we would talk about Galway or sing the old songs, or I'd read Uncle Sean's poems to them, but that always choked them up. Other times we'd just sit and look and wonder if we'd done the right thing, coming to this strange land so far from home.

Granddad organized his family to live within their means, and soon we had our own home—a duplex, they called it. Granddad and

Grandma on the ground floor and Mam, Dad, me, and the twins upstairs. The rest of the family followed suit, and we all lived within a mile of one another. I liked the new neighborhood better than the old one, but it was further from the sea. Our Sunday walks now took us into the woods. I swear there were more trees in Boston than in all of Galway.

My new school, St. Justine's, had one nun who was from the old country, Sister St. Bridget. She helped me learn the new sports of baseball, basketball, and football. She also discovered I could sing.

"Remember, John Dunne. First you're an American, second you're Irish. You're in a new country, and you have to learn the new ways."

*March 17—St. Patrick's Day*

The church hall was packed with every parent—almost—and scores of aunts, uncles, cousins. It was standing room only. I peeked through the curtain during the intermission. I was starting after the curtain went up, and I wanted to make sure that Granddad and Grandma were there.

They were, about six rows back on the end. Mam was sitting with some of her friends. Dad was standing at the back with the husbands.

The men pretended to be gallant and let all the ladies sit. What they really wanted was to be able to make a quick exit as soon as this was over and get down to the bar for a quick couple of drinks. The women could escort each other home along with the kids.

"Oh Danny Boy, the pipes, the pipes are ca-a-lling from glen to glen and down the mountain side."

"You could hear a pin drop when he'd finished," Mam would describe later as she relived that historic moment for her. "Then they started shoutin', more, more, more!"

I could still hear them myself and Sister St. Bridget pushing me out, saying, "Go along, John Dunne. You have got to do another song."

I didn't know what to do. We had never talked about a second song. What should I sing?

"'I'll Take You Home Again,' Kathleen," I mouthed to Miss Dempsey on the piano below. She shook her head. "Tommy O'Hara's singing that later," she whispered. "How about 'How Are Things in Glochamoraugh'?"

I started to sweat. I couldn't remember the words to it. Wait a minute. Wait a minute. I raised my hands, and the hall fell silent.

"Soldiers are we, whose lives are pledged to Ireland…" I broke into the "Soldiers Song," and I could feel the Irish pride radiating from the group. Slowly they started to join in, and soon the noise was deafening.

They started to stand, old and young alike. I stole a look at Granddad. He was standing straight and proud, taller than I'd ever seen him. No sign of his age, head erect, shoulders square, and tears streaming down his face. I'd never seen him cry before, not even at Uncle Sean's funeral. I'd never seen any man cry before. I knew if he did it, it was all right for a man to cry, sometimes.

I was wrong. The men didn't dash off to the bar that night. They came back to our duplex and seemed to want to stay together.

Granddad had said he just wanted to be quiet and went to sit in the front room. Grandma quickly had a pot of tea made and poured himself his pint pot and asked me to take it to him.

"Ah, John, m' boyo. Y' did us proud. Y' were proper glorious tonight. Here, blow on this for y' granda." He had poured some of the tea into a saucer and wanted me to cool it down for him.

"Y' made me the happiest man on this earth, so y' did. Y' said y'd do it and y'did. Promise me this now, will ya?"

"Anything, Granddad, anything," I said between blowing.

"Promise me y'll never sing the Soldiers Song again, ever."

"But why, Granddad?"

"Oie can't tell you why. But promise me y'll never sing it again for anyone as long as y' live. And promise me that y' will never tell anyone why. Just say that's a special song, and oie only sing it for m' Granda when he asks me to. When oie'm gone, tell 'em that it was the last song y' sang for me and y' don't want to spoil the memory. Will y' do that for me?"

"Yes, I will, Granddad."

"Good, that's it then. Oie know y' never will 'cause y' said y' wouldn't, and y' always do what y' say y'll do. Off ye go now, an' let me have a sleep."

Going back into the other room was stifling. The heat was almost unbearable, and everybody was talking at once.

"Sure, and wasn't that as sweet as anything John McCormack could have done tonight?"

I turned at the sound of the strange voice. It belonged to a face I hadn't seen before, but was vaguely familiar.

He was about twenty or twenty-one, tall and skinny, about six feet, with dark brown hair about the same as mine. His hand was rough as he took mine to shake it. He was like hundreds of jaunty Irish lads who had come to America to "seek fame and fortune."

"Sean Donovan's the name, oie'm y' cousin from Ireland. Your granda and my granda were brothers. We met at my da's funeral. I just got in on the train from New York last night. Oim stayin' at Aunty Madge's."

He looked awfully tough with strong shoulders that carried a jacket two sizes too large for him. It made him look "a typical mick straight off the boat."

Looking at me with searching eyes that made me uncomfortable, he said in a quiet voice, "Y' sure changed my plans for tonight. Oie was expectin' we'd all be 'oistin' a few down by now. Y' put the bloody damper on that, so y' did."

"What did I do?" I asked defensively.

"Holy Mother of God, y' sing the most stirrin' songs. Y' get 'em all nostalgic for Ireland. They'll not want to be rubbin' shoulders wi' no Proddies tonight. Sure, and if they did, there would be some blood spilt, sure enough there would. It's a gift y' have, laddie. But it can be a bloody dangerous gift."

"How can singing a couple of songs be dangerous?"

"Not any couple o' songs. Just the ones that get the blood up, intensify the pride. Jesus, Mary, and Joseph, we Irish are the most romantic race in the world. If the Brits on'y knew, they could put the whole country t' sleep if they played the right lullabies on the wireless all the time. Enough o' that talk. Are ye gain' to sing for us ag'in?"

"I will if they want me to," I said, brightening a little.

"What will you sing then…Danny?"

"My name's John, not Danny," I said and then realized he had meant the title of the song. "Oh, I'm sorry. I see what you mean," I apologized, trying to recover. "Yes, I'll sing 'Danny Boy.'"

He laughed quietly, not loud enough for anyone else to hear.

"I know y' name's John. But just for that, my nickname for you will always be Danny Boy." I jutted out my chin. I was about to show my smart aleck cousin, even though he was ten years older and bigger than me, he would call me by my proper name.

He deftly put his hand over my mouth, smiled a magical grin, and said, "It'll be our secret, Danny Boy. Nobody will ever hear me call you that. It'll be just between you and me, okay?"

I didn't like it, but something told me not to argue with this character, so I nodded, and he lowered his hand.

A few minutes later they had me singing and were all singing along, thankfully. I was getting tired so it was almost a relief when Dad's head appeared at the door. With a quick backward jerk of his head, it signaled the end of another glorious night.

On my eleventh birthday Granddad gave me a prayer book. The inscription read,

> To Sean,
>
> Happy Birthday. May God keep you in peace and happiness for all your days.
>
> *Your loving brother,*
>
> *Pat.*

"Oie want ya to keep this safe now, John. It's the only thing oie have left to remember y' uncle Sean with. Oie gave it t' him for his first Holy Communion." The tears rolled down his cheeks as he sat in front of the fire, smoking his pipe.

"Thank you, Granddad. I will. I will keep it safe."

"You're the apple o' my eye, John."

"Thank you, Granddad..." I hesitated. Dare I ask? "Granddad..."

"Sure, and what is it? Spit it out."

"What happened to Uncle Sean? Why doesn't anybody talk about him?"

"'Cause everybody loved him. He was our hope, so he was. Then to be...that way..." The words caught in his throat.

"When he what, Granddad?"

"When he got killed, when he got blown up."

The pain on his face showed in every line. The short white hair stood in stark relief against the back of his chair. He had slumped down as he was reliving the tragedy.

I wanted to ask him how, but I daren't.

Granddad lifted himself to an upright position and wiped his moist nose on the back of his sleeve.

"That's why y're never to sing that song again. The Soldiers Song. He was singin' it the day he left the house. He was off to a meetin', a meetin' of the Sinn Fein. They blew 'im up. The murderin' thugs."

My heart was beating so wildly. My uncle, a martyr for the cause. The rotten Proddie dogs had killed him. Well, I'd get a few of them when I got a chance.

"Was it the Proddies, Granddad?"

"No, John... It was his own kind that did it."

"It was an accident. The bomb went off by accident."

"No, John... They eliminated him. He was too much for peace. He was too much of a leader. And them as were at the top saw him as a threat. A threat to what they had set their hearts and minds on. So he had to go."

"But Gran—"

"No buts. Listen to me. It was his nearest and dearest friend what did it to him, went with him all the way to the meetin', they did, together. At the last minute, this friend—Sean loved him like a brother, so he did—this friend made an excuse to turn back and left

Sean to trip the booby trap. Y' aunty Kath found him. He died in her arms saying his prayers."

"Do you know who betrayed him, Granddad?"

"Oie do. He told your Aunty Kath who it was. She said that he'd told her not to tell me unless oie swore that oie wouldn't take vengeance nor would oie have any of my sons take vengeance for him. She made me swear it. Oie swore to her oie'd never ask anyone to avenge his death." His pale eyes were rimmed with red as he looked at me and hugged me. "It was his dying wish for us all to come to America. That's why we're here."

"Listen t' me now. When oie die, they'll be looking at you and sayin', 'Wouldn't he be a foine one to be helpin' us.' Oie've told 'em, 'Stay away.' Oie want you t' have nuthin' to do with the murderin' thugs.

"You, why, you're goin' t' go t' St Blaze and then t' a foine university. Y're goin' to get an education. You can be anythin' y' want to be. Stay away from the IRA. They're the ones who killed Sean, not the Proddies. You have never let me down, John. Oie know that you'll make me proud of you, whatever you do in life." He finished as though he wanted to say more, but he was too upset for me to ask any more questions.

Granddad died a few weeks later. The wake was enormous. It seemed as though hundreds of people came to Grandma's house to pay their respects and then stay and reminisce and drink and argue. I wasn't comfortable about Granddad being in the front room, laid out there, people filing past and shedding a tear then going in the next room and getting merry. All the visitors were like the rest of the family and friends: poor working-class people, except one man who was dressed very posh. His black suit shone, not from wear like my Dad's did, but because it was silk. He was tall and distinguished, very handsome, and spoke softly. His brogue was still there, but he'd lost most of it. Everyone was very polite to him, but behind his back they looked at him with a look that was a mixture of fear and envy.

"Who's the man with the gold chain in his waistcoat, Uncle?" I whispered to Uncle John.

"Richard Fuller. He owns Fullers Building Contractors. I wish he hadn't come. Y' gran's beside herself. She doesn't want to be rude, but Da never had any time for him."

"Why didn't Granddad like him?"

Uncle John shrugged and moved away.

It was then that Fuller, as though he sensed he was the topic of conversation, turned and took in the whole room with a magnetic smile. His strong teeth flashed against his weathered face. He looked powerful, every inch a self-made man. His bright blue eyes danced as he called across the room to Grandma.

"Maggie, I'll be off. If there's ever anything you need..."

Grandma waved in a neutral way.

"God bless all in this house," he bid as he left.

*Someday I want to be like that,* I thought. Someone who people took notice of, with beautiful clothes. I slowly moved to the window and watched him cross the street toward a huge black Cadillac. My Granddad had had a powerful friend in Mr. Fuller, if not a friend, someone who at least had respected him enough to cane to his wake.

Uncle Bartley had taken over as the head of the family; he was the oldest and the most fearsome—fearsome to others that is, not to me. We had walked for miles together on Saturdays and Sundays. He always taught me something new. He was the closest thing to Granddad there could be.

"Uncle Bartley, who was that man, Fuller?" I asked.

"Sure, he's the Irish-American dream come true. Didn't 'e come over the same month we did only two years ago, and now he's runnin' one o' the biggest buildin' contractin' companies in Boston. The company had nothin' but labor trouble when he first came, but he sorted them out an' then bought the company from the former owners. Has 'is own name up there now. One day you'll be able to start your own business. This America is the land of opportunity, but you've got to get an education. I've been talking with your Da, and we've decided that you should go to St. Blaze. Y' Granda wanted that for you. It's a foine school, and it'll set y' up for university."

On the second day of the wake, Sean announced he was going back to Ireland after the funeral; he hadn't found work.

"Danny Boy," he said out of earshot of anybody else. "Oie'll be seein' y. Probably the next time you'll be big enough to take a poke at me like y' wanted to on Saint Paddy's night. If y' do, oie sure hope y' don't punch as well as y' sing, or y'll knock me bloody block off."

By the third day the level of storytelling had reached its peak. One of Granddad's dearest friends from the old country had taken the chair in the center of the living room and held the attention of everyone.

"Sure, an' Pat Donavan was one o' the best fist fighters oie've ever seen. Oie've never seen 'im licked. In 'is younger days he was the 'terror' of the building sites. Some o' the Clerk o' Works used to want 'im on the site just t' keep the other lads in line," Kevin Shaw said sadly.

"You're right. Oie never saw the man afraid o' anythin'. Sure, an' 'e didn't know what fear was," said another.

"You're wrong there, boyo. Oie've seen him scared," Kevin laughed. Everybody turned at this heretic statement.

"Y' never have seen m' Da scared," protested my Uncle John. "Himself was never afraid o' man nor beast."

"Calm the sen. Oie'm tellin' you 'e was scared once. Oie was there to witness it. If himself were 'ere t' tell the tale, he would."

"When did it happen?" challenged Uncle John.

"T'was years ago. We were just a couple o' young lads. We were working on the scaffold on the new bank building on O'Connell street in Dublin. Well, oie looks down an' sees this sight oie'd never seen afore, and me with m' big mouth yells, 'And who'll be 'avin' three rounds with the black fella then?' Sure, and oie had never seen a black man afore."

The older men were nodding, agreeing that black people were rare in that part of the world.

"Well, this blackie stopped dead in 'is tracks." He looked up and yelled back, 'Yes, who will have three rounds with me?' Jesus, Mary, and Joseph. What have oie done? This man was a giant. Even from where oie was standin', twenty feet up, he looked big. And he was lookin' straight at me. Well, as y' know, oie've always been known as a match maker. So oie sez, 'This fella will, Pat Donavan. He'll have a go.'" Every eye in the place was riveted as he unfolded his story.

"Oie thought Pat was going to knock me right off the scaffold. Without a word 'e started down the ladder, wavin' t' m'self to follow. When we got t' the bottom oie almost shit m'self. This bugger must have been one o' those Watusi warriors. He was seven feet if he was an inch." He paused for the effect. He was a masterful story teller.

"Pat steps up to 'im an' looks 'im square in the eye, which was hard to do. This soddin' chap was head and shoulders taller. 'So you'd be wantin t' have three rounds, would y',' Pat sez. The black fella nods slowly, settin' 'imself to let Pat take the first punch." He started to digress. "Now, I think if Pat had a slugged 'im right, then he could o' whipped him. But he didn't."

He stopped. They were all on the edge of their chairs.

"So what happened?" they all demanded at once.

"Well, Pat sez, 'So you'd be wantin' t' go three rounds, would y'? Well, let's be off t' the Grapes. Oie'll buy the first round, Kevin will buy the second, and you can buy the third." His final words were lost in groans and laughter.

"Sure, you're a bigger liar than Tom Pepp, so you are, Kevin. Nobody will ever believe another word."

"Oie only tell the God's holy truth, cross my heart." The twinkle in his eye showed his enjoyment.

Kevin turned to me.

"Sure, and y' granda was a diplomat. He was no coward. But he did know what fear is. Not like y' namesake over there." He pointed to Uncle John. "He's the crazy one, the jail bird."

"Don't be gettin' on about that." Everybody started laughing as Uncle John started to blush just as I would blush sometimes.

"You're a jail bird, Uncle John?" I teased with a smile. The men loved it; they liked a fresh audience for their stories.

"Oie didn't even spend one night in there," he said to me. Turning to the group, who were nudging each other and laughing, he said, "You lot ought to be ashamed, fillin' this poor lad's head with those stories. It was all a big mistake."

"Tell 'im about it. Try to clear y' name," they laughed.

"Well, it was when we went t' work in Cork that time. One day when it was pourin' down rain. We'd been huddled in the site but all mornin'. It got to about eleven, which happens to be openin' time. We said t' Billy Richmond, the gaffer, we'll be off for a bite to eat."

"And a pint or two," they interrupted.

"Well, lad, if you're rained off but you stick around, you get sub-pay. But if it stops rainin' an' you're not there t' start work, y' don't get it. Well, we'd told him we'd just be at the Fountain, only a spit away from the site. We had a pint and a pork pie. Joe Moffat poked his head out and said it was still pourin', so we had another. Before we realized, it was three, chucking out time." The rest of the audience were enjoying it as much as I was. Even Uncle John had to smile.

"Wouldn't y' know, it had stopped, the sun was shining. We headed back to the site. That's when the trouble started. This bugger Moffat"—he pointed at Joe, who was pretending to fall off his chair—"this bugger goes up to the hut and sez to Billy Richmond, 'So what's the bahn t' do wi' us then?" Billy, the little snot, sez, 'You lot can bugger off. You should a been here two hours ago.' Well, one thing led to another. He got mad. We got mad. We ended up chasing him all round the building site until he locked himself in the site hut."

"Here it comes," they echoed.

"Well, we were both well-oiled and mad. We decided to teach Tim a lesson. We gathered up some old wood, rags, and paper and lit a fire under the site hut. Silly bugger over there"—he pointed at Joe Moffatt again—"wedged a plank at the door so he couldn't get out. He ended up jumping through the glass window. We never touched him. We figured he was scared enough. Anyway, he filed charges against Moffatt and me, and we ended up paying a fine."

The place was in an uproar. They had all heard the story before, but they loved it. I was laughing so hard myself I thought I would wet my pants.

"There's more, tell him the rest of it," they cried enthusiastically.

"Oh God, can't a fella ever live somethin' down? Well, they'll tell y' if I don't. When we got to court, we were charged with damaging public property. We pleaded guilty, and the judge sez, 'Fined ten pounds.' I didn't have any money with me, so I sez, 'Your Honor, could I have time.' Meanin' time to get the money. 'Sure,' he sez. Ten days in jail." This time I almost fell off the chair.

"Well, Moffatt had the money and loaned it to me, so I never did go to jail."

They had embraced me as one of the group. I had just turned fourteen, and I felt like an adult.

"Come on, John Dunne. Let's have a song for y' granda's memory. Y'll be givin' us 'Danny Boy,' won't y' now?" It was Laurie Muldoone from the back of the room. They all called for me to sing.

"O Danny Boy, the pipes, the pipes…" I nearly couldn't finish for the tears and the choking feeling. I could mentally see Granddad and Uncle Sean's faces smiling at me.

# Chapter 3

Saint Blaze was an all-boys school with a great reputation and tradition, we were told by the monsignor as he addressed us.

I looked around at the 150 new boys from all over the north eastern United States. Most of them were boarders; I was one of the lucky ones who was a day student. I went home every evening to my family while some of my new friends wept themselves to sleep with loneliness.

It was one of the most modern facilities in all of USA. It had a marvelous gymnasium, completely fitted with all the most up-to-date equipment, including a full-size indoor heated swimming pool. We had a football field and track. I often thought back to my old friends in Galway who would never have believed such a place was possible.

It had several laboratories, metal and woodworking facilities, drafting room, and the most splendid library.

The faculty all wore the black robes I had only seen in movies before. You recognized the prefects by the special gold braid around the collar of their blazers.

We listened very attentively to all the teachers who spoke to us. Then we were given cards: one to assign us to our home room; another for our seating assignments in the dining hall and which sitting we were at.

It wasn't the first time I'd had to meet and make new friends, but I still found it hard, though exciting, meeting all these strangers from other towns and states. Some I had only remotely heard of.

Most of the teachers spoke very precisely. They quickly corrected anyone who used bad grammar, but they never made fun of the accent, not like some of the other boys who obviously thought they were better than the others.

"Can I sit here?" I asked, feeling a little unsure of myself in this new environment.

"I am sure you can. The question is, may you sit there?"

The tall prefect grinned at my confused expression.

"You can sit there, I am sure of that, unless your legs don't have any joints. It is physically possible for you to do it. What you are asking, I presume, is for permission. In that case, the question should be, 'May I sit here?' Yes, you may."

The dining hall was bedlam. It was as though everybody was trying to shout at the top of their voices. A whistle was blown, and three prefects quickly took charge. They explained quite forcibly that, with their authority, they could demand almost anything of anybody, justifying their power by quoting the laws of the church:

> Let every man be subject to a higher power. He that resisteth the power resisteth the ordinance of God and they that resist, purchase for themselves damnation.

They explained that the almost-slave-like duties that the new boys had to perform were to help them to become more Christlike.

Under Roman law, a Raman soldier had absolute right to insist that a subject carry his pack for one mile. The Jews were such a proud race they had perfected the ability to pace off exactly one mile. They would then put the pack down. They had obeyed the law of Ceasar.

"Then came Christ who said, 'Go the extra mile.' It wasn't enough just to do what you were supposed to do. You should do more than that." That was where the phrase "Go the extra mile" came from.

Frankly, I thought the Jews were the smart ones. I could see, maybe, carrying a pack for a war-weary soldier just back from the front, someone who had been putting his life on the line for me and the rest of us. But I didn't quite see the parallel between them and these prefects who seemed to delight in subjugating us freshmen. However, the rest of the glamour outweighed everything else. It was good to be alive.

The school had been founded by the Jesuits, and challenge was part of every day. In schoolwork, in sports, and recreation, challenge was something you never shunned. You rose to the challenge. Sometimes I enjoyed the rewards and other times the misery of failure. The rewards were recognition, the misery of failure was physical punishment of the most severe kind. At the end of my junior year, I was credited with having coined "The Jesuit Principle—it is easier to receive forgiveness than get permission."

Barry Clegg had been the first friend I had made on the varsity football team. He was the full back who had made it possible for me to break all the rushing records at St. Blaze. I'd been uncertain what his reaction would be about my intention to ask his sister, Sheila, for a date. Barry hadn't objected; it wouldn't have made any difference if he had, but it was nice to have his approval.

She was at least a couple of years older than me, but I had seen her often at our preseason practice, never with a boy. At first I'd assumed that she was there because of Barry, and she probably had a steady boyfriend who was away at college. Then I noticed that she rarely spoke to Barry unless he and I were together. Others on the team laughed and joked with her easily, yet there was no gossip in the locker room or kidding about anyone going out with her.

I had begun to fantasize that it was me she was interested in. Every time we had wind sprints, I'd tear up the field to finish yards in front of the others. I'd look at her, and she'd be looking the other way. I'd go out for a pass and make a terrific one-handed catch, and again she'd be talking with someone else.

This time I'd just kicked a punt so hard I sent the ball way over the catcher's head. I stood and stared at her. She was looking for something in her purse. I willed her to look at me. She rummaged around in that silly little bag. Her profile was perfect: dark brown hair tied back in a ponytail, a small nose that wrinkled as she was becoming annoyed. Her strapless shoulders shone as the late afternoon sun bathed them, and the light breeze caught the powder-blue skirt, creating an almost-sculptured look to her figure.

She couldn't find what she was looking for. Snapping her purse shut, she started to walk quickly along the sideline. The hardened surface, worn free from grass by thousands of people parading there, broke slightly as her small heels dug firmly into the clay. Her ankles and calves were magnificent, and as her hips swayed slightly, her breasts rose gently in perfect harmony.

"Dunne!" I jumped as the coach's voice broke my trance.

"Yes, sir." I started to run toward him.

"Will you go and get it over with. Go and ask her for a date, then we can all get down to some serious practice." His face showed no amusement nor anger. I didn't know if he was kidding me or not.

If I ran after her and he was being sarcastic, I would be humiliated. Even if he wasn't, what if she said no? Everyone would know.

I stole a quick glance in the direction she had been heading. She had stopped and suddenly turned and looked at me. Was she looking at me or the coach or someone behind us? My neck did a one eighty; there was nobody behind me. God, I felt like such a fool.

"Meet the challenge, you asshole." Was that the coach or my own inner voice saying those words?

I ran so fast toward her she started to move out of the way.

"Sheila," I gasped. I hope she thought I was out of breath.

"Yes," she smiled.

God, I almost passed out. She'd said yes. You haven't even asked her the question yet, stupid. Go ahead, ask her.

"I was wondering…"

"Yes."

There she goes again. Please don't interrupt me this time.

"Well, I was wondering… Would you… I mean… Do you…"

"I'd love to."

"What?"

"All of the above."

"I'm sorry. I meant—"

"Is this a multiple-choice question or what?"

"Jesus Christ," I raised my eyes upward. "Will you go out with me tonight?" I lowered my head and looked at her beaming face.

"If Jesus Christ is too busy, I'm available. You'll have to pick me up at home though. Maybe we can catch an early movie. Just let Barry know what time you'll be there." She was moving slowly away but still holding my eyes. "See you later, John."

"Dunne!" The coach's voice again. I ran back to the group. "Well?" he greeted.

"Well what, Coach?"

"You've kept these guys standing around while you pursued your love life. Don't you think you owe us all an explanation? What did she say? Are you going to take her out or not?"

"Yes, I am going to take her out."

"Alllrrriigghhtt," the group growled together.

"Now, gentlemen. I would prefer that further bulletins on Dunne's amorous exploits be issued on your own time. *Get back to work.*"

The locker room was buzzing with questions. What did I say? What did she say? Barry watched me with faint amusement as I told them how I smoothly ran over and said, "Hi, Sheila. How'd you like to take in a movie tonight?" How she'd acted a little cool at first, but she'd folded under my magnetic smile.

Barry and I left the locker room together.

"Sheila asked me to tell you what time I'd pick her up. Tell her about five fifteen."

"I'll tell her, and I'll ask her to verify that bullshit you handed out in the locker room."

He was laughing out loud now. He knew how hard it had been for me. I'd pestered him for what would be the best approach, and he'd been no help at all.

"Your nickname will be Peg-Leg Clegg if you do. You, you're my best friend, and I've had no support from you at all."

"Everyone's been betting on how long it would take you to ask her. She told me weeks ago to tell you to ask her out."

"Then why didn't you?"

"I told her I'm not playing Cupid. You'd taken just about every other decent-looking girl in town out. She'd have to wait her turn until you got down to the second string."

"You, Barry Clegg, will never have hemorrhoids. You know why? Because you are the world's perfect asshole."

"I know. I glory in your praise. Look, one thing. She asked me to tell you this if and when you got around to asking. When you call for her, Dad will almost certain to be there. Whatever you do, don't let him know you are Irish."

"What?"

"I know, it's stupid. We're Catholic as well, but he has a thing about first-generation Irish. Please yourself as far as I'm concerned. Walk in singing 'When Irish Eyes Are Smiling' if you want to."

It was the first time I'd called for a girl at her home. Mrs. Clegg greeted me warmly at the door. I was nervous, and she sensed it. Her bright eyes gave me an appraising glance. I must have measured up because she took me by the elbow and guided me toward the living room.

"Don't worry, he'll not bite you," she whispered. "Harold, this is Sheila's escort for this evening, John Dunne. Why don't you make John comfortable while I go and hurry Sheila along."

I wanted to ask her to stay; she had put me at ease immediately. As she retreated, her smile kept sending me nonverbal reassurance. Her walk was just like Sheila's, and her figure was only slightly more generous around the hips. The dark hair done in a French twist highlighted the classical bone structure of her face, one that had matured without aging. A forecast of what Sheila would look like in years to come—elegance and beauty.

Mr. Clegg was a stern-looking man. He wasn't as big as Barry but much more handsome. His steel-gray hair and clipped mustache made him quite menacing until he spoke. He first made me feel comfortable by talking about football, then he questioned me about school. In only a few minutes he had made me completely relax.

Sheila, at last, made her grand entrance, and Mr. and Mrs. Clegg said goodbye to us both at the door.

"Have a good time. And Sheila, watch this young man. These Irish lads can charm anybody with their blarney." He was laughing as he waved.

Neither of us said a word until we were halfway to the bus stop, then I started to laugh. The combination of the tension, relief, and just the sheer humor of it all hit me. She started to laugh too; it was infectious. By the time we could control ourselves, the little hint of eye makeup that she had so delicately applied had smudged. She noticed the trace on the back of her hand.

"Now look what you've made me do," she giggled, removing a small compact from her tiny handbag. "Oh, I look awful."

"You look divine. You're the most beautiful thing I've ever seen walking." I put my arms around her and pulled her toward me, leaning against the high wall behind me. "Now what was all that about? Your father knew I was Irish all the time."

"I'm sorry, John, that was my fault. Some time ago I'd heard Daddy telling Mother about someone, and he called them 'thieving micks.' I just assumed he didn't like Irish. I had told Mum that you were that Irish boy who played football with Barry. She said, 'I don't know what your father will say about you going out with a mick.' That's why I asked Barry to warn you. But I was hoping—did you really mean that, when you said I was beautiful?" she finished breathlessly.

"I'm not in the habit of saying things I don't mean. If you ask me if I really mean something again, I'll give you two real black eyes. Now, if you want to fix your face before we meet our public at the royal bus stop, Your Highness, get a move on."

The repairs took all of thirty seconds. We ran to the bus stop just in time. We sat on the first two seats that were available. She took my hand in a grip that was almost too tight.

"No one said that to me before," she whispered.

"What, that they'd give you two black eyes?"

"No, you know what I mean."

"You've also got the sexiest voice," I whispered back. "From now on, you're only allowed to speak in a whisper."

The grip relaxed, just a fraction. She was fun, she was a great looker, and we were going to have a great time.

The Ritz was the most modern cinema in town. It had accommodated courting couples by installing double seats in the rear three rows. You could sit with your arm around a girl and not have the arm rest digging into your ribs. As the lights dimmed, she snuggled up, dropping her right shoulder slightly under my armpit, her head rested on my shoulder. She smelled good. She slid one arm around my back, and her other encircled me. She was almost purring. I was the happiest man on earth. Was I a man? Dare I try something? I started to perspire and think of all the consequences. It wasn't worth it. I didn't need it.

*Didn't need it—are you crazy?* I said to myself. *You're going to have to someday, then you're going to wish you'd had some experience.* Well, not with this one. It was getting hotter in the theatre, and I was really starting to sweat.

"Just a minute, Sheila, let me take my jacket off. It's awfully warm in here."

She unwound herself as I stood up to take off my jacket. The bulge in my pants was there again. Thank God the lights were out. In an instant she was back in the same position. I looked down at her and kissed her on the forehead. She raised her head and offered her lips. I gently brushed my lips across hers. They were moist and warm. She raised her left hand and placed it on the back of my neck and firmly drew me down to a stronger commitment. Her mouth was just slightly open, and I opened mine a little. It was the greatest kiss I had ever had. My whole body was quivering, and so was hers.

"Would you like an orange drink before the feature starts?"

"No, thank you, I'm just fine."

"Well, I'd better go to the bathroom before the beginning. Don't want to miss any of it, do we? You sure you don't want anything?"

Get control of yourself. You've been out with other great kissers before. Yes, but not like this one. None that sent me completely round the bend. Maybe I could let my hand "accidentally" take hold of her breast and see how she reacted. Yes. But…what if the reaction was a slap on the face? Then what? I didn't want to lose this one, not like that. I wanted to see her again; she wasn't like the others.

Back in the darkness of the theatre, she had settled into a position that made it seem as though our bodies were molded for one another. We kissed not as intently as before but with just as much tenderness. She did want to see the movie; it wasn't like some of the shows where the movie was so poor the only reason for being there was to neck. During the action scenes, she reacted to the violence, grabbing hold of me as though I would protect her. Occasionally she moved to get more comfortable. When she did this, her right breast would brush against my side, setting off fantasies that would surely send me straight to hell.

After the show we went across the street to the Youth Center and had a couple of lemonades.

"Can you dance?" she asked. "Come on, let's do it."

The first dance was fine. It moved fast enough, and I had learned to maneuver around the floor at church socials. The next dance was a waltz, and she moved in close. I thought our bodies had been molded together in the movie theater. This time it was in the vertical position, face-to-face. The lights were dimmed, and a spotlight hit the mirrored ball hanging from the ceiling. Millions of lights sparkled and radiated around the room. The floor became crowded, and the music softened to a slow "Moonlight in Vermont."

Her body was so close, all over close, I thought I was going to explode in my pants. My shirt was wet through with sweat. I looked at her, and she looked as cool as the moment I picked her up. She gazed into my eyes, and I kissed her lightly on the lips. Her arms encircled my neck, loosely at first, her fingers combing into my hair. Then, as before, she gently but firmly pulled my head forward and kissed me.

"Let's get out of here," I said hoarsely.

"Who's talking sexy now?" she teased. "Okay, let's go."

"We have plenty of time. Let's walk home," I said.

"Sure, let's walk."

We talked about all kinds of things and nothing. It was the first time we had had any conversation. She worked at Clegg, Bates and

Taylor, her father's construction company. She called it "Slog, Dates and Failure."

"They make you slog away at work, trying to meet impossible deadlines, and they're never satisfied. Get it?"

"Slog for work, Dates for deadlines, and nobody ever does anything right, so you're a Failure," I interpreted.

"Daddy is all right, but those other two are like a couple of nuns—they'll never be satisfied." She started to laugh and saw the shock on my face.

"Oh, I'm sorry, John, I forgot. I feel terrible. It was just what someone said in the office today. God, I'm sorry."

She hadn't meant anything by it. It really was an innocent remark. I changed the subject quickly.

Sheila had gone to Wellesly Prep, a private school for girls, then to Pine Manor College and got her associates degree in accounting. She wasn't very bright, she said. She had left school and gone to work for her father, who was a partner in the company and very strict with her. He was meticulous with her training. Not only did her work have to be correct but he expected her to know and understand what she was doing and the reasons for doing it.

"It's like he expects me to take over someday. I don't know, Barry should be the one, he's the man. Daddy says he'll never be able to grasp it all. Yet in front of Barry he always talks as though I'm so immature. Then when we are alone, or at work, he talks tome almost as though I am the only one he has any faith in, the only one he can trust. It's confusing."

"Perhaps he feels that Barry needs to feel superior, to build his confidence. Or he's afraid if he treats you with importance, it might overwhelm Barry. He obviously believes in you and your ability. Prove him right. There is no reason in the world why you can't be the president someday. Think about it. Sheila Clegg, President of the biggest construction company in Boston… in the whole United States…in the world."

"That's silly. I'll probably get married and have three or four babies and spend the rest of my life changing diapers."

"Is that what you want to do? If it is, then that's what it will be."

"I think it would be nice to be able to do both."

"Then you probably will—do both, that is."

We had reached the end of the street. It was a posh area with tree-lined sidewalks and gardens with flowers. Some even had sculptured shrubs that looked so elegant.

Most of the way we had walked hand in hand. Now I put my arm around her. She slipped her arm around my back under my jacket. We swayed gently toward her home. I didn't want it to end, but it was at least ten after ten.

"Did you enjoy tonight, Sheila?"

"It was terrific. I enjoyed every moment."

"Would you like to do it again?"

"What do you think?"

"I think I'd like a straight answer."

"Is this straight enough?" she said and kissed me fiercely. We locked in the tightest embrace. It happened right then. I exploded into my pants. Trembling with the sensation of the relief of the pent-up sexual frustration, I held her and held her. It was almost as I had fantasized it.

"When?" I gasped, hoping she hadn't felt the pulsating through that moment of mixed ecstasy.

"You say when, and I'll be available."

"Well, let's see, it's your turn to pay. Somewhere expensive. I know, why don't we just go for a walk in the park tomorrow evening?"

"I'd love it. I think I can afford that."

"I'll call for you about five thirty then?"

"I had the most wonderful time, did you?"

"The best, the best time I've ever had."

"Really?"

I raised my fist in mock threat.

"I'm sorry, but I wasn't sure you liked me enough to ask me out again, and—" I couldn't hit her, so I kissed her into silence.

# Chapter 4

Sheila and I became inseparable, and her father talked to me more than Barry. He offered me a part-time job. I would be working in the same department as Sheila. The company of Clegg, Bates and Taylor was one of the largest construction companies in Massachusetts. Mr. Clegg's father had founded the company fifty years previously.

Although he was a stockholder in the company, Mr. Clegg was not the boss. I learned later that his father had been in financial difficulties some years ago. He had taken in Bates and Taylor as partners and had lost control of the company. Mr. Clegg was in charge of accounting, Mr. Taylor of sales, and Mr. Bates of the construction operations.

I approached the principal regarding my opportunity to have a part-time job. Surprisingly, he was very supportive and helped me arrange my schedule. I could take two full afternoons a week off and leave at two o'clock on the other three days. This gave me approximately twenty hours a week. Clegg, Bates and Taylor only paid me minimum wages, but it was all spending money; I was on easy street.

Accounting fascinated me. I would ask Mr. Clegg lots of questions. I started to understand the difference between assets and liabilities, general accounting procedures, and the importance of having a well-balanced set of books for the Internal Revenue Service. Mr. Clegg explained the role of an accountant was not to just keep the books and say if the company was making or losing money. An accountant also needed to know and understand the law, to allow the company to take the best advantage of every tax situation.

I was impressed with how much Sheila understood. She had said that she wasn't very bright. I quickly found out that she was modest with herself.

Every year our main football game was against our archrivals, Avon. All the students made a big thing of preparing for the massacre. On the night before the game they built a bonfire and burned an effigy of an Avon player on top of it.

Sheila and I went to the celebration. We had been going together for several months now. There were hotdogs, hamburgers, coleslaw, potato salad, and desserts that would guarantee to help you gain ten pounds just looking at them; it was a feast for everyone.

The local community got into the spirit also and put on a firework display. It was well organized by the Youth Center director and two of his friends. They were very cautious about making sure that all the displays were done at a safe distance from the crowd.

The main display was over, and the fire was beginning to collapse; it would probably burn until morning. The crowd started to dissipate, very young children crying that they didn't want to go to bed. Their parents and the older people were glad to get back to the comfort of their homes. Only the teenagers really wanted to stick around. Suddenly, out of the corner of my eye, I saw a sparkling object arcing toward us.

Some fool had decided that Sheila and I looked too comfortable, standing with our arms around each other, basking in the radiated heat from the fire. I turned my back to the object, shielding Sheila. As I did, she slipped off-balance and started to fall.

The fizzing firecracker ricocheted toward her head, exploding as it hit her on the crown. For a couple of seconds I couldn't see a thing. As I reached down blindly for her, I could hear her screaming, "I'm on fire, I'm burning!"

I ran my hand over her, trying to feel what part of her clothing had caught on fire. It was her hair that had been burned. I could smell it.

Brushing my hand across her head, I could feel the hot, brittle ends. Sheila was terrified and shook violently. She was in shock.

Holding her as tightly as I could, I kept saying, "You're all right, you're all right."

People came rushing over. As my vision cleared, I could see that no serious damage had been done. I examined her hair, neck, and face. There were no visible marks on her skin. She was trembling uncontrollably.

One of the girls who had come over to us said, "It was that damn fool, Billy Webber, who threw it. Showing off for the rest of his gang, I guess."

Billy Webber was one of the local toughs, about eighteen years old. He loved to terrorize old people and other teenagers. He would harass anyone who was willing to be intimidated by him and four or five of his friends. I felt impotent to do anything but glare. I couldn't leave Sheila, and I didn't fancy my chances against the whole of Webber's gang.

Sheila didn't speak all the way home. Her parents were already in bed when we arrived. I wanted to waken them and tell what had happened, but Sheila insisted she just wanted to go to bed herself.

My bike was at Sheila's. Riding home, I had to pass the area where the bonfire had been. It was about half a mile from home and consisted almost entirely of cobbled streets. A racing bike on these streets was not the most comfortable vehicle. I made a sharp right turn and came across the open clearing where a bonfire was still burning strongly.

Webber and his gang were coming toward me. Had I been traveling at a decent speed, I would have been able to brush past them before they reacted, but I was traveling too slowly. Two of then grabbed the handlebars, causing me to fall off the bike. As I fell, I continued to roll and got to my feet immediately.

That had been the critical moment, and they missed it. I had fully expected them to jump on me while I was on the pavement. If they had, I would have been beaten to a pulp. Now with half a chance I could outrun them.

"Okay, Dunne. Some of 'em were sayin' down at the bottom of Battery Park Lane that ya said ya were goin' to beat me up," Webber challenged as I steadied myself.

"I never said any such thing."

"Ya callin' me a liar?"

Obviously, this was a no-win situation. He was going to have a fight with me whether I wanted to or not. He outweighed me by at least fifteen pounds. Even if I got the upper hand, the others would soon step in to help him. Trying to maintain my composure and glancing around the group, I had a flash of inspiration.

"No, I don't want to fight you. But each of you is going to give me five dollars for the damage that you just did to my bike."

The look of astonishment on their faces was priceless.

"What did you say?"

"I said, you are each going to give me five dollars for the damage that you have done to my bike."

"And you and who's bloody army's goin' t' make us?" they sneered.

Pointing to the three older ones, I said with a smile, "If you don't give it to me now, you'll give it to my uncle, Bartley Donavan, at work tomorrow."

Their mouths were so wide open I could have reached out and pulled their tongues as they gaped in amazement. I had recognized them as laborers from the building site at which my uncle worked. There were very few people who didn't have a great deal of respect for his ability in street fighting. All four of them looked at Webber.

"You never said he was a Donavan."

"How the hell did I know?"

"Well, we're getting the hell outa here." They turned and fled, leaving Webber and me face-to-face.

Something shiny appeared in Webber's hand.

"I'm goin' to carve your fuckin' face to shreds," he hissed.

Now it was my turn to run. I bolted toward the bonfire, hoping some witnesses would stop him, but no one was there. I could easily outrun him. I was one of the fastest sprinters over fifty yards in the state. Over a longer distance I was in much better shape than he was, but I couldn't just abandon my bike.

I had to let him stay close enough to think he could catch me. When I got him far enough away from the bike, then I would turn and sprint back and get the bike.

I reached the fire about six yards ahead of him and decided to circle it and tire him out. Running clockwise around the fire without even thinking, I swooped down and picked up the unburned end of an old chair leg. The other end was charred and still glowing.

Stopping abruptly, I turned and jabbed the hot end at Webber. He slithered to a halt. The sight of me now with a burning club had turned the tables. He was basically a coward at heart. He turned and ran back around the fire in a counterclockwise motion.

I swung the club in an arc and caught his trailing ankle. With a loud scream he started to go down. I had hit him harder than I had intended to. His body started to turn over as he fell, and as he landed, his momentum rolled him toward the fire. Shrieks of pain and agony deafened me as he rolled, facedown into the burning embers.

I took hold of his feet and dragged him out. Pulling off my jacket, I smothered the flames on his clothing. It was the most ungodly sight, his face. It was charred beyond recognition.

"I'll be back in a minute!" I shouted as I raced to the telephone box and dialed the emergency number.

"Fire, police, or ambulance," came the immediate response.

"Ambulance, please. My name is John Dunne. I am reporting a burn victim. There has been a severe burning accident. Someone fell in the bonfire near St. Blaze school. Send an ambulance immediately." I hung up and hurried back to the scene.

Webber was going through the most awful shaking I had ever seen. I considered lying on top of him to try to stop him. What were you supposed to do in a case like this?

"There is an ambulance on the way!" I yelled, not knowing if he could hear me. "Just try to breathe evenly." I didn't know if that was what you should say. I felt I should say something.

His body was totally out of control. As I looked at him, I couldn't feel any pity or guilt. He had been ready to take a knife to my face. He had caused Sheila a terrifying experience that same evening. Within three minutes, the ambulance was there, and the attendants took over with brisk precision.

"Are you a friend?" they asked.

"I know him, but we're not friends."

"Do you want to go with him to the hospital?"

"I'll follow on my bike," I volunteered.

"St. John's then, emergency entrance."

"See you there." I strode toward my bike.

The emergency room was filled with other burn victims. Webber received top priority. A policeman was taking statements from family and friends of victims.

"I was riding my bike home. As I passed the bonfire, I noticed him—Webber, that is—running past the fire. He tripped and fell into it. I pulled him out and called the ambulance. That's all I know."

I didn't know where he lived, but the policeman did. Webber was a familiar figure to them.

"I feel sorry for the poor bastard," said the policeman. "He's a nasty piece o' work really, always in some trouble. Last time I heard, he was on probation for assault with a dangerous weapon. Doesn't look like he'll assault too many people from now on. Hell, he's lucky to be alive."

Webber recovered enough by midmorning to confirm my story that it was an accident. The next day, the report was in the local papers. I had become a real hero in the Clegg household.

When I called on Sheila the next day, she was still pale and withdrawn. Her mother fairly glowed with praise for my heroic act in saving "that poor boy's life."

Sheila wanted to go out, so we went for a walk in the park. It was cold and damp, but I had to have sane privacy to tell her the whole story.

Sitting silently on a bench, she let me finish telling it.

"John, I don't believe you."

"What do you mean, you don't believe me?"

"I don't believe that's what happened. It's just too much of a coincidence that you would run into them. I think that you were so angry at them for what they did to me, you went and found Webber and took revenge on him."

"Sheila…"

"I don't care," she cried as she smothered me in moist kisses that were salty from her tears. "I don't care, I love you for it. He is a monster, he only got what he deserved. If you hadn't done something, I would have lived in terror for the rest of my life."

She was shivering. I couldn't tell if she was reliving the awful experience or if it was the dampness in the air. I was feeling cold myself.

"Look, let's either go to the movies or let's go back to your place and watch the TV."

"I don't want to go to the movies. Let's go home."

The house was deserted. Sheila's mother and father had gone to a dinner dance. Barry had gone to visit a cousin in New Hampshire.

"Why didn't you say that your mum and dad were going out?"

"Oh, I forgot," she replied in an offhand way. "Light the fire please. Would you like a cup of tea or coffee or lemonade?"

"Lemonade please," I answered, turning on the TV and the small lamp on top of it.

Lighting the fire was simple—just turn the gas valve and strike a match. The authentic artificial logs glowed like real ones. I thought of the terrible job it was back in Galway, with all the dampness. I was just turning off the overhead light as she returned from the kitchen.

"So this is how the rich folk live," I commented as she deposited two glasses of lemonade and two Twinkies on the coffee table.

"Don't be silly." She was attempting to smile, but she was still troubled.

"Sheila, I want you to understand how it really was with Webber—"

"I don't care. I don't want to—" She advanced toward me, reaching out to kiss me and shut me up.

This time she was going to hear what I had to say. I raised both hands to stop her and push her back. As she accelerated, her breasts stopped my hands. I jumped back as though I had received an electric shock. She then grabbed my hands, replacing both of them on her breasts, and continued to advance.

The backward motion caused me to trip over the arm of the settee. She followed and tumbled on top of me.

"Please, please don't, please don't ever mention it again. Please, John, please just kiss me," she moaned. "I know you did it for me. You've shown me that you love me, now show me some more."

With her laid on top of me, I was wedged. I couldn't move without pushing her on to the floor. She held my hands tightly to her breasts as she kissed me with more fervor than ever before.

It was most uncomfortable, not the way I had fantasized. The first time I had had my hands in "forbidden territory" with consent. The only other time I had had a "feel" was with a plump fourteen-year-old in the swimming pool. I accidentally touched her while we were fooling around. She hadn't objected, but neither had she responded.

I didn't know what to do. Sheila wriggled around to lie alongside me. She kept my left hand firmly on her right breast and started move my hand in a small circular motion. I started to massage the beautiful, firm flesh. I felt her nipples harden while simultaneously I started to harden.

"Oh Sheila, I've wanted to do this ever since I first saw you. I love you."

"And I've wanted you too," she breathed.

Looking down, the tiny pearl buttons seemed ready to pop open. Dare I go further? I was afraid that if I made one wrong move at this point, she would stop and I would burst. My thumb and forefinger started to unbutton the blouse. She snapped all the buttons open and lifted the bottom of her bra to expose the whole breast. My eyes were blinking with the sweat, but I was too close not to see the perfectly formed beauty, the nipple erect. She brought her hand to the top of my head and gently pulled me down to kiss it. It seemed so natural now, I caressed her and gently sucked.

Her whole body quivered with delight.

She was moaning ecstatically, "I love you, oh, how I love you."

Her hand moved steadily down my back, around my buttocks, and started toward my crotch. If she touched me, I would come for sure. I swiveled around on to my belly so it was impossible for her to reach me.

My left hand dropped to her leg, just above the knee. She was writhing, her legs were splayed wide open. My hand advanced. As it reached the top of her stocking, I felt the unfamiliar suspender from her garter belt. I paused and gently stroked the inside of her inner thigh. Our breathing was coming in short gasps, and Sheila was going wild. Almost angrily she grabbed my hand. I misinterpreted and panicked. I started to pull my hand away, but she pulled it back to the top of her legs. Her panties were wet. She started to press my hand against her and start it massaging her.

She raised her buttocks, and with one hand she slipped off her panties. My fingers were stroking the moist pubic hair then searching inside her. I started to steadily move my fingers in and out.

She responded by forcibly pushing me on my side and started to unbutton my fly. I couldn't wait any longer. I stood up quickly, ripped open my pants, removed one leg, and lowered myself into position.

"I can't get it in," I gasped.

I was thrusting in every direction but the right one. She reached down and placed the head at the entrance.

"Don't push too hard. Gently, gently…"

I could feel the moistness of the entrance. I thrust gently as she ordered.

"Arrgggh," I cried. I had come.

I hadn't even got it all in. I didn't know if I got any of it in at all. I could have died of embarrassment.

"I'm sorry, Sheila."

"Sorry for what? You were wonderful."

"But I came too soon. Before I even got it in."

"Well, you'll do better next time. But you were absolutely wonderful. That was better than anything I'd ever dreamed of. Much better than anything my friends have described to me when they've done it."

"You mean you girls talk about what you do with your boyfriends?"

"Some of them do. I've never had anything to talk about. In fact, I was on the verge of thinking that you didn't really want me. Sexually, that is. I thought you just wanted me as a friend."

"Sheila, I've been crazy about you. I've dreamed day and night about doing this. I've been afraid that if I tried something, you might be insulted and wouldn't want me anymore."

"Well, thank God you did tonight because I was losing patience with you. Now, do you mind letting me get up? You're heavy."

I pushed myself up with great reluctance. She swung her delightful legs around to sit on the edge of the settee. She deftly replaced her bra over her gorgeous breasts and started to button the lower buttons of her blouse.

"Is that why you have been so moody lately?"

"John Dunne, I had got to the point that I just didn't want to be alone with you. You would hold me and kiss me and tell me you loved me. You would work me up to a fever pitch and then nothing. Do you know how many times I have wanted to scream at you?"

"Have you any idea how many times I wanted to scream at you?"

"You have screamed at me. Every time you held me I could feel you. You didn't scream in words, but your body said enough. How could you feel that way and not make a move?"

"I was scared of rejection, if you had said no…"

"Kathleen O'Donnell told me that you did it with her."

"Kathleen O'Donnell is a bloody liar. I never even took her to the movies. I saw her in the park a few times, but I never did anything but kiss her. You've got to believe me." Why was I defending myself?

"I know she's a liar. She just wanted to make me jealous."

I had slipped on my pants and reached down to pick up the exciting garment she had cast off a few moments earlier.

"Are you going to put these back on?" I grinned, dangling her panties in front of her, the flicker of the firelight causing the satin material to shimmer. "Or can I keep them to show Kathleen O'Donnell and the boys?"

"John Dunne, you wouldn't…" She looked as though she would burst into tears.

"Of course, I wouldn't," I said, taking her gently in my arms and kissing her lightly on the forehead,

"I've never talked about you or any girl for that matter. Not that there has ever been anything to talk about. I certainly will never talk about you." I stroked her back and said, "I would like to tell the world about you. You are the most beautiful creature ever created, and I love you with all my heart." Offering the delicate panties, I said, "Here they are, you'd better put them on, or you'll catch cold or something."

"Well, I will if you really want me to," she said coyly, "but I was rather hoping that you might want to have your wicked way with me again," she finished, laughing hysterically. I was blushing from embarrassment as she slipped away to the bathroom.

I took out my handkerchief to try to wipe up the mess of my ejaculation from the settee. I wasn't doing too good a job as she returned with a damp cloth.

"Let me do that," she said as she leaned over me, starting to sponge at the sticky spot. "Look at what you have done to my pretty skirt." She twirled to display the damp spot on the back.

"Oh my God, what will you do?"

"I'll just wet it thoroughly and tell Mummy that I sat in something."

"Are you sure you haven't done this before? You seem to know all the things to do."

"Don't you ever say that again. I have never been with another boy, ever. What about you, with your reputation. I bet you have been with lots of other girls. None of them have actually admitted they have been with you, but most of them act like they know something I don't know."

"My reputation," I scoffed. "Does my performance tonight make you believe I've had any other experience? I wish I'd had some so it could have been better for you. Believe me, I was a virgin. I probably still am a virgin because I don't think that counted and probably so are you."

"I am," she admitted, laughing, "but you're not leaving me tonight before we change all that." Giggling, she fell on top of me. "So I'm really the Delilah that championed Samson?"

We laid for a while, embracing one another, not saying a word. I gently stroked her back and her neck. She ran her fingers through my hair and started gently biting my earlobe. I ran my hands across her buttocks, something I had never dared to do before. She pressed hard against me and sighed.

"Did you really mean it when you said it was wonderful?" I asked, still full of self-doubt.

"It was marvelous."

"Yes, but I didn't even…" not knowing how to complete the sentence.

"That didn't matter. For me, it was fabulous. You were so tender and caring. I had three orgasms."

"You did? When?"

"The first time was in the park, the second time was when you started sucking on my breasts, and the third time was when you massaged me. Down there…on my tender spot."

"Maybe I should have talked more to some of the other chaps about their conquests. I feel so ignorant, so dumb. Not only don't I not know how to do it, I don't even know what I'm supposed to do."

"I don't know that much either," she confessed. "Won't it be fun though finding out together?" She giggled in that most inviting way.

"It will, it sure will," I laughed, losing some of my self-consciousness.

"Do you want to watch some TV?"

She stood up and walked toward the TV standing in the corner. My thoughts were flying all over the place. I started to say something, but the words were choked off as she turned and undid her belt. Her dress dropped to the floor. She was naked from the waist down. Bending one leg slightly, as though posing, she slowly started to unbutton the blouse.

"Or are you ready for round two?"

I was already hard. I felt like I would come again just looking at her.

The blouse slid to the floor. She bent forward slightly as she undid the hooks on the bra at the back. Tantalizingly she let the bra slip away to reveal all. She lowered her eyes.

"Well?" she demanded.

"I'm ready, I'm ready." Standing, I frantically started pulling my shirt over my head.

"Wait a minute, don't be in such a hurry, I want to watch you. You watched me. Now one button at a time."

I tried. I really tried to do it slowly, but my mixture of excitement and embarrassment was so acute I couldn't stand it. I was blushing, and sensing my embarrassment, she stepped closer and started to help me. We quickly finished the disrobing, and I drew her to me.

"Sweetheart," she interrupted my passionate kissing, "we will have to be careful this time. It was a good thing in a way that we didn't do it properly the first time. I'm sure we would have made a baby if you had come inside me."

"Were you scared?"

"Scared? I was absolutely terrified."

"Then why did you let me?"

"I didn't care. I wanted you so much. I knew what I was doing, and I was prepared to accept the consequences. But this time we must be more careful. Promise me, when you feel yourself coming, you will pull it out."

"I promise, I promise," I breathed.

I was getting harder and harder by the second. Her arms encircled my neck. Lowering her gently to the floor, I pulled a throw cushion from the settee and slid it under her buttocks.

Her back was arched, and her pelvis raised. I knelt between her legs. She reached for the end of my penis and directed it to the spot.

"Gently, please gently. It's going to hurt me. Gently."

I could feel her stiffen her muscles, not allowing me to penetrate, as I started to thrust.

"Relax," I said, "I will never be able to do it if you are all tight."

"Sorry, but I'm so scared. Please don't hurt me."

"If it is going to hurt you, then we won't do it," I said.

"Oh yes, you bloody will," she said, gritting her teeth. "If you quit on me now, I'll scream. Just be gentle, okay?"

She started to relax, and I decided to massage her a little before I started again. Tenderly I stroked her mound of pubic hair and slowly ran my fingers over the entrance, progressively allowing my fingers to creep into the soft moist crevice. I located what she had described as her "tender spot" and started to slowly massage it, quickening the movement until she was breathing so fast I thought she was going to burst with the pressure she was building up inside.

"Arrggh," she almost screamed, "now, now, put it in now!"

I moved into position and felt that I was right and gently started to push. She was still very tight, but the lubrication provided by her juices made it less painful for both of us.

"Gently, please."

"Yes, darling, gently," I breathed as I pushed a little harder. I felt her muscles stiffen again. "Relax, relax, I won't hurt you."

She relaxed for a moment, and I pushed again. This time I felt a shudder go through her. There was a faint cry of pain and then a tremendous sigh as she placed both hands on my buttocks and pulled me into her.

It was the most unbelievable feeling. She was so warm inside, and we were locked into the most intimate of all embraces. I could feel it coming. How long dare I stay like this? I had only made a half dozen thrusts, and I was already coming.

She was holding me so tightly and obviously didn't want me to move. I pushed away just in time as my ejaculation spewed all over her belly.

"My God," I said, "you nearly got it all that time. You were the one who was scared. Couldn't you tell I was coming?"

"Thank you. I must have lost my mind. I was scared, but it felt so good I wanted to feel everything. I'm glad you didn't though."

She reached up and pulled me down on top of her. I could feel the sticky substance between our bellies. The thought of how close we had come caused me to shiver, contemplating the consequences.

During the passion of the lovemaking we had generated our own body heat. Now, even with central heating and the fire warming, I felt a slight chill.

"Come on, let's wash this stuff off us and get some clothes on. We'd better not tempt fate. Daddy might have too much to drink and come home early, or Mummy might get bored and feign one of her headaches."

I glanced at the clock. It was nine thirty. Two hours ago we had been sitting on a park bench. Tonight's experience had seemed to be light years in the future. We went upstairs, carrying our clothes, arms around each other. We went into the bathroom together. After we had cleaned up, we stepped across the hall to her bedroom to get dressed.

"Next time we do it in bed," she stated. "That carpeted floor is all right in the movies or in books, but it's too uncomfortable for me."

"I'd do it on a cedar shake roof in the snow."

"Not with me, you wouldn't. You'll have to find someone else if you want to do dirty stuff. Another thing, this is private. I don't want you trying to feel me up in the movies."

"Sheila, I love you more than anything in the world. The last thing I would do is cause you any embarrassment. I will always treat you as a lady in public." She smiled gratefully. "And in private I'll treat you like the slut you really are." I laughed as she threw a shoe at me that hit me in the stomach.

We went down stairs and watched a variety show on the TV, which neither of us were really interested in. I decided to leave around twelve thirty before her mum and dad came home.

# Chapter 5

It was late February. I had rushed through my lunch and left the school dining room just in time to catch the bus that would drop me at Clegg, Bates and Taylor. I always seemed to be in a hurry everywhere these days.

I started to cross the street, pausing to allow a car to pass me before crossing. It drew up alongside and gave a short toot on the horn.

It was Sean at the wheel. He'd come back to the States just before last Christmas. He had stayed with me in my room for the first month, and we had become great friends.

"Hello there, m'boyo. Get in."

"I'll be late for work. I have to catch my bus, it's coming now."

"I'll take you. Come on, jump in."

I climbed into the passenger seat and the car accelerated down the hill.

"Where did you get the car, Sean?"

"It's a company car, sure it is. Aren't I the executive now? One o' these days a bright lad like you, you'll have a car like this."

Sean and I still saw each other a lot. He and my main talked for hours at the kitchen table. He got along well with my uncles, the ones that were my mother's brothers. He was witty and charming.

Occasionally when he would get drunk, they would criticize him.

"Sure, and that Sean, he can't hold 'is beer. He's pissed out of his mind on four beers." They would laugh. "Thank God he got 'imself an education. He can't fight worth a shit. Young John 'ere could whip the fucking pants off him, and there must be, what, six years between 'em. Let's see now, John, how old are you?" Uncle John asked, turning to me, the perpetual observer of the "Brothers Council."

"I'm eighteen in two months, Uncle."

"Aye, and that weak-bladdered sod, Sean, must be twenty-four. Sure, and y' could kick the shit out o' 'im, couldn't y' now?"

"Wait a minute, 'e's not such a bad sort a chap," Stevie interjected before I had to answer.

I wasn't at all sure I could take Sean on in a fight. He was still a little bigger than I was, not much though. Still he had the psychological edge, being older.

"Oie'm not sayin' he's a bad chap. Just that he can't drink or fight. Sure, 'e's got the brains, didn't he go to University in Dublin? A major in Economics, if you please. Oie'm sayin' that if it come to a fight, oie would rather 'ave John Dunne at my side than Sean. As a fighter, sure enough 'e's a bloody washout, so 'e is."

"Y're right, no doubt about it. But he has 'is winnin' ways. He is bloody foine company. He's a great storyteller. Oie just love t' listen t' him tell the stories of back in Ireland. Tellin' us about the cousins back there in the old sod."

"Well, oie just know, he'd never last a day on the site if he had t' carry the hod. He'd be knackered in half an hour."

"Well then, isn't it to 'is credit that he doesn't 'ave to carry the hod like us lot. He can work in the office wi' other shiny arsed clerks. Oie understand he's got 'imself a very important job now."

"Aye, but he's in wi' a right lot. Oie wouldn't work for that bunch if they paid ten times—well, twice," Bartley corrected himself. "I wouldn't work for them if they paid twice the wages. Da always said they were a bad lot. Oie'll 'ave nuthin' t' do wi' them, Da said."

Sean and I had lapsed into silence as I had been reflecting on the view my uncles had of him. We were almost at the office.

Sean broke the silence.

"There's a fellow in your office called Ramsbottom, isn't there?"

"Yes, there is, he's in the accounting department. Do you know him?"

"No, I don't know him, but this friend of mine runs a messenger service." He took a deep breath. "Well, I owe him some money. He said that if I could help him out this afternoon, he would let me off the money I owe him."

Then came what I had learned was the "pregnant" pause. I didn't say a word. I knew he was working up to something, and I wasn't going to bite.

"Well, this friend—oie hesitate to call 'im friend. He breaks knuckles and things if y' know what I mean. He sez if I would pick up a package from these offices from this fellow, and I just wondered if you knew him."

"Yes, I do," I answered, wondering why he was telling me his troubles. How did a bright person like Sean get mixed up with people like that? He ought to have more sense.

"Well, there's coincidences. Oie need a big favor. Would y' be helpin' your cousin Sean out a bit?"

"What is the favor?" I asked flatly. He was getting smarmy, and I didn't like it.

"Well, oie'm doin' this errand on the side, y' see. Oie 'ave to do it, or oie'm in big trouble. Well, oie just can't go into Clegg, Bates and Taylor's offices as large as life and pick up a package."

"Why not? We have messengers come in all the time."

"Well, y'see, John, it's this way. Oie work for a competitor. The Fuller Company. Oie don't know who might know me in there at Clegg's. If someone recognizes me, two things could happen. One, they could throw me out. Two, they could call Fuller's and ask what oime doin' there. If Fuller's found out, oie'd really be in the shit. Oie could lose m'job. Y' wouldn't want to see me fired, now would y', Danny Boy?"

"What's the favor?" I said testily.

"Well, oie was wonderin', if oie called Ramsbottom and told 'im t' give the package to you, you could nip downstairs and give it to me. Save m' goin' inside."

"What about my job, Sean? What if I lose my job?"

"Sure, an' nobody'll miss y'. Isn't you that's like a bloody whippet? Fastest thing on two legs in all of America. Sure, if some of the horses oie'd backed had been as fast as you, oie wouldn't be in the spot oie'm in now." He smiled.

He was flattering me, appealing to my vanity. I wasn't the fastest in all of America, but I had recently run the hundred-yard dash in 10.30 seconds. On the football field there weren't too many faster.

It didn't seem like such a big thing.

"All right, when do you want me to bring it down?"

"Three o'clock on the button. You see that shop on the corner?" He indicated the candy store. "Upstairs is a Bookies, oie'll meet y' in the doorway. God love y', it's goin' t' work out beautiful. Oie'll be able to get a bet down on the three o'clock race. Oie've got a dead cert, Danny Boy, and the way this buggers been running, oie'll be makin' a fortune."

God, when would he ever learn? Ever since we had become friendly, I had shown him how to read the form books. I had learned from Uncle Bartley who was also not the greatest tipster in the world. Every time we all got together my uncles would have a horse they fancied.

"Sure, and this one here, hasn't he been placed the last three times out. He's due for sure, his time has come today," either Sean or one of my uncles would say.

"The last three times out, the distance was six furlongs and seven furlongs. It says here that it tired at the end. This race is a mile, and it's carrying the same weight and has the same jockey, it doesn't have the stamina," I said. "And what's more, *it* is a filly, which is a she."

"A mere fucking detail, clever bugger. I'm tellin' y' this sod can run whether *she* has balls or no balls. I can feel it in m' bones." It was always the same and always an excuse. I didn't fare much better, but then I didn't bet the amounts that they did.

"There is no such thing as a dead cert, Sean."

"There is when you know the fix is in. I have it from the horse's mouth. Listen, oie'll call Ramsbottom and ask him to give you the package. You can give me the package, and I'll get my bet down. I'll put a dollar on him for you. The odds should be at least fives so it would be five bucks for you."

"Okay, three o'clock. If you're not at the corner store at precisely three, I'm going straight back to the office, and you can come and get it yourself, understood?"

"Understood, understood." He nodded.

The afternoon went as usual. I helped out and took messages to different departments.

At ten minutes to three, Ramsbottom came to me with a bulky brown envelope and said, "You're going to give this to the messenger?"

"Yes."

"He should be there now. Off you go, careful no one sees you."

It wasn't that much different from many of the packages I had delivered to other places. I slipped it under my arm and walked out of the office. Taking the stairs two at a time I raced to the corner. It couldn't have taken me two minutes. Sean was standing in the doorway.

"God bless you and keep you, Danny Boy."

"Well, that's that then," I said. "I'm off back."

"Just a minute, just a minute. Oie know you're going to be mad with me. Oie just learned oic'vc got to bring another parcel back here at four. Oie was just thinkin' if you could meet me here at four, oie could pick up my winnings and give you yours. Then you could take the parcel back."

"What!" I said, "You can't be serious."

He gave a helpless shrug of his shoulders.

"Danny Boy, just one last favor. Oie promise oie won't ask any more, please."

He really looked worried, and it had only taken me two minutes to run down. The truth was he had that way with him that made it very difficult to refuse.

"Okay, four o'clock, don't be late, or I'm not waiting."

"Four o'clock it is then."

No one had missed me, and I got busy with same column adding that Mr. Clegg had given to me. Checking the clock at exactly five minutes to four, I left the office and repeated my high-speed sprint to the corner store.

No Sean. Where was he? I had told him I wasn't waiting. I checked with a clock in a jeweler's window, and the time said four minutes past four. In one minute I was leaving. I watched the second hand trace around the face of the clock three times. I started to return to the office when suddenly Sean drew up in a car.

"Sorry, Danny Boy, oie know you're mad at me, but here's your winnings and the package. The odds were ten to one."

He was gone, leaving me standing angrily on the street with a brown envelope just like the one I had given him and a ten-dollar bill.

Returning to the office as quickly as I'd left it, I almost bumped into Ramsbottom.

"Thanks," he whispered. "Everything okay then?"

"I suppose so."

He casually took the envelope and walked away.

The next few days were busy. Work was hectic, and school was beginning to reach that point in the year when all I could think about was quitting and going to work full-time.

It was February 20. The announcement in the Boston Globe said there was an inquiry being made into the professional and business practices conducted by Clegg, Bates and Taylor.

The charges were that they had conducted themselves in unethical and illegal ways in order to secure both local and national government contracts. The main focus of the inquiry was around the new low-income projects being built on the south side.

Sheila was waiting for me at the bus stop.

"No work today," she said unhappily. "There's a right bloody mess going on at the office. Everybody's been sent home."

"I read a little about it in the morning paper. What's going on?"

"The county auditors arrived this morning with the police to seize the books for the firm. It's caused a lot of excitement and concern amongst the employees. They have search warrants for the safety deposit boxes at the bank and a search warrant for our house. Can you believe it? Daddy is walking around in a daze. The nuns are even more worried than Daddy." She always referred to Bates and Taylor as the nuns. "Of course, they don't know anything about accounting.

They kept saying, 'Yes, but what if they find something?' Daddy kept saying there's no problem, there's nothing to find. John, all the accounts are in good order. I don't know why they are all so upset. Let them examine the books, everything balances. They can check every entry if they want to. I know that Daddy's books are clean."

"It's upsetting though," I said, as reassuring as I could. "Having search warrants for your home, that's pretty drastic."

"Yes, that's the worst thing. If they had just come in quietly and done the books, that wouldn't be so bad. It's the scandal, in the newspapers, all the bad publicity. Six customers called already and said to put a hold on their work until after the inquiry is finished. These are bids for new work. We could lose those contracts. It could be very costly."

That evening Mr. Clegg told me that "under the circumstances" they would not be able to keep me on as a part-time clerk. Perhaps when everything was cleared up, they would be able to take me back.

"Do you know, John, they have interviewed every employee in the accounting department?" Sheila said indignantly. "It was awful, all thosc questions, just like we were common criminals."

"Easy does it, Sheila. They are only doing their job. The charges that have been made are very scrious. The tax payers have a right to expect them to do a thorough job. Don't worry about it. Everything will be all right. I'm just sorry for all the employees having to go through this questioning, but I understand why."

"Have the police interviewed you, John? You never said anything about it if they did?"

"No. No one has contacted me." I wasn't sure if I was eager to be "grilled," as they said in the cops and robber books.

"They probably won't question John," Mr. Clegg explained. "When John started with us, I couldn't add anyone to the payroll in the accounting department. We were over budget. I hired him in the maintenance department as a "part-time" janitor. As far as the auditors are concerned, he never worked in the department. They can't possibly interview all the hundreds of people that work for us. They'll just stick to the accounting staff."

"Think yourself lucky, John," Sheila said. "It's not much fun, is it?" she said to her father.

In the continuing weeks when I visited Sheila's, I noticed that Mr. Clegg was becoming more and more withdrawn. He wouldn't discuss the subject even in casual conversation.

Reading the newspaper reports, apparently someone had notified the authorities that the company had been involved in "payoffs." Highly placed members of the city councils were mentioned and some in the city engineering and architect's offices. It was alleged that these payoffs were to ensure that Clegg, Bates, and Taylor knew ahead of time what the low bid would be. This virtually assured them of the contract. After the contract was awarded, the engineers and architects would make changes that had to be paid for as extras. This allowed the firm to charge exorbitant prices for these "unscheduled" changes. It was estimated that hundreds of thousands, perhaps millions, of dollars had been paid out through this scheme. The "secret source" claimed that there was a separate set of books, but no evidence had been found so far.

# Chapter 6

The birds had started to build their nests high in the trees this year. As the milder weather started to treat Boston kindlier, I had tried to persuade Sheila to do something different. I offered to repair her old bicycle, and we could go for a ride in the park or around the lake.

After a lot of cajoling, she finally agreed to trying "just a couple of miles on Sunday if the weather's nice, then we'll see if I'm up to the long stuff."

Excitedly I dug her old Schwinn out from under the rest of the rubble in the garage. The main thing it needed was a good cleaning and oiling. It also needed some new brake pads, a battery for the lamp, and a spring to make the bell ring. Making out my list, I committed to fixing it on Saturday morning, the day before our ride.

I arrived at eight thirty Saturday.

"I have everything here to make you ready for the tour de force. It shouldn't take me more than an hour or so."

"Sure," she said with a twinkle in her eye, "I can't wait to go for a ride."

"That's the spirit."

Going into the garage, I set the bicycle up and removed the wheels and cleaned everything. I finished off with a light clean film of oil. Having almost finished, it was looking very sharp. I ran into a snag.

One of the nuts on the front brake shoes had rusted solid, and I couldn't budge it. Looking around the garage for some penetrating oil, I discovered that although there were paint cans with every color in the rainbow, there was no penetrating oil. I went into the house as Mrs. Clegg was about to leave.

"I'm going down town shopping, Sheila. Don't you forget to do the breakfast dishes, and both of you, don't get up to any mischief."

"Before you go, Mrs. Clegg, does Mr. Clegg have any penetrating oil?" She looked at me as if I'd asked for some mystical substance. "One of the nuts is rusted fast, and I don't want to shear it off. I need something that will loosen it."

"If there isn't anything in the garage, I don't know where you might find something like that. Wait a minute, perhaps down in the basement. Daddy keeps some old tools and things down there. Sheila, show John where to look. I'm late, got to go. Sheila, you're going to the basketball game to watch Barry and John. Your daddy is going straight there from the office. So I'll see you tonight for supper."

Sheila followed her mother to the door and waved her goodbye as she closed the gate. Now I understood the twinkle in her eye. Her enthusiasm hadn't been for my fixing up the bike. It was because she knew we were going to be alone for about two and a half hours. Barry wouldn't be coming home. He had a job down town on Saturday mornings and would go straight to school for the game.

"I've always fantasized about being raped by a black man," she laughed.

"What?"

"Look at yourself."

Glancing in the mirror in the hallway I saw what she meant. I was covered in oil and grease. I must have wiped my hands across my face several times. It was streaked with black. I feinted a lunge at her, and she let out a little scream.

"Stop it, Mom's not out of earshot yet. She'll think you really are trying to rape me. Get away from me with those filthy hands. If you touch me, I'll hit you with something."

I had her backed against the wall, a millimeter between our noses. Both of us leaned forward so that nothing else touched. She puckered and kissed me lightly on the lips.

"You get that job finished fast, and I'll show you what good little boys get, okay?"

"Okay," I sighed. "Show me where the stuff is in the cellar."

"You had better clean sane of that oil off before you do," she said, producing some cleaning liquid from under the sink. "Daddy keeps everything so neat and tidy. Nobody but nobody ever touches any of his things down there. He'll have a fit if you make a mess. Make sure you put everything back just as you found it."

I washed my hands thoroughly and then followed as she led the way down the steps.

"If there is anything, it's probably over in that corner by those old tool boxes." She motioned toward the far corner. "I'm going to leave you. I'll finish those dishes and prepare myself for a fate worse than death."

"Hold on, I have a game to play this afternoon, and I had better have something to eat soon. If I wait too long, it won't have settled in my stomach. Can you fix me something light?"

"Anything you want, Master. What would you like?"

"Do you have any custard pies?"

"No, but I can get some. I'll just run to the bakery and pick up a couple."

"Don't do that. Don't go to any trouble."

"It's no trouble. Anyway, you're probably going to be a while. You don't want me breathing heavy down your neck. I'll be back soon." She went back upstairs.

I sorted through the multitude of cans with various contents. A quick examination of the cans revealed no luck. I decided to check out the tool boxes. The first two showed nothing I could use. The third and largest box had a revelation that changed the rest of my life.

The top item of the toolbox was a heavy manila envelope which was labeled *Dunne*. I couldn't believe it. Why would a folder with my name on it be in a toolbox down in the Cleggs' basement?

I speculated for several minutes on what it might contain. It wasn't sealed. It had one of those red cloth tapes that tied around it to keep it closed. My curiosity got the better of me, and I opened it.

Inside was another envelope, a large bulky one addressed to Mr. Jones c/o of a PO box in Waltham. The envelope contained an accounting book, a ledger. It was about seven inches by twelve inches and an inch thick. I recognized it. It was one I had been given on several occasions at the office to make entries in and balance the columns. It was smaller than all the others in the office. What is this doing here, and why not at the office?

My initial thought was that Mr. Clegg must have created some work for me that didn't really apply to the business. Just practice, so to speak, so I could learn the fundamentals of accounting without taking the risk of my fouling up the company's real books.

As I looked closely at the entries I had made in the neat printing that I was so proud of, the names suddenly screamed out of the pages. When I had done them, they meant nothing, just names. Now these were names that had been in the headlines of the local and national newspapers. Names associated with the "alleged" misdeeds of the scandal at Clegg, Bates and Taylor.

This was the evidence that the authorities had been looking for. I leafed back through the pages. The last ten pages were all in my handwriting. The prior ones were in another hand. Going back over almost three years I mentally added up the amounts.

If my limited knowledge of bookkeeping was accurate, the payouts were something in excess of three million dollars. I wanted to throw up. I felt betrayed, used. How could a man I had looked upon as a second father have done this and made me a part of it?

Obviously, I was perfect for the job. Nobody ever checked my work or cared particularly what I was doing in the office. I could admit it to myself now; most of the people that worked there had said as much. The job had been created for "the future son-in-law."

Every word was true, all the things that had been said in the newspapers. Every syllable was absolutely true.

I replaced the folder exactly as I found it. My mind was racing. How could I confront him? What would I say? Closing the tool box, I sat for a moment and tried to collect my wits. Sheila will be back in a moment. I can't tell her.

Returning to the garage, I started to take out my anger on the frozen nut. It loosened, and I was just finishing replacing it when Sheila came out of the back door.

"If you didn't look so scruffy, I would take advantage of you right here on the garage floor," she teased.

"Not now, Sheila, I've got to finish this."

"Umph," she reacted to my rejection, "all right, but don't be long."

I deliberately took my time and didn't finish the bike until about twelve thirty. After eating the custard pies, I made an excuse to leave, that we had to arrive at the gym early for a special practice. I left Sheila both frustrated and bewildered.

"I'll see you at the game."

"I'm not coming," she spat.

"Suit yourself," I replied, feeling like hell.

I hadn't exactly lied about having to be there early. The match was against one of our toughest rivals, Longmeadow, and we were going to have to play our hearts out to beat them. They had lost only one game, and so had we. Whoever won this afternoon would probably be the conference champions. I had to keep my concentration on the game, but I couldn't. The whole thing kept coming back into my mind. The company's growth over the last few years had been something of a phenomenon. Bigger and bigger contracts—they had been doing millions of dollars' worth of business, yet the profits on the books really only showed a small margin. Profits hadn't gone into buying new equipment either. They leased most of that. I have to think about the game. We have to work as a team today.

Alan Battle was their captain, and he had been needling me that they were going to beat the tar out of us.

Sheila did show up at the game, and it was a tough one. Midway through the first quarter we took a commanding lead. Then they came back and equalized. Alan was having a good game. I felt that we were beginning to gain the psychological edge. They had tried to make it more physical, and we were winning that fight also. A couple of times Alan had got away with charging, but he had hurt himself doing it. Alan Battle wasn't one who could take a lot of physical punishment.

He kept glowering at me and saying, "You're going to get it, Dunne. We've got your number."

Then I made my big mistake. We ran the same play one too many times.

We had gone into a special drill that was a favorite. Barry would deliberately throw a high shot to bounce off the back board. Everyone would leap for the shot, and I would float up as they descended and tip in the rebound.

My fingers had just felt the satisfying slap as I made the basket when I felt the hard shoulder driving under my left rib cage. Whoever it was had started his leap as I was coming down. At the same time someone else caught my legs and pulled them sideways. I was spinning like a top when I crashed into the boards and made a one-point landing on my shoulder.

The feeling of the collarbone breaking was the most vivid pain I had ever felt. It was as though I was in slow motion. I could feel the jagged broken ends threatening to puncture the skin. Staggering off the court, I was mad as hell.

I saw Mr. Clegg approaching from the top of the bleachers.

"We aren't waiting for an ambulance," Mr. Clegg declared. "We'll go in my car. It'll be much faster." He led me helplessly to the large Buick.

Sheila was already in the back of the car, crying. "Stop that, Sheila," he rasped.

The hospital was as uncaring as usual. I was a fairly frequent visitor for minor scrapes. This was my best, or worst, so far. Efficient, though; I had to give them credit. In no time at all they had put an "X" bandage around both my shoulders to pull them back into position. Gave me a plastic container with some pain killers, and I was free to go.

Mr. Clegg dropped Sheila at their house before he ran me home. I entered the empty house as he drove away. Taking two more painkillers, I lay down on my bed and fell asleep.

# Chapter 7

The luminous hands on the alarm clock showed twenty past seven. I couldn't get up; my arms wouldn't push me into the sitting position. I had had this same experience once before after I had dislocated both shoulders. They had been sore, but with a little massage, I had been able to lift myself. This was quite different. I swung my left foot out of the bed and hooked it under the frame. It took all my strength to lever myself into an upright position. My God, was this what I had to do for the next four or five weeks? Everyone was out. I made myself a corned-beef sandwich and munched on it alone, thinking more and more of having to face him.

Unable to ride my bike, I walked as briskly as I could to Sheila's, arriving at the end of the street about half past eight. As I approached the house, a voice behind me called.

"Hey, John, how are you feeling?" Mr. Clegg had been out to the corner store and was catching up with me. "Gosh, you look a bit pale. Are you sure you're all right?"

"Yes, I'm fine." He reached out to open the gate.

"Before we go in," I said hesitantly, "I want you to know that I know about the ledger. The second set of books you had me keeping for the payoffs."

He looked as though he'd been hit with a sledgehammer.

"You!" he gasped. "You, so it was you who's been spilling to the press. You'll ruin me. You'll ruin all of us."

He moved back a few paces and began gulping for air. His face turned quite ashen, and suddenly he looked much older. Then he clutched at his head and staggered toward the door. He collapsed on the front steps and laid there, his breath coming in harsh, quick spurts.

I rang the doorbell and stood helplessly. I couldn't do anything all strapped up like this. Barry arrived and immediately panicked. He started yelling for his mother, and Sheila to came at once.

"Get him inside," I said, taking command. "Sheila, get something to keep him warm. Mrs. Clegg, call for the ambulance. I think he's had either a heart attack or a stroke or both."

Barry was very strong and was able to drag him into the house. He lifted him on to the settee. Mr. Clegg came around a couple of times before the ambulance arrived. Each time he became conscious he looked at me, and terror appeared in his eyes. He gestured frantically for than to get me out of their house.

They all thought he was deranged, but to quiet him, I left the room and stayed out of sight until the ambulance arrived. Sheila and her mother went in the ambulance, and Barry and I followed in the car.

"What happened? Did you see him have the attack, or did you find him on the doorstep?"

"I met him at the gate. We were just talking when suddenly he turned very gray."

"He's been so upset lately, what with all the problems at the office. He's had a heart condition for years. I hope he's going to be all right. Mum just doesn't know how to cope without him."

He had already been taken into the special care unit when we arrived. We all met in the waiting room.

"What was he so upset about when he looked at you?" Sheila said to me.

"Maybe it's because I'm so pale. With this hump on my back, maybe he didn't recognize me in his condition."

"He looked like he had seen the devil himself when he looked at you. I've never seen Daddy frightened before, but he was absolutely terrified."

We waited for two hours, and I was beginning to tire. Although I wanted to stay, I could tell that I couldn't last very much longer. I indicated I was going to leave, and Barry insisted on driving me home. He continued to speculate on what had precipitated the attack, but I didn't enlighten him.

When I stopped at the house the next morning, Barry answered the door but didn't welcome me in.

"How is he? Has there been any improvement?"

"He's resting as comfortably as possible. He's had a stroke and is paralyzed from the waist down. His speech is very slurred." He stepped out to the front step, closing the door behind him.

"We left the hospital about seven this morning, and Mum and Sheila are in bed. The doctor gave them some sleeping pills. He—Dad, that is—did manage to say some strange things. He blamed you for the stroke. He said you had caused it, that you were the most evil person on this earth. He couldn't tell us why, but he made us promise never to associate with you again. Sheila was heartbroken, and Mum and I couldn't believe our ears. But because of the state he was in, we all agreed. What is going on? Why would he say a thing like that?"

I stood there in silent disbelief. The most important thing in life was being taken from me, and I couldn't do a thing about it. Unless I told the whole story. If I did that it might just kill him.

"I don't know. I have no idea. He must have some wild imagination."

"Well, for now at least we have agreed to abide by his wishes, not to see you. Perhaps when he's well again we can get him to talk about it. We can then find out what is bothering him and clear the whole matter up."

Sadly I walked away. I could feel Barry watching me as I opened the gate.

"It's not fair," I said, turning to look him in the eyes. "I have done nothing to deserve this."

His expression told me he believed me. He turned and went back in the house.

# Chapter 8

The next days and weeks were hell. Without Sheila, my life had become a complete void. Most of the time I would spend at Grandma's, playing cards with my uncles and aunts, and I would enjoy their stories.

Uncle John and Aunty Florrie weren't speaking to one another. I thought it was interesting that although she was mad with him about something, they would still come to Grandma's. They had a real sense of duty to her. Of course, if they hadn't come, they'd have had to supply a good excuse for Uncle Bartley. Since Granddad had died, Bartley was the head of the family, and everybody looked to him for advice and decisions. He flattered me by always discussing the problems with me.

"Y 'ave a good head on y' shoulders, and y' listen good. Even if y' don't know a thing about it, it helps t' talk to someone. An' y' don't go washin' y' dirty laundry wi' people outside the family," he had told me in one of his sober moments. He'd been watching John and Aunt Florrie all evening.

After Florrie had made several bad plays, Grandma got a little impatient. She was very competitive and didn't like to win unless the game was played well.

"So what's eatin' away at Florrie this evenin'?" she asked the open question to everyone.

"Nothing, nothing at all, Ma," Aunty Florrie said, obviously trying to control herself.

"Sure, and there is too. So what's this big lump been doin' t' y' now?" Grandma turned on Uncle John, who started to blush. "What 'ave y' been doin' t' this lass o' yours?"

"It's nothin' Ma, 'onest."

"Is it the belt y'd be wantin'?"

I started to giggle and only just stifled it. Uncle Bartley had given me a warning look. The thought of Grandma taking a belt to her twenty-five-year-old son seemed ridiculous. He was twice as tall, but he wilted under her look.

"I just had a bit o' bother, that's all."

"A bit o' bother, is it? A big enough bit t' make this poor lass almost in tears." Turning to Florrie, she said, "Now come on, out with it, what's 'e done?"

Florrie started to cry. "He shames me so, Ma, so he does." She blubbered a little and then went on. "We were out with my brother Jack and his wife. Having a nice night of it, we were. A few drinks around the neighborhood, then we finished up at La Florentine's. We'd had a few dances, and Mary and I went to the ladies to freshen up a bit. When we come back, our Jack and this cleft head are mixing it up on the dance floor. That was bad enough, sure he's had more than one fight when I've been out with him. It was what he did. They'd started the pushing and shoving and yelling, 'Come outside' to these two chaps, when this one says"—she hooked her finger at Uncle John—"'All right, you want a thrashin', here, y'll get one.' With that, he whips off his jacket, and underneath he had no shirt on."

Now I couldn't stop myself. I started laughing out loud.

"It's no laughing matter, John Dunne," Grandma hissed at me through her clenched teeth.

"Sorry, Gran—"

"Go on, Florrie," she said, ignoring me. My other uncles were all grinning behind Grandma's back.

"Sure, and the very reason he had no shirt was what he was fightin' about. He only has one good one, and that was dirty. We can't afford a new one until he gets back t' work. The fellas they were arguin' with, they work at Fuller's. They are all on overtime while our lads are laid off."

The tone of her voice had got stronger as she finished. I got the impression that she understood the reason for Uncle John's being mad at the dance when he stripped off his jacket. It was the shame of all Boston, knowing that he didn't have a decent shirt to wear that hurt her the most.

"So y' shamed y' wife did y'?" Uncle John hung his head. "It's interestin' t' me that y' would have the money t' go boozin' but no shirt t' y' back." Grandma glared at Uncle John as Auntie Florrie jumped to explain.

"Well, Ma, you have t' have a night out now and then. And it was Mary's birthday."

"He shouldn't go pickin' fights anyway. 'E's always ready with his fists, so he is."

"Yes, well, I know, but it was these chaps from Fuller's that started it." Florrie was now defending. "They were grigging our Jack and John about bein' on unemployment. Y' can't blame 'em for gettin' mad." She had now justified his actions to herself.

"Anyway, he might not have had a shirt, but he had the best set o' muscles in the room." She started laughing, and everybody joined in. The tension had been relieved, and Uncle John and Auntie Florrie gave each other a kiss.

They hugged one another for a few minutes until Grandma said, "Are we goin' t' finish this game?"

"Yes, Ma," they all echoed.

"Eyes down lookin', then," she said as the cards skimmed across the table.

I let some time pass before I asked the question, "How is it that Fuller's have their men on overtime, and you are laid off?"

"Since the Clegg, Bates and Taylor scandal, Fuller's have had the lion's share of the work. We wouldn't work for Fuller's, and they probably wouldn't hire us on," Uncle John explained.

"Why's that?"

"Well, y' Granda always said we should have no business w' the likes o' them. Sure, and himself always said that they were just a front for dirty money."

"A front for what?"

"For the IRA," he whispered. "Don't you ever breathe a word now," he added as the rest of the roam stared him into silence.

"That's just silly talk," Grandma interrupted. "Y' Granda was a very proud man. Years ago, back in the old country, him and Fuller had somethin' of a fight. Anyway, he'd never have, nor let any o' this lot, have anythin' do with 'em. That's the way the Irish are, they carry a grudge for at least five centuries. Then they drag it out, polish it, and fight about it again."

"That's strange. Cousin Sean works for them, you know."

Uncle John said, "Aye, well, that's different. Y' see, the old Fuller and y' uncle Sean, they were pals. In fact, old-man Fuller was with Uncle Sean when he died, on the way t' the Sinn Fein meeting together, they were. So y' see, Sean has a job for life, so he has. Say what y' like about 'em, they look after their own."

"How did it happen, Uncle Sean, I mean?"

"Oh, it was a terrible accident. Weren't they goin' t' this meetin', and Fuller had t' go back for somethin' just afore they got t' the meetin' place. When he got about twenty yards away, the booby trap went off. Sean must have thought someone else was inside and had already disarmed the trap. Stupid, it was, so it was."

I could feel the chill coming over me. Grandad had not told me the whole story, nor had he told his sons. If any of them had known what I knew, they would do the same addition that I had done. Fuller had been the childhood friend who had killed Uncle Sean. Grandad hadn't said so, but that was it.

"I swore I'd never take vengeance nor any of my sons take vengeance…" "I swore I'd never ask anyone to take vengeance…" I could still hear him and see his face, as he had said those words. Well, it wasn't five centuries since that happened. Fuller, I thought. And Sean working there as large as life—he couldn't know the truth.

"That's enough of that talk now, on with the game." Grandma was watching me. She knew that I knew—Fuller was the one who had betrayed and killed Uncle Sean.

"John Dunne, y' Granda always said that you would be the man we'd all be proud of. He always said John's so bright one day he'll be at the very top of whatever he chooses. Don't follow the example of these wild ones. Get your education and prove y' Granda right. Leave the stupid fightin' and politics to the crazy ones. Do y' hear me?"

"Yes, Grandma."

The voice was eighteen, but the mind was thinking back to years ago. Seeing that tall, powerful figure I had seen at the wake, the handsome face with the winning smile and cultured voice, I remembered the looks the other men had given him behind his back. They had envied him his material success, but they feared him. I also remembered Uncle Sean, how he'd sat me on his knee and held my hand as we sang.

Had Granddad been afraid of Fuller? Probably, but that wasn't what had stopped him. It was his promise to his murdered brother's wife. Every line in Fuller's face stood out so clearly in my mental image. His smile had changed to one of mockery. He was laughing at me.

"Don't worry, Granddad," I vowed silently. "I'll get them. I'll make him pay someday. You couldn't tell me yourself, but now I know. I'll take revenge for you and Uncle Sean."

# Chapter 9

The weeks stretched into months and years. Sheila was always on the horizon. Her father had never fully recovered from his stroke, and he was adamant that we should never see one another. Barry and I saw each other quite frequently, but he never spoke directly to me unless he was forced to. He was civil but not friendly.

I had been offered football scholarships by Notre Dame and Penn State but chose to stay close to home with an academic scholarship from MIT. The money wasn't as generous, but my love of engineering made up for any lack of funds. I completed my undergraduate and master's degree in six years and took a position with Land, Smith, and Grace, a small machine-tool builder whose reputation for quality and precision had impressed me. They were also gracious enough to allow me to accept a part-time teaching position one day a week; the extra income was attractive, and I still had ambitions to get my PhD.

Sean and I had built a close rapport. He continued to push me with his "What did you learn today?" The habit was a good one.

I enjoyed his company enormously, but socially, with girls, he was hopeless. He could amuse then and entertain them, but when it came to dating, he preferred his beer. As a result, we saw each other only on his frequent trips to Mam's house.

Lands', as everyone affectionately referred to them, indicated their willingness to sponsor me in a special six-month program at Harvard Business School. The course was designed for senior executives, most of whom had been in the business world for years. It meant getting someone to substitute for my teaching on Wednesdays, but it was worth it.

I took advantage of their offer, and with only two months left to complete the course, I was looking forward to June and being able to take a break from continuous education.

I seemed to have done nothing except work, study, eat, and sleep for the last few years. I hadn't minded, though; every subject was enjoyable. The subjects all had meaning and purpose. All of the education had a practical application.

Harvard was quite a different environment. I had never been exposed to such a mixture of people. The businessmen came from all over the world: Indians, Pakistanis, French, German, Italian, Swiss—even the native-born people were different. I found them fascinating. I had met many new friends, in particular, Neville Lipez.

Neville was an attorney who had come back to the law school for additional education. He practiced with one of the largest law firms in Boston.

Neville was about six feet three inches, swarthy skin, handsome features. He could have done an advertisement for Charles Atlas. He had invited me a couple of times to have a drink with him. Occasionally we would stop at one of the downtown "body shops" and pick up some of the local girls. After the dance we would go back to his house. His grandfather had left him a substantial amount of money. He decided that at twenty-five he ought to be independent and have his own home. A cleaning lady came in twice a week to clear up the rubble he had created. He enjoyed his bachelorhood immensely.

Neville's place became a second home; it was close to the campus, and as I hadn't yet been able to afford to buy a car, I slept there most nights while I was attending business school.

The relationship with Neville matured, and we became constant companions. We both enjoyed similar interests and had a mutual respect for each other's values and tastes. He was an exciting companion when we were out on the town, but most evenings we would stay home and just sit and talk.

One evening in mid-May, I was leaving the campus when I heard the horn of a car. Barry Clegg was waving to me, beckoning me to join him.

He had the old Buick, and it was looking a little worse for wear. I walked over to the car.

"Get in, John, please," he said rather urgently.

"Are you sure?"

"Please get in. I need to talk to you."

"Okay" I got in, and we pulled away.

"John, I really don't know to start with this. Let's go and have a drink."

We drove out of the city to a small bar in Chestnut Hill. The bar maid served us two beers, and we retired to a corner. Barry produced a piece of paper from his inside pocket.

"What do you know about this, John?"

It was one sheet of the ledger book that I'd kept at Clegg, Bates and Taylor.

I looked at the paper then at him. I drew a deep breath. Before I could answer, he said, "I recognized your handwriting, John. I've seen it many times when you made up the playbook for the team. You've always had a very distinctive hand. The way you print so clearly, it isn't a common way of writing. This is your handwriting, and I found this in our basement."

"Well," I hesitated, "when your father had me working at the office part-time, he had had me keeping this ledger. At the time I had no idea what it was. I just made the entries from slips of paper that he gave me and totaled the columns. I made sure they balanced and turned in the work. I didn't know that it was anything different than what the other people were doing in the office. I felt that it was less important because I was the office kid."

"You do realize what it is?"

"Yes," I said, "and I probably know where you found it."

"You do? How?"

I told him about the Saturday when I broke my collarbone and how earlier that day while repairing Sheila's bike I accidentally discovered the ledger book. I also told him how that night I confronted his father with it, and it had precipitated his father's stroke.

Barry looked at me for a long time.

"So that's why he told us all we were never to see you again. Now I understand."

"Not quite," I said, remembering when he clutched his head and accused me of blackmail. "Not quite. Apparently somebody else knew about the ledger and had been blackmailing your father."

He nodded his agreement.

"Your father assumed it was me. At the time, if you recall, it was during the investigation." I took a swallow of my beer. "Whoever it was that gave the reports to the newspaper must have been blackmailing your father. I speculated that your father had refused to continue to pay. So they spilled the beans to the press and the authorities. But they must not have had any evidence to show because none was ever produced. Your father had been smart enough to get the evidence out of the office before the auditor descended to grab the books." I leaned back, relaxing after being able to share the story after all those years.

"There has always been something unhealthy about Dad's relationship with the other two partners in the firm. I have always suspected that somehow when Grandfather took them in, he did it under a lot of pressure."

"The nuns," I said.

"What?" He gave me a blank look.

"They used to say that Bates and Taylor were like two nuns, they'd never be satisfied."

"Oh, I never heard that. It's true, though. They have been constantly badgering father to sell his stock. Almost on a monthly basis. They came over to the house, it usually starts out pretty friendly, but it always finishes with them getting mad."

"Why would they want to buy his stock? I understand that business has been pretty bad for the firm since the scandal."

"God, no! Business has been great this last year. This year we'll make the biggest profit ever. Even during the worst time, the first six months after the audit, they didn't lose money. In fact, Sheila made the comment to Father that maybe the audit wasn't all bad. We found out who our faithful customers were, and through belt-tightening, we were still able to do pretty well."

"You didn't have the extra profits drained off by the blackmailers either nor presumably the payoffs," I pointed out.

"That's true. Of course, Sheila and I didn't know that until now. You know, Sheila is really mad at Bates and Taylor. They both took terrific increases in salary. They gave her one, but nothing like what they took. She's running that office now. She has taken over completely all Father's responsibilities. Naturally she reviews everything with him in an evening. It's a tremendous job she's done. I'm really proud of her."

I realized then how much I had lost touch with her. Sheila had always shown a keen interest in the business, but I hadn't envisioned her being able to handle that big a job.

"I'm working at the firm now," Barry continued. "I hate accounting. I've been trying my hand in the construction department. My father is incapacitated, but he still owns a third of the company. Sheila and I ask questions on his behalf, and I don't get any answers that I understand. Sheila understands the business far better than I do, and she's not satisfied either. Another thing. Why hasn't father destroyed this ledger?"

I had thought about that.

"I think it's his protection. A lot of people could get hurt if it was ever found. That may be what Bates and Taylor fight with him about. If they know that he still has the ledger, he has them in as deep as he was. Another reason would be, since his stroke, he hasn't had access to it."

"Yes. It was a most effective hiding place under normal circumstances. Your finding it was a freak. I would never have gone down there if he were still active. He was the handy man, the Mr. Fix it. I had never even put a screw in until he got laid up. Now I do everything around the house."

I liked Barry, but I almost said "poor baby." This great kid had never had to hustle. I had probably done more physical work since I was seven years old than he would do in his entire lifetime.

"Who do you think was blackmailing him?"

I paused and started to review. Seven years was a long time, but it came back easily.

"I think I know who might be involved." I told him how I'd been asked to drop off a package. Then pick up a package. It seemed pretty innocent at the time. "Ramsbottom was the one who gave me the package to deliver." I didn't say it was Sean I'd given it to. I just told him I'd been asked to deliver it to some chap down at the corner store.

Barry clenched his fists on the table.

"I want to have a confrontation with Bates and Taylor. Ramsbottom will give us an explanation of what it was all about. I'm going to show them the ledger and tell them that it if I don't get this cleared up, I'm going to the police."

"Don't you realize what that could do, Barry, if it all comes out? You involve the police, and you have to involve your father. There is no doubt he was involved up to his neck, like it or not. He was fully aware of the payoffs that were being made. In his present state of health, it could kill him."

Barry hesitated, his sense of justice and fair play wrestling with his concern for his father.

"You're absolutely right. What can I do?"

"I don't know if there is anything you can do while your father's still alive. Even after his death I don't know that anything useful would be accomplished by going public. I don't think you have much of a chance of catching the blackmailer. If you do, what proof do you have that he did blackmail them? The blackmail stopped, I presume, when the story broke. That would have been the threat—the exposure. Now that's done, there is no more threat. The blackmailer can't hurt you unless he can tip off the police to the location of the ledger. He would expect your dad to have destroyed the incriminating evidence.

"The only people in the world that know it still exists are the two of us and your father, and Bates and Taylor. The only reason to keep it and not destroy it is to have a lever with Bates and Taylor." I paused. Much as I wanted him to do something, I couldn't accept the consequences. “Think of what it will do to the family, your mother and Sheila. It would ruin the business. That business is going to be a source of income for you all in the future if it is left alone. Don’t you think I’ve thought this through a hundred times? I’ve had to live with it for the past seven years.”

“I understand.” He used the words, but the tone carried frustration. “Sheila’s still in love with you, you know. She still carries that photo I took of the two of you when we went to the Cape.”

I didn’t answer. I had tried to develop calluses over that part of my memory.

“Well, if nothing else, I’m going to tell Sheila. I’m going to tell her that there is no reason for her not to see you.”

“You know why she can’t see me. If your father found out, it might cause another stroke. Neither you, Sheila, or I want that.”

“John, I can’t just do nothing. I have to get to the bottom of this.”

“I understand how you feel, but what can be done?”

“I’ll think of something.”

“Barry, before you do anything, please talk to me about it. It could be disastrous.”

He agreed. We finished our drinks, and he drove me home. My parting words were a plea again for him not to make a move without discussing it with me. Again he agreed.

With Harvard Business School behind me, I received a promotion. One of my new responsibilities at work was developing new attachments for the machines. We were constantly being contacted by outside inventors who had some new gadget. They wanted us to manufacture the product under license and sell it with our machines. They, of course, would receive a royalty on every one produced. My job was to review these ideas and determine if there was any merit to them. Some were fascinating but had no practical application. Others were useless. A few ideas found their way in that were potential gold mines.

Fred Braden was one of those intense types that his enthusiasm either made you love him or hate him. He had a concept that seemed to have a revolutionary approach to tracing shapes with a lathe. I was so impressed I convinced my boss and received the go-ahead to develop a working model of this new tracing device. After several weeks of negotiations, we got together and started to build one. It failed; however, I still felt that the principle had merit. We agreed to try again—and again and again.

We had about reached the end of our rope. I was beginning to be embarrassed by the failures, and my boss, Guy Williams, was becoming impatient at the amount of time and money we had sunk into it.

It was during one of our heated review meetings that I received a personal phone call, which was most unusual.

"Hello," I said, picking up the receiver.

"John?" My heart tightened. I wasn't quite sure. I daren't breathe. "John, is that you? This is Sheila." She spoke faintly.

"Yes, it's me," I croaked.

"John, I've got to talk to you. Please don't be angry with me. Please give me a chance, just to talk."

"Sheila, I'm not angry with you," I said quietly. "Of course, we can talk. When do you want to get together?"

"I can't do it today. How about Wednesday?"

"I teach at college on Wednesdays—"

"That's even better. Can we meet somewhere downtown for lunch?"

We agreed to meet at the Kardomah Restaurant in Quincy Market shortly after twelve.

Returning to Fred, I was in a semitrance. He could see I was shaken up.

"Are you all right?" he asked. "We can do this another time if you want."

"No, I'll be fine. Just a bit of a shock. Let's get back to work."

It was no use. I couldn't concentrate. After about half an hour Fred suggested that he should once again go and review his calculations and design. We would get together next week. I didn't sleep for the next two nights. She was in my mind constantly. I oscillated back and forth, thinking about how I would give hell to Barry for saying anything then how I would thank him for bringing us back together.

I took an early train on Wednesday and made arrangements with one of the professors to take my afternoon classes. Concentrating on the morning classes was sheer hell. At last they ended, and I got to the Kardomah about ten past twelve.

She was standing just inside the entrance. She wasn't particularly hungry, and I had already told Neville that I would be meeting with her at his house.

"Just to talk things out," I explained after he made a suggestive remark.

At last we were alone together. We looked at one another across the few feet that separated us.

"I've missed you so much," we both seemed to say at once as we moved together. "I've missed you too."

We hugged each other tightly for a couple of minutes, then Sheila pushed gently away.

"Before we start, I need the answer to some questions, and I need the answers before I get all flustered with you holding me. Please sit down over there and fill in the blanks for me."

"No," I said.

"What?" She was bewildered.

"No, I will not sit over there. I haven't been near you in four years, and I'm dammed if I'm going to be ordered around. I'll sit next to you, and I'll answer what questions I can. But I'm going to have my arms around you. You will have your arms around me."

"That's not fair. You know I can't concentrate like that."

"Well, you're just going to have to try," I said, sitting down and enfolding her in my arms. She responded in spite of her words of protest.

"Barry has told me an awful riddle. He said he had talked with you, and you had explained everything to him, that he had found something and that he could straighten the whole thing out." She held herself back and looked in my eyes.

"I did talk with Barry last week. He called on me after work and told me he could straighten things. Tell me, exactly what did he say?" I had to find out just how much she knew before I added anything.

"It was on Sunday. Charlie...you know, the fellow I have been going out with—well, Charlie and I had been sitting with Daddy. He likes us to read the newspapers to him. Suddenly, without saying anything to me, Charlie asks Daddy if he would mind if he asked me to marry him. I was speechless. We'd never discussed marriage. I like him a great deal, but I could never consider marrying anyone while I'm still in love with you." I squeezed her to reassure her.

"Daddy was thrilled. He said it was a great idea. Such a fine young man with a great future, he said. He called Mummy and told her the news. You know what she's like. She gushed over Charlie, and I sat there like I was an outsider. I wanted to scream, but I haven't seen Daddy so happy since his stroke, so I said nothing. When Barry came home, he was furious. He didn't say anything in front of them, but afterward when we were alone, he blurted it out. He called me stupid and an idiot for agreeing to marry someone I didn't love. He said he knew what it was that Daddy was angry with you about. That it was all wrong, and he was going to straighten it out. Then he wouldn't talk anymore. That's when I called you on Monday."

I leaned back to make a little distance. "Barry told me much the same thing," I said. "I have done nothing to harm your father—I know that, and I want you to know that. Whatever it is that Barry has found out has convinced him. Why don't we let Barry do what he has to do? While he's doing it, can't you take me at my word and believe me?"

"You know I already have. I wouldn't be here if I didn't. Oh God, how much time we've wasted. How I've longed for you to walk in and drag me away. I even told Mummy that I was going to see you, and she nearly went out of her mind. She said it would kill Daddy, and if that happened, it would probably kill her. She thought that you must have done something, or you would have tried to contact me. Why didn't you? John, why didn't you try to get in touch?"

"I did try. Every time I called you were not in or couldn't come to the phone. After a while I had to assume you had accepted your father's wishes and really didn't want to see me anymore."

"I wanted to see you, John, in the worst way, then you seemed to disappear, and I never saw you for ages."

The rest of the afternoon was spent gradually catching up on each other's lives, what we had been doing at work and socially.

The natural physical attraction was undeniable for both of us. We both tried to resist each other at first, but our resistances were so low once we started, we went wild.

Sheila was insatiable. I had had a few affairs in the last seven years, but I believed her when she claimed there had never been anyone else. She never asked me, and I didn't volunteer.

Sheila ran me almost home and dropped me outside Luba's restaurant, a local haunt that made delicious food and with three separate bars and dining room catered to a wide spectrum of people. We had agreed that after she had talked with Barry, she would break the news to her mother and father that the wedding plans were off, and we were back together. She would call me in the morning. She waved as she pulled away.

# Chapter 10

I stepped into the air-conditioned coolness of Woes. I would have a quick drink with my friend Dave Thomas. Dave was the assistant manager there. As I climbed onto the barstool, I had a feeling of well-being. Everything was going to work out at last.

"Hi, John. What's new?" David greeted.

"Everything's classified information at the moment, Dave." I grinned.

"Great, we'll hear all about it on the six o'clock news then." He switched on the TV above the bar as the local channel logo was fading to black.

The local anchor man gave the highlights of the major news stories from around the globe and the nation then handed over the spotlight to the pretty blonde co-anchor who tried too hard. Mary Ann Baker was one of the bright spots on the local news. Her diction was good even if her delivery was a little too dramatic. If she ever could stop competing openly with her sidekick, she would get the recognition she deserved. She had the potential to be on one of the networks.

"Thank you, Tom. Now to the local scene."

Her face was altogether too grim.

"Lighten up, Mary Ann." I smiled to myself, willing her not to take herself quite so seriously.

She ignored my psychic pleas as she continued, "The top story this evening is of the disastrous auto accident, which claimed the lives of two Boston men."

The camera cut to the scene of a car being lifted out of a river as her voice over commented.

"This scene is the aftermath of a tragic accident, the sixth this year at the same spot, Harpers Turn. Both occupants were found dead at the scene. Their vehicle appears to have gone out of control and crashed through the barrier, tumbling into the river. Apparently both had been drowned. Identification on the bodies showed them to be *Barry Clegg* and *Joseph Ramsbottom*."

My heart literally stopped for several beats. I was struggling to breath, and yet my concentration on Mary Ann's somber face was total.

"Barry Clegg was the son of Mr. and Mrs. Harold Clegg, of Clegg, Bates and Taylor, the well-known construction company. Mr. Harold Clegg has been incapacitated for several years with a stroke. It is also a sad coincidence that Mr. and Mrs. Clegg, earlier today, had announced in the Boston Globe, their daughter's engagement to Mr. Charles Laughton. A Newton man was today arrested when he…"

David's customary wide grin quickly changed to a sober expression.

"You knew him, didn't you? Wasn't he your blocking back at St. Blaze?"

"Yes," I whispered as he placed a beer in front of me.

"Goddamn dangerous road. There's been dozens of accidents right at that spot. Nobody's been killed before though. They must have been going at a hell of a speed to crash through that barrier."

I was hardly listening to him. My thoughts were spinning. This was not an accident; it was too much of a coincidence—both of them together.

"I need to be on my own right now, Dave," I said, leaving the bar and going over to the alcove in the corner.

Something had happened. Barry obviously had talked to Ramsbottom, and they had had the confrontation. Now they were dead. It was murder. Why had he done it? Barry had promised me he would discuss any action before he made a move. He probably saw the engagement announcement in the paper, and it was a surprise to him. Sheila hadn't mentioned it. Her mother must have placed it without telling either of them. He had probably tried to call me at work and couldn't reach me. He wouldn't have been able to reach Sheila either.

That must have been the reason for his rash action. The bastards had killed him. Those ruthless, high-finance racketeers had wiped him off the face of this earth.

Guilt swept over me as I remembered the unkind thoughts I had had about him never having had to hustle. "I had probably done more physical work since I was seven than he would do for the rest of his life." Little did I know then how short that life would be.

"Excuse me, sir." Looking up, I saw the apologetic face of the waitress. "Sorry to disturb you, but there is a gentleman in the other room who would like to have a word with you. He said he's sorry, but he can't come in here 'cause he's not dressed properly. He's in the bottle-shop bar."

"Thank you." I rose and walked to the other bar.

Sean was standing just outside the door.

"Ach, it's a sad day for everybody, sure it is."

"They bloody murdered him, Sean. They killed them both. I can't believe it." An overwhelming surge of anger came over me. Remembering the events of over four years ago, I grabbed him by the lapels and pulled him savagely into a corner by the door. "You had a hand in this somehow." I saw him wither with fright.

"Jesus, Mary, and Joseph, don't look at me like that." I relaxed my grip on his lapels. "Sure, and y' put the fear of God into me. Y' look like y' could do murder yourself. Saints preserve us, oie had nothin' to do with it."

I grabbed him by the scruff of the neck and dragged him out into the street. The memories coming back of how my uncles had said years ago I could whip him. I'd had some doubts then, but not now. There was no doubt in his mind either. He knew I could pulverize him if I decided to.

I pushed him up hard against the wall. He was sweating with fear and started to plead.

"Holy Mother of God, please, John, please let me explain. Oie think I might know something, but I had nothing to do with it at all, please believe me."

I motioned for him to start walking up Cavendish street.

"Start talking."

"Well, all oie know is hearsay. At Fuller's they talk a lot about Clegg, Bates and Taylor, being as how they are competitors. They really were very happy when all that scandal was going on. Fuller's picked up a lot of extra business as a result of that. Mr. Fuller and Flynn, that's the general manager, are always saying how the partners at Clegg's are at each other's throats, that they will destroy each other given half a chance. That's all oie know."

So Fuller's were on the sidelines, cheering for each side to destroy themselves, were they. The thought confirmed that Bates or Taylor or both had been involved in Barry's death.

I took a shot in the dark.

"This has something to do with that parcel you had me carry for you that day, Sean."

His eyes darted wildly from side to side.

"Sure, and that was just an innocent bit of mischief on my part. Oie'm sorry that you got involved, but oie don't know what was in the parcel, honest."

"What happened to it during the time I gave it to you and you brought it back?"

"Oie took it straight to the drop like they told me to and then picked it up forty-five minutes later. Oie just followed instructions, so oie did."

"Don't talk in riddles, Sean." I was ready to smash him in the face. "What drop? Who are they?"

"Sure, an' oie have no idea who they are. They on'y spoke t' me on the phone. The drop was at the public library across the street from our office. Go in t' the nonfiction department, so 'e sez. Put the package on top of the Encyclopedia Brittanica and bugger off fast. Then come back in forty-five minutes."

I let go of him, and he almost fell to the ground.

I had to call Sheila. I didn't care who answered the phone. I had to get moving.

"You don't talk to anyone about our conversation tonight, Sean. You meet me in the Waltham Reference Library tomorrow night at five thirty. Remember, not a word to a soul, or I'll tear your tongue out."

He nodded nervously. I could tell he was terrified of me. I had never realized that I could look frightening to someone, but he certainly was afraid of me.

I left him standing there, and as I walked away, I thought I could hear him sobbing. I had to find a phone to call Sheila.

"Oh, John darling, thank God you called. You heard about the accident. Daddy's had another stroke, and Mummy is with him. There is a policeman here who wants me to go and identify Barry's body. Can you believe they announced it before anyone had officially made an identification? I'm at my wit's end. I don't know what to do."

I agreed to go with her along with the police. They picked me up en route.

It took only a brief second for both of us to see Barry's face to make the positive identification. Sheila fainted at the sight of his handsome features, which had been badly mutilated. He must have either hit the steering column or the dashboard and then gone through the windshield.

They called a doctor for Sheila. While they were attending to her, I had a conversation with the doctor who had examined Barry. He remarked that it must have been a terrible crash. Barry must have attempted to get out of the car at some point during the accident because his left hand had been crushed. The doctor speculated that he must have trapped it in the door as the car plunged into the water.

*Or they might have tortured him*, I thought. Why would they do that? Perhaps to find out if anyone else knew about them. Maybe to tell them where the ledger was. He'd had the one page of the ledger that he showed me. Had he shown them, or was it in his possession when he died?

I asked the policeman if we could pick up Barry's clothes and personal effects. As there was no question about it being an accident, there were no objections.

I quickly examined the contents of his pockets, which had been placed in a brown manila envelope. A pocket diary, no entry for today's date, a wallet, everything apparently intact, comb, pen, a couple of keys, etc., nothing unusual and no page from the ledger. I checked the pockets of the still-damp jacket; nothing had been left inside.

Except—wait a minute. There was something in the top pocket. The flap from an envelope. It had been folded in two as though the comb had been pushed down on top of it, and it had wedged at the very bottom of the pocket.

769-3232 was all that was written on the sticky piece of paper. Maybe it was nothing, but I'd find out. I knew now that although I couldn't prove to anyone it was murder, when I had checked one thing out, I would know for sure myself. If it was murder, I had a plan to prove it.

A voice in the outer room was familiar. When I looked out, Mr. Taylor and I recognized each other immediately.

"Dunne, isn't this tragic? Mr. Bates and I were in Washington when we heard the news. The police contacted us at our hotel, and of course, we immediately drove back. Poor Ramsbottom, he didn't have any relatives that we know of. The police have asked me to identify the body. How are the Cleggs holding up?"

I told him the situation, and he looked most distressed. His concern seemed genuine.

"It's sad to meet again after all this time under such dreadful circumstances. You know, I'd always expected, hoped, that you would come back to work for us after you left school. What are you doing these days?"

I gave him a brief chronology of my career to date, and he expressed his admiration for my accomplishments.

"We need engineers as well as accountants, you know. If you are ever interested in coming back, just give me a call."

"You said you were down in Washington. On business, I suppose?"

"Yes, we have a big potential defense contract with the Pentagon. It's getting down to the nitty-gritty. If we pull this one off, it will be the biggest job ever for the firm. We have been down there all week. You know, some people think it's all glamour, staying at fancy hotels and eating in fine restaurants. Most of the time we never get out of the conference room long enough to enjoy any of the benefits."

If Bates and Taylor had been down in Washington all week, then they were not whoever Barry and Ramsbottom had seen today. They could have arranged for someone else to take care of them. That didn't make sense.

I had to think that the whole thing had happened spontaneously. It must have been triggered by Barry seeing the announcement of Sheila's engagement. That happened only today.

No, they were not the ones. Who had killed them? Barry and Ramsbottom had their meeting with someone else. Who?

Taylor's warm greeting and friendly attitude made it difficult for me to believe that he could be involved. I had to keep reminding myself that these people, whoever they were, were not going to parade around with horns sticking out of their heads. They were probably very ordinary-looking people, possibly pillars of the community.

Mr. Taylor was called into the same room that Sheila and I had been in a few minutes ago. He returned in what seemed only seconds, looking as though he was about to be violently sick.

Shaking his head, he sat down and held on to the chair.

"My God, what an awful sight. He was such a quiet, unassuming sort of fellow. He'd worked for us for about ten years. Nobody really seemed to get very close to him. It's sad, no family, lived all alone. I wonder, well, the firm will take care of the cost of the funeral. Least we can do, he was a good man..."

"Miss Clegg's ready to go home now, sir," the policeman interrupted.

"Thank you, Officer." I turned to Bates.

"Well, I wish we could have met again under better circumstances," I said to Mr. Taylor. He nodded faintly as we left.

The drive back to Sheila's was quiet and uninterrupted by conversation. She was totally exhausted. The powerful Dodge seemed to understand the urgency.

The lights were on in the house when we arrived, and the Cleggs' family doctor, Dr. Latimer, was waiting. He explained to the officer and myself that he brought Mrs. Clegg home from the hospital and had given her a sedative. He anticipated that Sheila would be in a similar state and was waiting to give her the same treatment.

The police officer said good night and sped away. I helped get Sheila up to the bedroom and discreetly withdrew as the doctor administered the sedative.

As soon as I left the bedroom, I went down the stairs two at a time then raced through the hall and the living room to the steps down to the basement.

The toolbox was in exactly the same place and the folder was there. I quickly removed it, stuffed it inside my shirt, and went back upstairs to the living room to wait for the doctor. In a few moments he appeared and said they were both resting comfortably. We left together.

Dr. Latimer made a couple of attempts at conversation as he drove but probably interpreted my unenthusiastic responses to my personal grief. He was kind enough to drop me at Neville's, even though it was substantially out of his way.

Fortunately, Neville was in bed. Although I disturbed him, he was obviously too tired to get up. At last I felt safe in opening the folder. Undoing the official-looking red cloth tape, I opened the flap and allowed the contents to slide out on to the kitchen table. There was the larger brown envelope addressed to Mr. Fred Jones, also a smaller white envelope addressed to Mr. H. Clegg Esq. at his home address. I hadn't seen the smaller one before.

My first priority was the ledger in the larger envelope. I held my breath as I removed the contents and opened the ledger.

*The page was missing!* That sealed it in my mind; it was murder. If the page had still been enclosed, there could have been some doubt. It was highly likely that Barry had taken it with him to the confrontation. It wasn't in his effects. I was convinced it was murder.

I sat for several minutes, absorbing the truth of my suspicions before I turned to the smaller envelope. Inside was a letter. My hands were trembling as I unfolded the crisp white parchment.

> *Dear Mr. Clegg,*
>
> *Sorry to have to write this note. You have been a good boss, and I have let you down. I have mailed the ledger that you have been keeping on the payoffs to a post-office box in Waltham, and the key is enclosed.*
>
> *I want you to know that I was forced to help them; they blackmailed me like they have blackmailed you. They beat me up several times. I know that I was wrong and so were you, but these people are the worst. They are totally ruthless. They'll kill me if they ever find out that I did this.*
>
> *I just heard that they are going to tell the newspapers and the police, and I expect that by the time you get this letter, the reporters and auditors will be all over the place.*
>
> *You can probably leave the ledger at the post office for a few days until it all blows over, but don't leave it there too long. When it doesn't show up, I mean when the police can't find it, they'll start on me, and if they do, I know that I won't be able to hold out.*
>
> *I rented P.O. Box 399 under the name of Fred Jones. I hope it's safe there.*
>
> *You have been a kind and generous man to me, and I feel rotten about what I have done. Please forgive me.*

The note was unsigned, but I could almost see Ramsbottom writing it. He had been terrified of them, whoever they were. So that's how the ledger had been hidden. The US Postal Service had been the hiding place. No wonder nothing had been found. That post-office box would have held the contents for a year perhaps, maybe more if the rent had been paid regularly.

The stamp had been canceled on both envelopes the same day, February 20, seven years ago. They had been mailed simultaneously. Barry hadn't mentioned this letter when we talked. Could he have found it somewhere else? In his father's desk, maybe? It might have been there all the time. I was so shocked when I found the ledger the first time I hadn't looked for anything else. Barry might have missed it also. That wasn't important; it just solved the mystery of why it was never found during the search of the Clegg's home and offices.

My mind wrestled with the evidence. All of it speculative. What would the police say? They probably didn't have enough to make any charges stick—and to whom? Bates and Taylor had an alibi.

If I went to the police, I would have to show them the ledger. The damage would be done to the Cleggs, but nothing would have been done to catch Barry's killers. The little slip of envelope flap was still in my top pocket. I took it out and looked at the number. 769-3232. This was my only clue and a slim one at that.

Leaving the apartment, I walked to the corner pay phone. It was almost twelve thirty. Inserting my dime, I dialed the number.

It rang. I assumed that because it was the middle of the night, it might take someone a while to hear the phone. I just let it ring. *Ring, ring, ring, ring, ring, ring.* I was about to hang up when a voice answered.

"Security."

What was that? It had to be some business number, and I had reached the night security.

"Hello," I said, "is Ashby there?" making up a name on the spot.

"Ashby? Sorry, no Ashby here. You must have a wrong number."

"Now, wait a minute," I said firmly. "I was asked to call Ashby at this number urgently. It's the middle of the night, and I want to talk to him."

"I'm sorry, but there's no Ashby or anyone like that name here."

"Who is this? Who am I speaking to?"

"Williams, security. This is the Fuller Company, and you have come in on Mr. Flynn's private line. There is no Ashby here. You must have a wrong number."

"Indeed, I must. I'm so sorry to disturb you. I must have transposed the numbers wrong, sorry…" I trailed off and hung up.

So Barry had called Fuller's, and Mr. Flynn was the person he had spoken to, I thought as I strolled slowly back to Neville's door.

Back in the kitchen I made some coffee and spent the next several hours going over the names in the ledger. In the last few years, so many more of the names had become familiar to me. When I was just a kid in school, I hadn't recognized the political names. Now most of them had faces. I formulated a plan that I felt might work.

I arrived early at work the next morning, which gave me time to make a phone call in private.

The call was to Gerry Dirkson. We were old friends. We also had played football together. More important at the moment was the fact that Gerry's father was a chief inspector with the Boston CID.

I would need someone I could talk to as a friend, someone who would take me seriously. I decided to call him at home.

"Hello."

"Hello, Mrs. Dirkson, John Dunne here. Is Mr. Dirkson in?"

"I'm sorry, John, you missed him by about an hour. He is on his way to work." She went on to explain that they planned on leaving for the weekend as soon as he got home.

"You can try him later, John. But if you miss him, he'll be back first thing Monday morning."

Barry's accident was the main topic of conversation in the office. Some of the others knew that we were at school together. Any association beyond that was unknown to the general office. The day started as usual with a brief staff meeting and my short report on another failure, a bristling look from Guy Williams, and a snide comment from one of the others.

"Dunne's project is getting to be about as funny as a rubber crutch."

Everyone laughed at my embarrassment and then we returned to our desks.

I hadn't cleared my desk on Tuesday after I broke off discussions with Fred. I had simply slid everything into the drawer. As I started to take out the papers, a magnifying glass that I kept in the drawer slipped on top of a photograph. The picture was the "sample" Fred had brought in with his original proposal.

Something caught my eye. I raised the magnifying glass, and the grain on the sample started to get bigger and bigger. It was wood. I don't know if the joke about the rubber crutch had given me a subliminal message. I felt that maybe, just maybe, here was the problem.

I called him immediately. "Fred, the sample, the photo you brought in with your original proposal."

"Yes?" he responded,

"Was that made out of wood?"

"Well, yes, it was."

"Fred, I think I might have the answer to our problem. The whole system is affected by the vibrations. The harmonics have to be taken into account. Let me refigure and get back to you."

It took until noon to completely go over everything. I made sketches of the new parts we needed and took them down to the Experimental Department. Fortunately, I had worked in that department while I was in the shops. Getting cooperation was much easier for me than it would have been for anyone else.

After looking at the sketches, the Experimental Department supervisor declared, "We'll try it Tuesday, but if it doesn't work this time, you've had it. I'm sick and tired of this sucker. It seemed like a good one at first, but the bloom has gone off the rose, John. If it fails again, ditch it, okay?"

"Okay," I grinned, knowing it would work now. "Do you mind if I use your outside line to call Fred? I'll tell him to come in Tuesday."

"Be my guest. I'm going for some lunch," he said, leaving me alone in his office.

I had two calls to make, the first one to Fred. I could have made that from my phone in the engineering-department office. It was business, but anyone could hear your conversation; and under the circumstances, I didn't want too many people to know about the new idea until it was proven. The second call definitely had to be private.

I called Fred and raised his spirits substantially. I told him of the changes. He couldn't express his excitement forcefully enough.

"Don't break out the champagne until after Tuesday. See you then."

The mental picture of Fred's happy face quickly disappeared as the larger problem came back into focus.

All night long I had wrestled with my decision. I should stay out of this. Make a simple report to the authorities and walk away. Why should I feel any responsibility? I had done nothing wrong, except wanting to shield Sheila and her family. I had suggested to Barry not to go to the police. His decision had cost him his life.

If I went to the police, what could I tell them? That I had played amateur detective and had "reason to believe" there was no hard evidence. But I wanted to get then. I wanted to get them for Barry, but I also wanted to get them for another reason. My Granddad had lived with a secret. He'd only told me part of the story, but he had told the other part to his sons.

I had to go through with it. I coughed to clear my throat and raised the phone to my ear. I dialed the number I'd dialed the night before.

"Hello," greeted a cheerful voice.

I hung up. I'd better check with Sean. What if he wouldn't go along? I'd have to do it with him or without him, but I want him with me in this. I needed him. I'll see him tonight at the library.

# Chapter 11

## Blood Money

Sean and I met in the reference library as I had instructed. I was there early and had got copies of the old newspapers. I read everything that was related to the Clegg, Bates and Taylor scandal. Almost every name that was mentioned as being potentially involved was a name that I had copied from the ledger.

There were many names that weren't in the articles, but every name in the articles was also in the ledger, except two. Those two I remembered were on the missing page that Barry had had.

As Sean wove his way through the various tables and shelves, the spring in his step diminished. He always had the air of someone who was carefree and gay. Now he realized that I meant business.

God, how I had come to love this man and be angry with him. During one of our rare arguments, I had told him forcibly about the things that really irritated me about him. He had shrugged and said, "Oie've always said, the measure of a man's love for someone is not so much all the things you like about a person, rather it's just how much shit you're prepared to put up with from him."

Well, I wasn't going to put up with any shit now. He could tell. I could see it in his whole body. The moment of truth had arrived.

I greeted him pleasantly, "Good evening, Sean. So what have you learned today?"

"Sure, and today oie've learned what it is t' have a tormented soul. Haven't oie said the rosary ten times if oie said it once?"

"Living with your conscience does that sometimes."

"Conscience, it is, that's part of it. It's also mortal fear. Oie never slept a wink last night. Oie could see y' face glaring at me, it was. Oie've never seen such anger, all over somethin' oie did years ago."

"You used me, Sean. That little scheme of yours"—the whispering by both of us added to the tension in the deserted room—"It'll on'y take y' a couple o' minutes, Danny Boy. Sure, and aren't you the one who can run like a whippet…" I mimicked the words he had used.

"Aye, well, true enough, oie did. But oie was under pressure too. It seemed not that bad at the time."

"Why didn't you make the delivery and pickup yourself?"

"Well, oie thought Mr. Clegg might know me, and oie didn't want to run into him."

"You always said that you'd never met him. How would he know you?"

Sean squirmed. He didn't want to say any more.

"How would he know you?" I insisted. He still remained silent.

Standing up, I looked at him with disgust.

"Sean, you and I are through. Don't ever try to contact me again. If you do, I will give you the biggest—" I knew that I was threatening him with the worst possible consequences. Not a beating, but the thought that he would be ostracized from the family. He knew in his heart that he was accepted by the rest of them only because of me. If I cut him off, he would have nobody.

"Mother of God, don't say that. Oie'll tell you."

"You were blackmailing him, weren't you? Weren't you?"

"No, yes, no, please, oie'll tell you, oie'll tell you. Honest, Oie never got a penny. Oie was just the messenger boy. Oie was pretty sure that is what was goin' on, but no one ever told me. Oie was just to meet him, always in a dark spot. Oie was to wear dark clothes with a scarf around my face and a hat. Oie never spoke. Oie just held my hand out, and he'd give me a packet, and oie'd run like a bugger. He never got a good look at me, but oie was afraid that he might just cotton on if he saw me at the office that day."

"Who was it that you gave the money to? I presume it was money, who did you give it to?"

"Oh, oie'm sure it was money. Oie never met the fellow. Oie was told that it was money the first time. This 'voice,' he called me on the phone at Fuller's. He said that being a good Irish lad, oie would be wantin' to do something for the 'cause.' He said that there was this fellow that was goin' to make a contribution, and he'd like for me to pick it up for him."

"What cause?" I said, wanting him to say it.

"The bloody IRA, which bloody cause do you think? Well, Danny Boy, you just don't tell those buggers to go sling their hook. So oie said oie'd be doing it. Well, he says how to dress so no one will recognize me. To put the packet in a locker at work with a combination lock on it. Sure enough, this locker was there with a loose lock. Oie put the packet in and closed the lock, and that was that. Anyone could have got it if they knew the combination."

I tried to keep myself from sneering. "How long had this been going on?"

"The week of Uncle Pat's, your Granda's, funeral was the first time oie did it. Y' remember oie went back home after the funeral t' Ireland. Oie wanted out. Oie'd said oie couldn't find work. Oie'd found it, but oie wasn't after that kind o' work. After a few months, though, oie had t' come back. Sure, there's nothin' left back have for me. Then the last time was the week before you carried the package for me."

I stared at him as he shifted around in his chair. Could I rely on him? Was he strong enough to take the truth? If I told him, would he be able to handle the job that had to be done?

"Sean, why do you work at Fuller's? You're bright enough to get a job at dozens of companies."

"Well, it's a good company. They've always treated me well." He wasn't sure about the change in my line of questions, but he welcomed it.

"Even though they get you involved in blackmail and possibly murder? The bloody cause. They treat you well, they sure do," I said sarcastically.

"Sure, and they 'ave nothin' t' do wi' that."

"Sean, Fuller's is a front for the IRA."

"That's just a bunch o' lies. Made up by the proddies, so it is. Just because they hire more Irish lads than anyone else. Sure, and the old man, Fuller, oie don't think 'e even 'practices' anymore. Not a crucifix or holy picture in sight."

"You're blind, Sean. You don't want to see. Why did they hire you? Then you start getting these anonymous phone calls."

"They hired me 'cause oie'm' bein' who oie am. Sure, old-man Fuller and my da were boyhood pals back in the old country. Fuller was good t' my ma. Didn't he send money t' her, the widow that she was, till the day he died? He always said there would always be a job for any relative o' Sean Donavans at Fuller's."

"Blood money."

"What are y' talkin' about?"

"The money he sent Aunty Kath. It was blood money. They were boyhood pals. That's true. Think about this. Why? If there will always be a job at Fuller's for a Donavan, why did my granddad not work there? Or any of my uncles?"

He started to answer, but I cut him off, "They didn't work there because Granddad said not to. Granddad didn't work there because he knew. He knew the night Sean Donavan and Fuller left to go to the 'meeting,' Fuller killed him."

I paused to catch my breath and watch Sean's reaction.

"Sean, they killed your da for the cause. They killed Ramsbottom and Barry for the cause. Mr. Clegg had a stroke because of what you did for the cause. How long are you going to cooperate and do the bidding of someone who killed your da?" I was still whispering, but I had to check myself. "Yes, killed him. Killed him for the *fucking cause*."

Sean jumped with the shock. He had never heard me use that word before, and I never had. Somehow all the other adjectives had failed. All the deep-rooted, in-bred prejudice, bigotry, and hatred had come to the surface. The subtle brainwashing I had been subjected to over the years now showed itself. Good, honest, well-meaning, God-fearing people had perpetuated it all under the guise of building pride in the heritage of the Irish-Catholic. The fine wine had turned to vinegar. I wanted that taste out of my mouth.

"God Almighty, oie've got t' have a drink," Sean said. "Oie have t' be able t' think straight."

"A drink isn't going to help you think. It will only help you to escape. Escape from reality."

"Well, let's be gettin' out o' here. They'll be closin' soon. It's almost seven thirty now," he said, steadying himself as he stood up.

The town was almost deserted at that time. We walked around the deserted streets.

I had said my piece, and I had to wait for Sean. I had to wait and see how he reacted to the revelation; to see how he would handle it.

Sean started out slowly, "You're tellin' the truth, Danny Boy. It all fits together now. Sure, and oie knew in m' heart before, but oie would always run away from."

He started to tell me about his ma, how she had taken the money that was sent; how she had been brokenhearted and had taken to drinking; how, when she had too much to drink, she would cry and talk about the "devil's own money."

Sean painted a montage that reinforced the knowledge we now shared. After over an hour of talking, I at last agreed to having a drink.

The Volunteers wasn't crowded. We had the small bar almost to ourselves. He never tasted the first beer. The second one he started to sip.

"Oie'm goin' t' have t' pay the piper, sure I am. What is it y' wantin' me t' do? Oie'll go t' the cops with y'. Oie'll probably be doin' a stretch, so oie will, and God knows what will become of me in there."

"You will not be doing a stretch. I have a plan."

As I outlined it to him, he got more and more nervous.

"The saints preserve and keep us. This is mighty dangerous stuff, and if it all goes the way you say, oie'm going up the river for a stretch for sure. Danny Boy, have a heart, give a fellow a chance."

"If you don't cooperate, you'll not only do a stretch, you'll possibly be implicated in the murder," I threatened. "I'm going to get those bastards with you or without you. But if you do exactly as I say, I am sure that we can present you as an unwitting messenger and get you off with a slap on the wrist. Now, can I count on you to do exactly what I've told you? Or do you want to take your chances?"

"Oie'll do it, oie'll do it."

"What is Fuller's home number?"

"Sure, and oie don't know that. Why?"

I ignored his question. "What's Flynn's home number?"

"496-2849. Why do you want then?"

"Because it's evening, and I can't call them at work right now."

I left him to go to the phone outside. He was taking a big gulp from his second pint.

This time there were no voices as I dialed Flynn's home number.

"Hello," greeted the same warm, cheerful voice.

"Flynn?" I said in a flat whisper.

"Yes, who's this?"

"Someone who knows about how you killed Ramsbottom and Clegg. I have the rest of the ledger, and I know all about the blackmail scheme." I was running an awful bluff.

"Who the fuck is this? Who is it?"

"Only someone who wants to share in the benefits."

"I don't know what you're talking about." He had started to recover. "Who is this? Is this some kind of stupid joke?"

The element of surprise had worked. I knew for sure that he was guilty. I had to convince him and scare him to death.

"Listen," I continued in the flat whisper, "listen good. You're out of the blackmail business. I'm taking over that operation. From now on, I'll collect the Clegg, Bates and Taylor money. Also, you're going to give me fifty thousand dollars to keep me quiet so I won't go to the police. Do you understand?"

"Look, who are you? I don't have that kind of money…"

"You're going to get that money, or you are going to hang by the neck until you are dead. How does that sound, Mr. Flynn?"

"Look, be reasonable. I can't raise ten thousand pounds."

"I will call you tomorrow. You had better have the money available, or the police will get the whole bundle and the goods I have on you." I hung up.

There was a curious exhilaration pumping through my whole body. I had had done it. Nothing was going to stop me now. God, that was a lot of money, fifty thousand bucks. Nothing though compared with the numbers in the ledger. Maybe I should have asked for more, convince them I meant business. They knew I meant business, I could tell. We had them; they were going to get theirs.

Sean had drained his glass and was indicating another round to the barman.

"Sorry, Colin," I said jovially. "We have to be off."

I jerked my head at Sean, much as my father had done to me thousands of times. Sean obeyed as I had done for most of my formative years.

"Couldn't we just have one more? Sure, and this schemin' and plottin' gives me a terrible thirst, so it does."

"I don't want you drunk and not able to go to work. You're critical tomorrow. I need you there to see what happens."

"Oie'll be there, Danny Boy, oie'll be there. It's a promise. On m' Granda's grave, Lord rest 'is soul. Oie want these bastards too. Oie know y' think oic'm scared, and so oie am. But oie'll do it."

I put my arm around him, and we embraced. He was drawing strength from my strength. I hadn't let any man put his arms around me since Brendan had kissed me. In a way, Sean reminded me of Brendan. He was the only other man that had ever shown concern and expectations from me and had also been able to help. All the others said they expected great things but then left it up to me. Sean had worked with me and challenged me. I owed him a great deal.

"Sure, and oie know that you'll protect me, Danny Boy. You'll see that no 'arm comes t' y' cousin Sean."

"I will, Sean. I will."

Arriving at the office early gave me a chance to prepare my presentation for the changes to the tracing device. The report that I gave at the staff meeting was greeted with muted groans. No comment from my boss, just a look that told me I was a source of irritation.

Later in the morning I made a pretense of stopping by the Experimental Department around noontime. I wanted to check on the progress of the tracing device, but I also needed to use the phone in private.

"Hello," responded a nervous voice.

"Flynn?"

"Yes."

"This is your friend from yesterday. You have the money?"

"Well, it'll take a day or two to collect."

"Good, I'll call you Monday and tell you how to deliver." I hung up and headed back to the engineering office.

Later in the afternoon Sean called, "Sure, and you were right, Danny boy. My God, you've got 'em scared. As soon as Flynn answered the phone, he waved to Mr. Fuller to pick up the extension in his office. Oie couldn't hear anything 'cause oie could only see 'em through the glass partition. But they were mad as hell when you hung up. They went into Fuller's office and stayed there for about an hour before they went out for lunch."

"That's all I needed to know, Sean. You meet me Sunday night and go over the plan again."

Sheila had called me at work and told me, as I expected, that under the circumstances she wasn't going to be able to break the news to anyone until after the funeral. The funeral was Saturday and we could meet on Sunday.

# Chapter 12

Sheila and I spent Sunday afternoon at Neville's, and he did a great job of getting her mind off the tragedy. I didn't protest too strongly when Sheila told me that she was going to give her parents a little more time before she broke the news. I couldn't spend more time with her than I was doing now even if she announced it on network TV.

At seven o'clock Monday morning, I at last spoke to Mr. Dirkson.

"Mr. Dirkson, John Dunne."

"Yes, Margaret said you had called last week. Sorry I couldn't get back to you. What can I do for you?"

"I need to talk to you. Most urgently. Today—this morning before noon."

"Well, I've got a busy morning. What with being away part of last week. Could you come by the office about ten thirty?"

"I'd rather see you outside the office, if that's possible."

"Is it official business?"

"You'll have to decide that, but I think it is."

"Okay. Where do you want to meet? I can be free by eleven."

"Meet me at the Grinning Rat." I'd given the nickname for a small pub near the Quincy outdoor market.

"You do move in classy circles, don't you?" he said with a touch of humor. "I'll see you there then."

I'd modified my original plan. I had wanted to go over the entire idea with Chief Detective Inspector Dirkson beforehand. But with the delay in contacting him, and further thought, I was afraid he might try to talk me out of it. I had decided to make it a fait accompli.

I made the excuse at the office that I had a dentist's appointment to have my wisdom teeth checked, and I was in so much discomfort I might not be back for the rest of the day. The car I had rented for the day was a welcome retreat from other people.

I made the call from a pay phone.

"Hello."

"Flynn?"

"Yes."

"Put the money in a Lords and Taylor shopping bag. Take it to the pay phone outside the Cavendish Hotel at precisely two thirty. I'll call you there and tell you where to deliver. I'll be watching. You'd better be alone."

"Yes, but—"

"No buts. I also want that page you have from the ledger."

"I don't have it."

"Then tell Fuller to give it to you."

I could almost hear him choke when I mentioned Fuller's name. I could hear muffled noises as though someone else was on the line. I hung up.

His LeBaron drew up along the curb. Chief Inspector Dirkson was an impressive man: distinguished and physically powerful. One could imagine anyone on the wrong side of the law being intimidated by this gentleman. Yet those in business could be comfortable with him because he looked like the president of a company. Everyone expected him to go all the way in the CID.

"Let's talk in the car," I suggested.

"Fine," he replied. "Shall I drive?"

"Just a little way," I answered.

"So what's it all about, John?"

I related the entire story to him, together with the speculations up to the point of calling Flynn's number the evening of the murder.

"John, you seem to have put together a case that is based on a great deal of circumstantial evidence. However, I think it is worth looking into. You can count on our discretion regarding the use of this." He indicated the ledger. "You realize that everything you have said could be denied. This ledger is mostly in your handwriting. There is no one to verify that you did it for Clegg, Bates and Taylor. In fact, the only way that it might be useful would be if it were found in either Clegg's possession or at their office. Or if you were to take the stand and give testimony that you actually did the entries there at their office." He made a facial grimace and shrugged. "That's not the case you're trying to develop. It's the blackmail and Barry's murder, isn't it?"

"What if I could give you absolute proof today?"

"I'm listening," he said, fixing his steady gaze on me.

I then proceeded to tell him the rest of the story—how I had called Flynn and demanded money and that they were going to pay off that afternoon.

"So," I said, "if they bring the money, that will be an admission of guilt, and you have yourself a solid case."

He was blazing mad with me. He told me in no uncertain terms that this was interfering in police business. He couldn't sanction such a plan. But after a lot of persuading and my reminding him that he could get to the bottom of a major local-business scandal in one afternoon, he agreed to do it my way.

I would call Flynn at the call box and tell him to deliver the bag to the Ivanhoe, a small restaurant on the southern outskirts of the city. The restaurant was only open for dinner, and nobody would be there until five o'clock. Dirkson knew the owner and would arrange for the rear door to be left open.

I would be there to collect it and then Chief Inspector Dirkson would step in and arrest Flynn. It seemed simple enough. Dirkson called the owner. He would make arrangements for us to be undisturbed.

He also explained that he had some other matters to attend to before our "little action," and he was going to have to leave me. We would meet at the Ivanhoe at two fifteen, and I would make the call from there.

Two fifteen arrived. I was waiting across the street from the Ivanhoe; Mr. Dirkson's car had not arrived. I called the restaurant and asked for the proprietor.

"Is Mr. Dirkson there?"

"No, I expect him any time. He said he'd be back by now."

"Thanks, I'll call back."

At two twenty-five, I called again. He still hadn't arrived.

At two thirty I called the number of the phone box outside the Cavendish Hotel. A familiar voice answered. It was Sean.

"Sean! What the hell are you doing there?"

"It's all gone wrong. Oie was told to bring the package. Flynn's been hobbling round all day, says he has sprained his ankle. Oie was told to bring this package. Oie don't like it, Danny Boy."

"Look, just keep your head. Do you know if you've been followed?"

"Ach, oie can't tell."

"Sean, I want you to drive around and make sure you're not being followed. Drive the wrong way down a one-way street if you have to. Be absolutely sure you aren't followed. Then come to the Ivanhoe restaurant. Park behind the building and come in the rear door. Okay? Sean, don't worry. Everything will be okay." I cut off any potential protest by hanging up.

I called the Ivanhoe again.

"No, he's still not here. Are you the gentleman he's meeting at three fifteen?"

"Yes."

"Well, everything is all set. Just come in the back door and take the first door to the right in the hallway. He'll be there. I'm sure he'll be there. Very reliable, he is. Me and the wife are going out to do some shopping, so you'll have the place to yourself."

I sat and watched as the lone couple left the small Ivanhoe parking lot as Mr. Dirkson's car was coming down the street. Thank God. I had almost begun to panic.

"He's on his way," I said urgently. "The messenger, that is, not Flynn. He has supposedly sprained his ankle, and he sent Sean."

"That will not be as strong a case. But if Sean can testify that he was given the money by Flynn, I think we can still make it stick."

The room was very small—only one booth that took up the whole room. Six could sit comfortably, eight at a pinch. The door from the hall was one entrance. The other was an exit door to the kitchen. I had intended to sit in the booth and have Mr. Dirkson stay out of sight behind the door to the kitchen. F would enter after the money had been handed over.

Chief Inspector Dirkson now took charge.

"There is no reason for me to stay out of sight. The only reason I agreed to your original plan was because of the possibility of Flynn perhaps recognizing MP and bolting. Now that Sean, who is in on the scheme, is making the delivery, that reasoning doesn't apply."

"Yes, but he may have been followed," I protested.

"All the more reason for me to be there. If he has been followed, they don't intend to let you get away with this. They have either tumbled to it or they plan on getting to you. No, I will be in the booth when Sean arrives. And just in case there is any funny stuff, you will remain out of sight behind the other door." He looked at me squarely. "John, I haven't had time to make a report about this. I haven't even told my colleagues at the station. We really should have more men involved. I am tempted to call the whole thing off. You call Flynn and say you have decided to reschedule, and you don't want to deal with anybody but him."

It made sense, and I could see he was trying to protect me.

"You're probably right, but it's almost time. Look, if Sean is alone, we can do that anyway. If he's been followed, it might make it awkward for him. They may think that he ratted on them. I think we have to go with it."

He reluctantly agreed.

Taking up our respective positions, we waited. It was only a few minutes before Sean entered the room.

"Please sit down," Dirkson said, "and give me the parcel."

"It's all messed up," I heard Sean say from my position behind the door.

"How do you mean? Did someone follow you?"

"Oie don't know. But oie do know it's all messed up."

"It's not all messed up. You just make a statement telling me who gave you the package. That should be enough evidence to give us a case."

"That's just it. Oie don't know who gave it to me. They pulled the old game in reverse."

"Tell me about it," Mr. Dirkson said patiently.

"Oie got a call this rnornin' from a voice that said oie was to pick up a package from this locker. Go to a pay phone outside the Cavendish Hotel and wait there till two thirty. Someone would tell me what to do with it. No one saw me face-to-face, and oie didn't see anyone either."

Damn! They had outfoxed us. I entered the room, and Mr. Dirkson looked at me with exasperation as he pointed to the plastic shopping bag Sean had placed on the table.

"One thing is for sure, though," Mr. Dirkson said. "They did it. It might not hold up in court, but they did it."

Suddenly the door burst open. We hadn't heard a thing from the outer hallway. He came in holding a gun, a look of surprise on his face. He had expected only two people to be there. He was about five feet, ten inches with a beer belly and wearing an old tweed jacket, the arms of which seemed to be ready to burst. He looked strong enough to tear the place apart with his bare hands. His face was pockmarked, and his nostrils flared, giving him a piggish look.

Mr. Dirkson's voice came out with a tone of authority.

"My name is Chief Inspector Dirkson, CID, let me have that weapon."

He almost did. He hesitated for just a moment then asserted himself, realizing that, with the gun, he was in charge.

"Sit down, copper. Keep your hands on the table. Now very carefully, two fingers only, put your piece on the table."

Dirkson obeyed him to the letter, his grim face watching those eyes.

"Good, now slide it over this way, slowly."

Dirkson steadily pushed the Smith and Wesson service revolver along the formica tabletop. Pig Face reached cautiously toward the gun and glanced at me.

"You, get your hands up and move over here."

The room was so small when I passed him, we touched each other. Sean had started to cry and say plaintive prayers to the holy family, the saints, and anybody he could think of. My hands were in the air and almost knocked one of the decorative plates off the wall. The plates had been a feeble attempt to make the room look homey.

"Shut that fucking wailing up, you asshole," the intruder hissed, turning his attention on the blubbering Sean.

It was an automatic reaction. My hand grabbed the plate. Tearing it from the hanger, I brought the edge of it down on his wrist. The gun fell to the floor and he let out a scream. He grabbed for the service revolver, but his desperate move only caused it to slither away and off the edge. Turning on me, his face was livid, it said loud and clear he was going to kill me and enjoy it.

Sean slid under the table and cowered, still crying. Mr. Dirkson came out of the booth quickly. It was now two to one, and we had him easy.

Pig Face produced a razor and took a swing at Mr. Dirkson, who swayed back just in time. I threw my arms around his neck and tried to get my knee into the small of his hack, but the room was very cramped.

*Bang*—there was a deafening explosion.

Mr. Dirkson tried to reach around to his back. The expression on his face was one I'd never forget. For an instant everything was frozen in place. I could see, as he pitched forward on his knees, that he was dead.

I still had my arms around the neck of the intruder. He was trying to pry them apart. At the same time, he was banging me back against the wall, swinging his head backward in a reverse butting motion.

As I struggled to tighten my grip, I felt something attached to my sleeve. It was the wire that had mounted the plate on the wall. The hook had caught in my cuff. He crashed me against the wall one more time. Again he went to move forward to make greater space, to give him more momentum for his next attempt to crush me. This time I let go and allowed the wire to slip into both of my hands.

His own forward momentum was increased when I released him, and the wire cut into his throat. It caused a strange gurgling sound. Quickly I brought the two ends across one another and jerked as hard as I could. I twisted the ends together. He knelt clawing at his neck. He was unable to breathe or say a word. He rolled over on his side and exposed Sean under the table with the gun in his hand, cowering in the corner.

I stood there, shivering. Everything had happened in less than a minute. God Almighty, what have I done? Gerry's dad was dead. A minute ago, two minutes ago, he had sat there, a powerful man.

All my body functions seemed to be in conflict. I wanted to run. I wanted to scream. Most of all, I wanted to bring him back. Turn the clock back. Do as he said, call the whole thing off.

Dumbly I turned my attention to the pig-faced intruder. He was still alive. Maybe we could save him.

Save him? I felt the cold wave of hatred spread through my entire body. I wouldn't save him if my life depended on it. This killer had come deliberately to get us.

The sound of Sean pulled my thoughts back to our situation. He hadn't moved. He couldn't get out from underneath the table without climbing over the two bodies. I had to take control of the situation. *What am I going to do?* I thought. *You are not going to panic.* I felt myself regaining my composure, though I was still trembling, and the adrenal in was still pumping as it never had before. *Think! Think! One step at a time.*

The decisions were made; now the action. I took the handkerchief from Mr. Dirkson's top pocket and said to Sean, "Take your finger off the trigger and give me the gun. Sean? Sean? I'm talking to you. Give me the gun."

His fingers relaxed their grip, and the gun rolled out of his hand. I picked it up gingerly, wiped it clean with the handkerchief, and turned to Mr. Dirkson. He was dead, no pulse and no sign of life.

The shot had entered in the lower part of his back. The angle it came from, it was a shot in a million. I looked at Sean; he was trembling and crying.

I turned again to our visitor. He wasn't quite dead yet, but he had lost the strength to reach up to his throat. He was quivering and gurgling.

I stepped back through the door and went into the bar. I took a glass, a bottle of whisky, and one of the cloths that the barman used to wipe the bar. When I got back to the room, Sean was struggling to get out from under the table. Helping him out, I started to try to calm him.

"Here, you need a drink," I said in a neutral voice as I poured him a shot. "Drink this down, go on."

While Sean was taking his medicine, I reviewed the situation once more. I waited, outwardly calm and concerned about Sean, inwardly wanting to get busy with the things I had to do.

"Have you finished? Do you want another?" I said soothingly to Sean.

"Yes," he whimpered.

"Come on then. This is the last one though."

"Oiem sorry. Oie don't know what happened. It just went off. A bloody copper, oh God, forgive me, what have we done?"

His attention had been totally on Mr. Dirkson's body. Then he turned and looked at the grotesque sight of our visitor. I thought Sean was about to throw up.

"We've got to get out of here. Oie think somebody heard the shot." Sean said.

"If no one is here by now, no one is coming. Sean, pull yourself together." I was going to have to take a firmer grip. "Let's have a look at this." Using the razor, I slit open the package. As I expected, no money. They never intended to pay, and they were willing to kill any number of people to protect their situation. They were a ruthless, dangerous lot who played for big stakes, and their tactics today couldn't be trivialized.

"Sean, this was an accident, it wasn't your fault. Anybody would have panicked given where you were. But you're right, we do need to get out of here. *We are not going to panic*." He was nodding his head in agreement. He wanted to be as far away as possible from that spot. "We are going to leave here, separately. You are going to meet me in the bar at Lochobers at four thirty. You make damn sure nobody follows you. Get going, slowly, just at your normal pace."

He stepped out into the parking lot. Nobody was around. He walked diagonally away, disappearing down an alley.

I waited about ten minutes. Wiping the glass and bottle, I replaced them in the bar. I checked out of every window to see if the way was clear. I hadn't seen anyone follow Sean, but they might have been waiting for Pig Face to emerge. I bent over and picked up the razor with one of the cloths. It wasn't as easy as I had thought. I had expected to make one smooth slice, but I had to hack a little to cut off the thug's ear. He didn't even twitch. He had completed his death throes. Wrapping the ear in the cloth, I tossed it into the plastic shopping bag and returned to the bar to wash my hands thoroughly.

I was just about to leave, and I remembered Mr. Dirkson's handkerchief. Stooping over him to replace the neatly folded linen, I felt terrible. I had orchestrated this, and it blew up in my face. He had been a good friend, and he was dead. The toll was mounting. Barry, his father's stroke, Ramsbottom, and now Mr. Dirkson. I wasn't going to give up; these bastards were going to pay.

I felt at the thug to be sure there was no life left in him. I then carefully placed the gun in his hand with his finger around the trigger. Disciplining myself to move as casually as possible, I picked up the shopping bag and stepped out into the street, gradually quickening my pace.

I made for a pay phone and called Flynn's number.

"Hello."

"Surprise, surprise, Flynn. You poor dumb bastard decided to double cross me, did you? Well, you'll hear all about it on the news tonight. You'll he happy to know that today's little episode has cost you five hundred thousand dollars." I hung up and hurried to meet Sean.

It was busy in Lochobers, the "Happy Hour" had started. Sean was there, pacing up and down inside the entrance with a whisky in his hand. He saw me, and I motioned for him to come to me. His eyes wandered longingly to the dark polished wood of the bar and then back to me. Draining the dregs, he joined me at the door. We drove down to the wharf area and parked in Anthony's Seafood restaurant parking lot, looking across the water to Logan Airport.

"I've already given Flynn the bad news." His jaw dropped a mile. "I told him that he would hear about it on tonight's news."

"Oiem as good as dead. They'll cotton to me for sure, Danny Boy, and the cops, if they find my fingerprints on that fuckin' gun—oie'll burn for sure. They'll never believe it was an accident."

"Sean, shut up and listen. You're safe, nobody will do a thing to you. I have an insurance policy. You will have to remember exactly what I say and mentally relive the experience that I describe for you. I'm going to repeat it many times so that it becomes a living reality. If you do that, you are completely safe." I only hoped he could concentrate.

"First, there are no fingerprints. I wiped everything clean, including the bottle and glass. They are in the bar. The gun is in our friend's hand." He relaxed a little. Now I had to start the brainwashing.

"Here's what happened. You got to the phone box and received instructions to go to the Ivanhoe, just as it really happened. When you arrived, you walked into the room. You saw no one. A hand came around you from behind, you smelt something funny, and all the lights went out. You woke up in a dark roam tied to a chair, and someone asking you questions from behind. They wanted to know why they had been double crossed. You didn't know. You told them how you had been told to pick up a package from a locker at work and deliver it. That's all you know.

"They told you that you would wake up in the car, to go home and speak to nobody, and report to work at noon tomorrow, returning the plastic shopping bag to the same locker. You will not even have heard a news broadcast or read a newspaper. You know nothing about what happened at the Ivanhoe. Do you understand? You know nothing."

Sean, to his credit, listened intently to what I told him even though he was bursting to say something.

"Do you understand?"

"Yes."

"Repeat it. What happened?"

He told the story letter perfect.

"Good, now you wanted to say something?"

"You don't understand these people. They're not like a court of law that listens to evidence. They'll just kill me because oie'm a loose end."

"No, they won't. I do understand these people. I'm made of the same stuff. They have a cause. Well, now I have a mission, and I am going to get them. We tried to draw them into a trap. They didn't fall for it. But we are going to do it again. This time I will tell them I will not have any surprises. I know them. They don't know me. You will be the bag man, this time and every time. If ever you are not available to deliver, that ends the protection for them. No, Sean, you are too important to them now. They have to take care of you."

"Again!" he shrieked. "Oh Most Sacred Heart of Jesus, save me. Did you say again? Every time, what's every time?" Sean jumped from the bench and paced up and down in front of me. "Jesus, Mary, and Joseph, I give you my heart and my soul. Holy Mother of God, pray for us sinners now and at the hour of our death. Our Lady of Perpetual Succor, pray for us."

"Sean," I said, standing and putting my arm around him, "we have lost the opportunity to get them legally. They didn't fall for our trap. Now a policeman has been killed. We can't go to the police with the story I told Mr. Dirkson. He only went along with me because he knew me. Even then I created a set of circumstances that made it almost impossible for him not to go along. I have to carry that cross for the rest of my life. Which makes it even more important. We have to get them for your da and for Barry. We have to make them afraid of us and get them to make a mistake that will lead the police to them." I made him look at me. "The bastards killed your da, Sean. Don't you ever forget that. They didn't kill him because he stole from them or cheated them or raped their women. They murdered him because he was for peace. And I swear I'll never have peace nor will you until they get what's coming to them." I had succeeded in rekindling the resolve in him.

"How will we do that?" he asked through clenched teeth and lips that were trembling with a combination of fear and determination.

"I don't know." I didn't. I hadn't a clue. But I would find a way. Somehow I would find a way. "They'll make a mistake, and we'll be ready. In the meantime, we have to stay on the offensive. If they think that they have scared us, we are lost. But if we come back with full force, they will cooperate. Now tell me what happened after you got to the Grinning Pat?"

I went over his story with him a dozen times until I think he really did believe it. The fantasy was more palatable than the truth.

# Chapter 13

The day that we had made Fred's tracing device work was a big day at Land's. I left my Guy Williams and Fred verbally puffing each other and excused myself to make a phone call.

I marveled at how easy it was for me to make the call. Now my mind was made up, I was committed, and the excitement level had started to increase. The closest feeling I had experienced before was the anticipation of the physical contact on the football field. I hesitated to dwell on the fact that any casualties in this action would be more than a broken collarbone.

"Hello," answered the now-familiar voice.

"Flynn?"

"Yes."

"Half a million dollars."

"Who the fuck do you think you are?" he burst out screaming.

"I'm the angel of death as far as you're concerned," I whispered in the flat monotone voice I had used before. "Did you read about your friends? That stupid thug and that dumb con. You were really stupid to bring the cops into this."

The newspapers had been full of the gory details, how a high-ranking police official had been killed. The police were pursuing several leads the article had said. I had decided to take the offensive with Flynn, as though I thought he had brought the police in.

"I never brought the cops in. Listen, you prick, whoever you are, you are playing in the wrong league. We are too big for you. You'd better back off."

"No, you listen to me, Flynn. *You're* the one in the junior league. You're blind, you have no idea who I am, and I know all of you. You saw the pictures in the paper—they didn't do my handiwork justice. In case you don't believe me, there is a present for you in the plastic bag I returned with that little Irish shit. I made him tell me all about how he gets his instructions. I want you to use him again. He's the kind of scared rabbit that will do as I say, and he won't try anything stupid. I told him to come back to work at noon and put the plastic bag back in the same locker he got it from. You can enjoy the little present, and I'll call you later with instructions."

When I returned to the work area, everybody was delighted. The first flush of excitement was over. Now we had to get the tooling designed and priced, the routine chores that go with every product.

Williams greeted me with a smile.

"Well done, Dunne. Fred here has asked me to go to lunch with him, but I have another engagement. Would you keep him company? Thanks a lot, old fellow." He beat a hasty retreat.

"Thank goodness he didn't accept. I only asked out of courtesy. He made me feel as though I'd asked for an invitation to the White House—I wouldn't have enjoyed my meal. Well, John, where do we celebrate?"

It was over lunch that Fred asked, "Have you ever thought of being your own boss?"

"Not really. In this business, you need millions."

"Not to do what I do. You know, we would make a terrific team—me with all my wild and crazy ideas and you to make them work. We'd be unbeatable. Tell you what, how about a partnership?"

I couldn't believe my ears. A partnership. In what? With Fred, this potty character? I liked him, and he had been lucky on this one project, but I didn't have a lot of faith in him as a serious design engineer.

"Fred, what are you talking about?"

"I mean we form a consulting company. I do the sales and marketing and maybe come up with creative solutions to problems. You do the design and detail, make sure they work."

He went into enthusiastic detail on how we could arrange the partnership. He already had a converted house and a workshop. He had several contacts in the industry. Once the reputation was established, success would bring success, he said. My native instincts were to hang on to the security of the big company, but he captured my imagination. Maybe being in business for myself wouldn't be that big a risk with what was going to happen in the next few days.

"Let me think about it."

"Yes, please do, think about it. Not too long though. All you'll do is think about the reasons for not doing it. You'll get cold feet."

Sean reported to work at noon on Tuesday. He had returned the plastic shopping bag to the locker. About an hour later he received a phone call from the mysterious voice, which patiently told him to relate what had happened.

Sean was told that he would have to deliver a package again later in the week, and he needn't be afraid. It had all been a mistake. From now on, he—Sean, that is—would be receiving his instructions directly from someone else. They would have to have a code name for the new contact—me—so that Sean would recognize who it was.

"Sean, I can't believe you would tell them that," I said in amazement when we met later.

"Sure, and oie couldn't think straight. Oie was shitting myself. There he was, askin' me for a code name, something that only oie would know. So I sez 'Danny Boy.' Nobody has ever heard me call you that. We've always been alone, y' remember, at your Granda's house after the St Patrick's concert was the first time."

That was several centuries ago, when I was young and innocent. I was still young but not so innocent. At the ripe old age of twenty, I was responsible for the deaths of four men: indirectly Barry, Ramsbottom, and Mr. Dirkson, and directly Pig Face, whose name I didn't even remember from the newspapers.

"It's too late now. You said it, and to change it might cause them to wonder. Remember, if I ever call you and identify myself as Danny Boy, you must never express any familiarity. We don't know if they have some way of listening in on your phone. It will be all strictly business."

"Right you are." He grinned. He seemed to have recovered some of his cockiness. "So what is the next step?"

"On Saturday I will call you direct. I suppose they are going to give me a number to call for you. The instructions will be very brief. Pick up the package, go to such and such a phone box in Bradford to receive further instructions."

Should I give him the instructions now? He'd probably be able to remember better if I did.

"Okay, here it is."

I proceeded to give him the details of the plan. I had constructed a complicated delivery to ten different lockers located at different parts of the city: bus stations, railway stations, meat lockers, self-storage places around the area. The first locker would contain several large plastic shopping bags, lots of newspapers, and the keys to the other lockers. Sean was to place the money in one bag and then camouflage the others to look like it with the aid of the newspapers. The idea was that if he was followed, they wouldn't be able to keep an eye on ten different locations. Only Sean and myself would know which locker the real parcel was in.

He repeated the instructions several times until I was sure he had it right. He was about to pocket the list of railroad stations.

"Just a minute. Let's not be careless. This list will be in the locker, and each key will be tagged for its location. We wouldn't want anyone to be going through your pockets and find this before you are supposed to have it, would we?"

Friday I called Flynn and told him I wanted to contact the carrier directly to give him my instructions. He informed me the code name was "Danny Boy." I acted as though I was suspicious and objected to the name but then accepted the idea. I was sure that they had something up their sleeves.

"Just make sure that the page of the ledger and five hundred thousand is in that package. Because if it isn't there and you try to get me again, I will he reading about you in the obituary columns within the week." I hung up without giving him chance to reply.

We played out the plan just as I had explained it, with one minor variation.

I called Sean at the appointed time and then again at the telephone box. He left for destination number one. The main thing I needed to know was what car was he driving. It was a green Chevrolet, license number FUG 769.

I waited patiently at the west end of the block that the YMCA was located in. Almost an hour passed before I saw the green Chevrolet coming down the off ramp from the expressway. I spotted it with at least two traffic lights to go before it reached the parking lot.

I walked in the main entrance and retrieved the small suitcase I'd left at the Y's reception desk and took up a position near the rear entrance. Risking only a quick glance around the corner to the granite-tiled entrance, Sean would be traversing in a few seconds. He was getting out of the car and trotting, as he had been told.

I laid the suitcase on the floor and snapped open the locks. A duplicate plastic shopping bag filled with crumpled newspapers was inside. Sean rounded the corner at an easy jog and almost did a beautiful sidestep around me.

"Sean, it's me." I grabbed him and looked into his startled eyes. "Quick, take this and give me that one. Ignore me and go along to the locker as though nothing has happened." He trotted off in a daze with his new burden, considerably lighter than the one I'd just taken from him.

Smoothly swinging the bag into the suitcase and snapping the locks closed, I was walking in the opposite direction before he had covered half the distance to the locker.

I headed across the pedestrian entrance toward the elevators. There were lots of people around, hurrying in and out in an effort to squeeze in a quick workout during their lunch break. It was difficult for me to tell if any of them had been following Sean.

Entering the elevator, I pressed the button for the fourth floor. The room I'd taken was on the sixth, but I would walk the last two flights.

As the elevator doors opened, I had a sickening feeling in the pit of my stomach. Things were not right. What was it?

I quietly opened the door to the stairwell and stepped inside. I was about to take the flight up, two steps at a time when I heard the sound of pounding feet and heavy breathing from below.

The stairs were constructed around some kind of central shaft, probably for the refuse disposal. There was no way to see who it was through the solid walls. Was it someone following me? It had to be. Why else would someone be in such a hurry running up a stairwell?

*This is the YMCA, you goddamn fool. Men come here for exercise. Maybe it's someone who just gets off running upstairs.* I stopped dead still. I could hear my pulse pounding in my head.

He paused to catch his breath and started to cough, one of those horrible coughs that sounds as though you are going to bring up something from your boots. He could only be half a flight down. I tiptoed to the corner and peered around the edge of the cement wall. He was dressed in street clothes and definitely not a regular visitor to the Y. Should I take him now or wait until he started up again? He took the decision out of my hands. He resumed his climb, not as fast and breathing very heavy.

At the moment he reached the top step, I whirled around the corner and hit him with my forearm across the throat. He was more solid than he looked. With his body leaning slightly forward, coupled with his momentum, all I had done was stop him in his tracks. I drew back and hit him with all my might in the stomach, and as he doubled over, I kicked him in the face. He tumbled backward down the concrete steps and landed with a dull thud at the landing below, facedown.

Running down the steps, I jumped from about the fourth one from the bottom and landed with both feet on his back. My heels must have broken every rib he had. I grabbed his hair with both hands and bashed his head into the floor about half a dozen times until I was sure he was senseless. Only then did I check to see if he was still alive. I wasn't sure, but if he wasn't dead, he wasn't far from it.

I started to check his pockets using my handkerchief to avoid fingerprints. I found an automatic pistol in one pocket and its silencer in the other then a cut-throat razor—these seemed to be standard issue for Fuller's mob. Nothing else was of major significance other than a driver's license that said he lived in Hartford Connecticut, and his name was Geoffrey Oakley. He was built a little like Pig Face, except he had been rather good-looking, in a rough sort of way. Too bad that face would never recover from the pounding I had given it. The razor slipped into my inside pocket and the gun into my belt. I stood for a moment, considering my next move.

First priority was to move this body before some unsuspecting stranger fell over him. He was heavy. The easiest way to move him was down the steps. I rolled him down each flight until we reached the basement level. I was pretty sure he was dead, and he would remain here undetected for quite a while.

I knew these bastards would try something. I hadn't been sure, but they were too ruthless to roll over and take what I was doing to then without putting up a fight. Had they sent the money this time? That would have to wait a few minutes longer. I climbed back up the stairs until I reached the first floor and then found my way to the pool area. I picked up a couple of used towels and returned to the basement area. Flynn and Fuller would have to be shown that I wasn't to be trifled with.

He was still there, undisturbed. I bent over and felt the pulse in his neck; there was nothing. I made sure. With his own razor, I cut his throat then, unzipping his fly, cut off his penis. I wrapped his organ in one of the face towels and then in another. There was more blood than I expected, and the first towel quickly soaked. The second towel made the bundle appear clean to the casual observer.

Once inside my room with the door bolted, I placed my bundle on a table and washed my hands. I then sat down for a full minute. When is this nightmare going to end? *You have set in motion forces that are enormous.* Flynn was right, I am out of my league. God, I hope nothing happens to Sean… He'll be all right as long as he does his rounds and visits every locker. I knew they were going to try something. I spotted that man in the lobby unconsciously because of the years of playing football.

Brendan had always said, "In any sport—football, basketball, hockey, whatever—always watch the opposition's eyes. They'll telegraph their moves with their eyes."

It had been a reflex action as soon as I had taken the "hand off" to check the "field." I hadn't realized how clearly I had spotted him until now.

My hands were sweating as I tried to unsnap the locks. Something I had done so easily downstairs was now a challenge.

Tipping the package out of the plastic bag, I dropped the towels containing his organ into it and went through the materials I had taken from him again. There was nothing of value, except for the beautiful automatic pistol with the silencer adapter. I examined the gun closely. German, fine craftsmanship. For a moment I considered keeping it. That would be dumb.

I carefully wiped each item to make sure there were no fingerprints and threw them in the plastic bag. Folded up, the whole thing was about as big as a large lettuce.

I turned my attention to the package. Opening it, I had my doubts, but this time they had hedged their bets. The money was there and so was the page from the ledger. Mr. Geoffrey "Prickless" Oakley downstairs had been their one last hope to retrieve it and get me.

I messed up the bed, ran the shower, soaped the face cloths, and generally made the place look as though it had been slept in.

The lift was so slow going down, and the walk across the main lobby seemed like a mile, but no one paid any attention. The cab swiftly pulled into the curb as I waved. It was one o'clock. The entire episode in the Y had taken thirty-two minutes.

"I need to go to an office supply store. Then the post office, then to Shawnut Bank down by the market. In that order, before one-thirty."

"There's Bailey's office supply just down here. It'll be difficult waiting, though."

"I'll pay for the ticket if you get one, and I'll make it worth your while," I assured him.

It took only a couple of minutes to buy a mailing box large enough to take the lettuce-sized contents. I addressed the label writing left-handed, which made it a scrawl but legible. At the post office I sent it, express mail, to the attention of Mr. Flynn c/o Fuller's.

We reached Shawmut Bank at twenty minutes past one.

The safety deposit box I had rented earlier received the half a million dollars and the page from the ledger was replaced in its original place with the rest of the evidence.

Fifty yards down the street from the bank was Leeds Luggage, where I had purchased the suitcase earlier.

"It really was too large, as I had said earlier this morning. I'd like to exchange it for that burgundy leather briefcase with the combination locks if I may," I reminded the salesman of my previous doubts about the transaction.

"Certainly, sir. No trouble at all. That will be fifteen dollars extra. Thank you, sir."

A brisk walk to the Kardomah, and I saw Sheila as she stopped traffic, looking for a parking spot. I leaned in the oven window and kissed her on the cheek. She was wearing a midnight-blue suit that contrasted with her flawless white skin, and her smile had the warmth I needed to raise my spirits. She looked as beautiful as I had ever seen her.

"Do you want a cup of espresso, or shall we go straight to Neville's and have instant coffee?" I asked.

"Let's go to Neville's and have instant something else," she said in a husky voice. My pulse rate had only just returned to normal, and now it was racing again as she slid over to let me drive.

# Chapter 14

If Maxwell House could ever have packaged the alternative that Sheila had for instant coffee, caffeine would have become extinct.

She had already told her mother that she had enrolled in art courses at the evening school with a "friend" Jennifer. She would be staying over at her house on Wednesday evenings. Also she would visit on weekends. She found Jennifer to be both intellectually stimulating and lots of fun.

She had not, however, broken off the engagement with Charles. In order to preserve the facade, she did have to see him on certain evenings during the week and at least one day on the weekend. I was extremely jealous. I tried to deal with the situation in a mature way, but it was evident she did have some deep feelings for Charles. She had told me he was a decent sort of fellow who treated her like a queen. Under any other circumstances he would have been a "good catch." She was going to feel terrible, breaking the news to him.

The newspapers were full of the bizarre murder at the "YMCA murder." None of the members were mentioned as possible suspects. It was reported the victim had been arrested for assault with a deadly weapon on three previous occasions. The press stories speculated it was a gang killing for revenge. They had paid up. I had to keep the pressure on. Sooner or later they would make a mistake, and then I would find a way to turn them in to the police. In the meantime, they had given me good justification for increasing my demands. This time I would leave Sean out of it. I was almost beginning to enjoy this game. They were really going to pay for what they had done.

"Flynn," I whispered as he answered the phone on Monday afternoon. "Did you get the memento I sent you?"

"Honest, I had nothing to do with that," he protested.

"Really? Well, whoever did have better be ready with half a million. It's going to be very expensive every time you misbehave like that."

"God Almighty, we don't have that kind of money. I had to beg, borrow, and steal every penny to raise the last lot. Look, I played it square with you. I don't know who tried to get at you, but it wasn't me."

"You have a very serious problem, Mr. Flynn. I don't care who did it. You were the only one I spoke to other than the little Irish shit. You are responsible. I will give you until Wednesday to raise another five hundred thousand. If you don't have it by then, you will never hear from me again. I'll never call you again. I'll just send you mementos of your kids one at a time." I couldn't believe I just said that. I almost started to apologize.

"You're crazy, you're not human. Please don't do anything to my kids."

"I'm very human, and I'm easily pleased. Just deliver the five hundred thousand without any problems, and I'll leave you in peace. Remember, I don't want to break you. You are the goose that lays the golden eggs. I'll call you Wednesday at noon." I broke the connection.

He sounded very tired when I called on Wednesday.

"Been losing same sleep, have you, Flynn?"

"It's not been easy, but I've got it. Look, you must believe me. I had nothing to do with last time, and if anything happens this time, you know I wouldn't endanger my kids."

"Relax, Mr. Flynn. This time you are going to deliver personally. This time you will be the only one to know where the delivery will take place. Be at this phone at eight o'clock tomorrow morning. Package the money in brown wrapping paper. Tie it with strong twine and seal the knots with sealing wax." He indicated he understood.

At eight forty-five he answered the phone on the first ring.

"God, I thought you would never call," he screamed almost hysterically. His nerves seemed completely shot.

"Go to the post office on Market Street and to the end pay phone in the lobby and wait for my call. Do it now."

He left immediately. I watched him from a safe distance as he dashed into the post office. I sauntered to the telephone box on the street.

Again he answered immediately.

"Underneath the coin box is an envelope. It's stuck there with scotch tape. Have you got it?" He confirmed that he had. "Inside is a label with an address typed on it. Stick the label on, go to the counter, and send it first-class."

"That's it?"

"Yes, and don't let me see you hanging around that address."

"No, I won't," he was saying as I broke the connection.

I walked back to the Fiat I had purchased with some of the funds from last week. I had taken delivery yesterday. It was a beauty: three years old, just about the limit of what I could afford if I had gone the financing route. Financial security was no longer a problem; in fact, an overabundance of cash was going to be my problem. Fred's proposal of a partnership started to look even more attractive.

Saturday morning I went to the post office in Newton and boldly picked up the parcel. It was just as I had instructed—brown paper wrapping sealed with sealing wax and the label with the address:

*Mr. Flowers,*
*P.O. Box 479,*
*Chestnut Hill, Mass.*

The label had been crossed out by the post office and had an additional label added.

*Forward to:*

*Mr. Flowers,*
*P.O. Box 135,*
*Newton, Mass.*

The safety deposit box at Shawmut Bank was not big enough. I had to rent a larger one. I decided to spread my business around and went to the First National Bank near the Corn Exchange.

Opening a checking account at First National with a modest deposit of a few hundred dollars, I left the checkbooks in the safety deposit box and kept a couple of checks from each book.

I had my regular account at the Waltham Federal, where I deposited my salary check. That was what I had to live on, being careful that I didn't live beyond my visible means.

But I had decided I would go into partnership with Fred. I had nothing to lose. Being in business for myself offered the benefits of letting me use some of these secret funds without anyone raising his eyebrows.

The week was a blur of activity meeting with Fred. He was very receptive to me being the financial, technical, and manufacturing person. He would be responsible for sales and creativity. I insisted that we had to make a real commitment to the success of our new company, and we would start by finding a manufacturing facility to lease.

Later that evening Neville gave me the name of a commercial realtor, Peter Lehman, who handled residential and business properties. We met the next day and looked at several small machine shops, all of them priced at around one hundred to one seven hundred thousand dollars. I had to be careful; although I could pay cash, people might start to talk about someone with that kind of money to throw around. The most promising one was, of course, the most expensive. The owner was retiring. He had seven employees, all of whom highly skilled, and several continuous contracts with local manufacturers. We negotiated the purchase for a hundred thousand down and an installment sale with the balance payable over five years—no banks involved. We signed the papers Tuesday. Now I was committed.

"Peter, this is going to sound strange to you. Neville had given me your name, and I know we are both good friends of his. However, I don't want him to know that I'm purchasing the machine shop. I want to set up a separate company to own it then lease it back to me and my partner at a fair rent. Can I count on your confidentiality?"

"Sure, it's not unusual at all for our customers to have different solicitors for various types of activity."

"Can you recommend someone who could do that for me?"

"My brother is an attorney, and he has recently started his own practice. He worked for the same firm as Neville but decided to hang out his own shingle. Here is his card, Paul Lehman."

That same day I rented an apartment about a mile from Neville's. I hired an interior decorator to furnish it completely on the understanding that it must be ready for occupancy by Friday.

There was a message at Peters' office, relayed from Neville: *Call Sheila—Urgent*

"Sheila, it's John. What's the matter?"

"Daddy died an hour ago. Mummy had only left him for a few minutes to go to the store. When she came home, he had collapsed. They rushed him to the hospital, but he was dead when they got him there. Please don't come over. Charles is on his way, and now is no time to create a fuss. It does mean I can't see you tomorrow. The funeral will be Friday, and I am going to leave after that to visit Jennifer for a few days."

"Do you want to meet Friday evening or Saturday morning?"

"Friday evening would be the best. I'm going to catch the five-thirty train into the city then—" Someone must have come into the room, and she was saying that for their sake.

"I'll be waiting for you at the curb."

"Yes, that would be nice," she said, almost bursting into tears.

I was very sorry Mr. Clegg had passed away. In spite of everything, I couldn't bear him any malice. I had tried to put myself in his position, to see things from his point of view. Whatever the circumstances were that caused him to become involved in payoffs to city officials, I was sure it was something that had been beyond his control. I found myself thinking about the happy times we had spent together, the drives home after work when he made me feel as though he had so much faith in my ability, his initial approval of my relationship with Sheila. He truly was a kind and generous man. I felt a pang of resentment.

My God, he could afford to be generous! They had raped the local councils for hundreds of thousands. On the other hand, the Cleggs didn't live in abject luxury. They were "well-off," even rich, by my standards. Of course, they were being blackmailed. Most of the extra profits had gone to pay bribes and then to the blackmailers.

I didn't want to remember him like that. I wanted only to think of the good times, wipe out the intervening years and remember that any estrangement between us had been a result of Fuller and his people. I was going to get them. His death, sad as it was, certainly uncomplicated our lives.

I hadn't seen her for almost two weeks. Although I had told her about the possibility of my leaving Lands' and the partnership with Fred, I hadn't mentioned anything about moving permanently downtown.

I couldn't tell her that I had bought the business. There was no way I could account for my sudden flush of money. Paul Lehman wanted to call the company Dunne Buildings Ltd. I settled for DB Ltd. and told everyone that the owner was a David Bernstein, a financier from Long Island.

The lease arrangement for the factory office and use of the machinery on an hourly basis, I flattered myself, was a stroke of genius. The terms I presented to Fred and Neville were very reasonable—low rates but not low enough to create suspicion.

No one needed to know who owned the business. As I was handling the financial matters, I would issue a check to DB Ltd. each month for the lease. With the income from the regular production operations, the repayment to the former owner should take care of itself. If it didn't, a supplemental deposit from my funds would.

The only snag was that DB Ltd. had no visible general manager. I had explained to Fred that one of the reasons that we had such a "Golden lease" arrangement was that I agreed to act as general manager until such time as "he" could find a suitable one.

Friday I picked Sheila up at the station. She was in rather low spirits, but she was thrilled that we were at last together.

"Oh John, it's been terrible with Mummy. She's getting over it now, but it was dreadful for her. All these years of nursing him, and he seemed to be getting better. He'd started walking again, you know. Just a little bit, but he was improving every week. Then to find him like that." She sniffled into her pretty handkerchief. Found him like what? I thought, *I wasn't aware of anything unusual about his death.* I had only read the formal announcement in the newspaper. There hadn't been any word about anything other than a stroke.

"What happened? How did she find him?" I asked.

"She had just gone to the store to pick up a few things, only left him for about twenty minutes. When she came back, he was nowhere around. He had been walking for short distances, around the house and around the garden. One of us was always with him, though, especially outside. We would have his wheelchair ready for him if he got tired. Well, Mummy panicked when he wasn't in the living room. She dashed from room to room and out into the backyard. He was gone, disappeared. Then she noticed the door to the basement was open, and she found him down there." She paused again to hold back the tears.

"That is sad," I said, feeling hopelessly inadequate and knowing what was to come.

"Mummy said he was on the floor, over in the corner by some old toolboxes. He had been going through his old tools and searching for something. His mind must have gone, John. He must have got some notion about fixing something and went downstairs to get his tools for the job. Anyway, he was still alive when Mummy found him, but by the time the ambulance arrived, he was in a very bad way...he was dead when they arrived at the hospital."

I tried to console her. It took some time for all the grief come out. Eventually she composed herself and said she felt much better.

"Thanks for letting me get that off my chest. The last few days I've had to keep a stiff upper lip." She smiled. "Everybody has been expecting me to have all the answers. Mummy has been so withdrawn and upset. I've had to carry the whole load. The business has been hectic. Bates and Taylor have been running back and forth to Washington on this big contract we've been fighting for, and I've had to hold the fort here. Even at the funeral, can you imagine, Bates and Taylor had to mention buying Daddy's stock. Worst of all, when

Dick Fuller came up to me to pay his respects—the old slug, he's been our fiercest competitor for years—he said that if I considered selling the company stock, he would like to make an offer." She took a deep breath and squared her shoulders. Talking about the business had brought spirit back into her voice.

"Well, I feel I've just been pulled back from the edge of a nervous breakdown—the relief, I can't tell you. It's all over now. No amount of crying will bring Daddy back. Let's go and have a good time and put all this out of our minds."

On the way to the apartment I filled her in on the facts of leaving Lands', starting the partnership, and getting a place of my own to rent.

I had arranged with the local Italian restaurant to prepare a complete meal with wine and leave everything ready to serve ourselves when we got there.

"I'm really excited about my newfound independence, Sheila."

"Does that mean you have no interest in getting married?"

"What? Of course, we're going to get married. I just meant it was a good way station—for a bachelor who didn't know if he'd have to wait until age eighty to marry his one true love. We need to talk about that, seeing as you brought it up."

"Yes, I know we do. We'll talk about it tonight. I love the apartment. It's very large for two people, but…it would be a bit cramped if we had some children."

"Ah, we don't want to talk about babies so quickly. I've just started a new business. We can't afford to be taking on added responsibilities any sooner than necessary."

Her face dropped. I thought she was going to burst into tears.

"Don't do that," I said. "Of course, we are going to have children and as many as you like and as soon as you like. I can't wait to see your mum with grandchildren on her lap. Speaking of your mum, have you decided when to tell her, or have you already?"

"No, I haven't. It was impossible. I told you how she was. Then at the funeral I found out she and Daddy had made arrangements with the Laughton's to attend a special charity dance next week. Daddy was planning to go in his wheelchair. They were going to make him the honorary chairman for the charity. Since he died, they've decided they want to make an even more special tribute. Mr. Laughton, Charlies' father, is going to say some nice things and give Mummy a posthumous award for Daddy. Which, of course, means that Charlie and I have to be there."

"One week from this Sunday I am coming to your house. You will tell your mother that you are breaking your engagement with Charlie and you are going to marry me. You are free, white, and over twenty-one, and if she has any objections, I believe I can deal with them. We are going to get married as soon as the law allows, and that is final. Is that clear, Sheila?"

"Yes, oh yes. Don't be angry. I get so frightened when you get angry."

"I'm not angry. I am frustrated. We have gone through seven years of not being able to be with one another, and now—well, I'm impatient. I'm not mad."

"You looked mad. I've only seen that look a couple of times. When you look like that, I feel you could really hurt someone. I'll never forget that night with Webber." She shuddered. "I really thought you might have killed him if that gang wasn't with him."

I hugged her. "Don't be silly. You tell your mother when you are ready. I've waited this long, and if I have to wait another five or fifty years, I'll still be here."

"Oh John, I love you so much. I will tell her a week from Sunday, the morning after the charity ball."

"All right, now how long are you visiting Jennifer?"

"Why? Do you have someone else coming in? This outside catering can be taken too far."

"Well, I didn't know…I mean, I wasn't expecting…"

"God Almighty, John Dunne, I need you more than anything else right now, emotionally and physically. You let me unburden myself, and that was great, but I need you to hold me and caress me. I need to escape from the horrors of the last few days. You're the only one that can do it for me." She took hold of my hand and leaned her head closer.

"I'm sorry. Look—a pact: no more talking about your mother, marriage, children, or the future at all until you leave, agreed?"

"Agreed. Let's just screw our brains out!"

"You slut—till when?"

"Monday morning. I have an appointment with the attorneys on Monday at ten. I wonder, can Jennifer stand me that long?"

"Jennifer maybe, but I might be admitted to the psycho ward before then."

"That would be interesting"—she smiled in a way I'd never seen before—"taking advantage of you in a straightjacket, very interesting."

I ushered her toward the stairs.

The weekend was exactly what Sheila needed to restore her mental attitude. The more she saw of the apartment, the more she loved it. She insisted on cooking Sunday dinner. We lazed around, made love, and I really began to see us living happily ever after.

# *Chapter 15*

Monday arrived too soon. I had intended to start work on one of Freds' patents and sketch up the parts needed to build it. Now I had offered to run Sheila into the attorney's office Monday morning. She had persuaded me to go with her.

Robert Staincliffe had been Cleggs' attorney for years. Burthold, Staincliffe, and Richardson were the oldest and largest firm of solicitors in Chestnut Hill. Burthold, the founder, had been Sheila's grandfather's solicitor, and the firm also represented Clegg, Bates, and Taylor.

"Mr. Staincliffe, good to see you again. This is my fiancé."

"Nice to meet you, sir." I could tell he didn't know if he had heard the name or not. He wasn't interested anyway.

Staincliffe was a cold fish, his eyes and his handshake matched. He was friendly, but one could tell it was false.

"Sheila, under the circumstances, it will be all right for your fiancé to be present, I suppose, but we are going to be talking about your personal finances, and you may wish to do that alone with me."

I stood up to leave.

"No, I want him to stay. We won't have any secrets in our marriage."

"Very well. Miss Hawthorn," he spoke into the intercom. Then to both of us, "Would you like coffee or tea?" We both opted for tea. "Three cups of tea please, then I don't wish to be disturbed."

He started to explain the will of Mr. Clegg.

Harold Clegg had left everything to his children to be divided equally. Of course, with Barry dead, Sheila was the sole heir. Her mother was to have the use of the house for as long as she lived or wished to remain there. She was also the beneficiary in a life-insurance policy that presumably would provide her with adequate income for the rest of her days.

Sheila was the beneficiary in another insurance policy for three hundred thousand dollars. She also received one third of the stock in Clegg, Bates and Taylor. The other two thirds of the stock were still in the name of Mr. Clegg, but had been "mortgaged" to Misters Bates and Taylor some seventeen years ago and would go to them to discharge the note.

He paused while Miss Hawthorne poured the tea and asked if Sheila had any questions. She didn't have any, so he proceeded.

"I have been instructed by Mr. Bates and Mr. Taylor to tell you that they are willing to buy our stock. They feel that according to the most recent independent audit"—he slid a portfolio over to Sheila with the name of a prestige certified public accountant on it—"that the fair market price would be three hundred thousand. However, in consideration for your family's long association with the firm, they are willing to offer you one five hundred thousand."

He paused again and stood up.

Walking slowly around the desk, he said, "Frankly, Miss Clegg, I think it would be a very smart thing to do. Sell them the remainder of the stock, and you'd be set for life."

While he had been moving around the desk, I had casually picked up the auditor's report. I also picked up some old papers that were part of the package that read *Mortgage*. Quickly I glanced at the face amount, the interest rate, and the redemption terms.

I had just gone through the same kind of deal buying my business. The language was different, but I could see that this was no ordinary mortgage note. I was also thinking that a mortgage was a mortgage, not a sale. He's not telling her everything. I pushed the papers to one side of the desk and accidentally knocked my teacup off. In my frantic attempt to catch it, I also knocked over the tray with the milk and sugar and teapot on it.

That majestic old desk must have been his pride and joy. The cold fish suddenly turned into a flying fish. Dashing to the door, he yelled for Miss Hawthorne. Just as quickly I picked up all the papers and gave them to Sheila.

"Tell him you can't make a decision now. You have to think about it. I want Neville to look at these. Insist you take them with you."

Miss Hawthorne appeared immediately. She had miraculously acquired the materials to right the terrible wrong.

While Staincliffe was busy supervising the mop-up, Sheila announced, "Thank you for putting me in the picture. Obviously, I can't make a decision right now. I'll think about it and call you later in the week."

"Wait, please, Miss Clegg, you can't take those with you. I need those papers to properly discharge the will."

"I need to study them closely before I make a decision of this magnitude. Don't worry, I'm the only heir, so I'm not going to change anything."

"Yes, but I'm your attorney, and it's my responsibility to advise you on these matters."

"You also act for Mr. Bates and Mr. Taylor, don't you?" she challenged. "Isn't that what is called conflict of interest?"

He was looking pretty uncomfortable when he said, "Well, yes."

*Good for you, Sheila*, I thought. Most people cowered before their attorneys as if they were mini Gods and blindly accepted whatever they were told or advised by them. Sheila was showing a side that I'd never seen before.

Staincliffe's mouth dropped open, and Sheila and I moved toward the door.

"I will be engaging a new firm. They will be in touch with you regarding my decision."

The flying fish went into action. He reached the door in double time and placed his back to it.

"It was so nice meeting you," I said, extending my hand. He automatically reached out for it. "You had better tell Miss Hawthorne to call the police," I whispered so only he could hear, "because if you attempt to stop us from leaving,"—I started to squeeze the limp hand, his face twisted in pain—"I will break every bone in your body." I relaxed the grip to the point that he knew that the intensity could be repeated swiftly.

"Well, I suppose that you are right, Miss Clegg. If you feel that it is in your best interests to retain another firm, we will be only too happy to cooperate with them."

I released his hand.

"Thank you, and good morning," Sheila said as she strode regally out of the office.

We reached the street before either of us spoke.

"I was so proud of you in there. 'Conflict of interest,' really. Have you been seeing Neville on the side? He always fancied you."

"I'm rather proud of myself. I'm so glad you told me to demand the documents. Bates and Taylor had already said at the funeral they wanted to make arrangements with the firm's stock, that they would be making an offer, but something didn't seem right. What prompted you in there to tell me to do it?"

"Just what you said, something is fishy. The stock, the mortgage. A mortgage is a loan against a security, which in this case is the company stock. If the mortgage is not paid, then the stock can be foreclosed on, and it would become rightfully theirs. Bates and Taylor haven't done that. Why? There must be some reason they haven't exercised that right. The terms of redemption are not clear to me. A legal interpretation is needed. That's why I think you should see Neville."

We met Neville for lunch, and he cleared his calendar for the afternoon. I protested that we didn't have all the money in the world.

"I haven't even accepted Miss Clegg as a client yet, so the clock is not running. Relax."

Neville reviewed the entire file and summarized the situation.

"Your grandfather, Sheila, was a wily old bird. He and Burthold pulled a fast one on Bates and Taylor. I speculate that he, your grandfather, got into a financial bind seventeen years ago. Not having the normal banking channels available—sometimes the construction industry is not the safest place to lend money—he had to deal with Bates and Taylor.

"However, he didn't sell them the stock. It had always been his intention to redeem the mortgage. They had negotiated all the rights and privileges of full partnership while they held the stock as collateral for the loan. But he had made the language such that any Clegg could redeem the mortgage, and there is no due date. So if you can pay it off either from your personal funds or by going to the bank, you will own Clegg, Bates and Taylor outright. You do now, actually, but you don't have control" He let that sink in.

"Now we come to the reality of the situation. They control the business, they have all the contacts. You could continue as your father did and take a planned approach to paying off the mortgage. However, from what you've told me about their overtures and the contact that Fuller made, it may be that they already have some scheme hatching to sell out to Fuller. Obviously, the deal would be stronger for them if they had all the stock, and weaker for them if Fuller got your stock—or should I say, the third that everybody acknowledges is yours. If you turn down their offer, they may sell to Fuller anyway—they could sell him the mortgage—that would make Dick Fuller your partner. For this reason, taking their offer might make the best sense."

I was crushed. I had hoped Neville would have some idea that would show Sheila was getting cheated. But here he was, saying basically the same thing that Stalncliffe had said. He had said it more clearly and honestly, but it was the same, possibly worse—she might end up with Fuller as a partner.

"Not only that," he continued, "even if you did pay them off and take over the firm entirely, you don't know how to run it. You know the accounting end, but—correct me if I'm wrong—you have had little or no exposure to the operational and sales part of the business. They could take their cash and start another company tomorrow. As I said, they have the contacts and the knowledge."

"So you are saying turn my grandfather's company over to them?"

"No, Sheila, what I'm saying here are the facts. You have to make the decision. I will act for you and do whatever you want me to do."

"How much will it take to pay them off?"

"Ask the math whiz. He's tried to teach me, but I would take his numbers before mine."

"Sheila is quicker at that than I am," I said.

"Let me have your adding machine," she said matter-of-factly.

The face amount of the mortgage was not an astronomical amount by today's standards, but in seventeen years, with interest compounded annually, I whistled at the resultant figure. Sheila asked me to double-check her calculations.

"Seven hundred and seventy-nine thousand and change."

"Can you raise that kind of money?"

"No. At least I don't think so."

"So what do you want me to do?"

"Nothing. I want to think about it. Daddy and Granpa gave their whole lives to that business. It's obvious they didn't want this to happen. There must be a way."

"Well, the only way I can see is, you raise the money to buy them out. You arrange with than to stay on, for at least five years, with the same basic benefits they have now so that you can learn the business. Also have them sign a noncompete clause, which means they will not start another similar business for at least another five years. By that time, you will be well established, and they will be too old. Frankly, I think your chances are slim to none."

She called her mother before we left Neville's office and told her a condensed version of the story. After a minor skirmish, she told her she would be home on Wednesday.

Two more days with Sheila under any other circumstances would have been an answer to my most fervent prayers. But this was a different Sheila. She was consumed with the idea of keeping the business. She couldn't sleep; she had no appetite. She was on the verge of exhaustion. Her sexual appetite of the weekend disappeared. That had been an outlet for tensions, but now the tension was back, bigger than ever.

By Tuesday noon she was so tired I put her to bed. I told her to call me if she woke up and wanted me. I couldn't just sit around waiting, so I called Ben.

Ben, the retiring business owner, had already agreed to stay on for three months. He would help us get started after we took over on August 1. Even though we were still a few weeks away from the takeover, I had already developed a great rapport with him. I decided to stop by and discuss with Ben some of the modifications to Fred's fuel-injection system. The basic design was good, but once again it lacked practicality. I persuaded Ben to help me make a couple of prototypes.

We both worked solid all afternoon and through the evening.

It was three thirty in the morning when we had all the parts and assembled them. It looked good, very professional. The parts had gone together with that comfortable feeling always associated with quality precision work. Now the question was, did it work? I wasn't an auto mechanic, and we needed to test the prototype in a practical way.

"We'll talk about this tomorrow," Ben said. He was clearly tired. "You're a slave driver. I don't think I'll last that three months—no, I'm only kidding. I haven't enjoyed myself so much for years. Good night."

Sheila was still pretty sluggish the next morning, and I had arranged with Fred to meet me at the shop. I left her for a couple of hours.

I introduced Ben and his son, Peter, to Fred for the first time. I explained how the fuel-injection system was supposed to work. Peter felt the best application would be on the truck they used for delivery. Not only had they kept a daily log of the mileage and gas usage, they even had a record of the weight carried on the truck for each trip. This would be important for making an accurate comparison. Peter also said if we wanted to test the system on a passenger vehicle, he kept a similar log for his own car. The habit of keeping a log was something that came automatically for him. Ben had disciplined him well.

Ben had said nothing to Peter regarding our arrangement to purchase the firm. DR Ltd. were a New York based investment company as far has he was concerned. So there was no problem letting Peter and Fred work together. Peter was a miniature version of his father. Once he got involved, he was full of suggestions for improvements. Thursday we would have a unit installed on both the truck and his car.

Returning home, I was dismayed at the state of Sheila. She had gone back to bed again and taken another tranquilizer. I made a quick trip to the drugstore and persuaded the pharmacist to give me some lookalike placebos. I felt she might become addicted if she took too many.

I called Neville.

"I've just had an idea. I have a contact that I met in New York. His name is David Bernstein—in fact, he owns the business we are leasing. I know he's interested in investments, particularly in a good company. I could talk to him, and maybe he would loan Sheila the balance of what she needs to pay off the mortgage."

"John, who's going to run it? She still needs Bates and Taylor."

"Well, you call her here in an hour. Tell her you think you may have someone who will loan her up to a half a million. If she can work the other details out, she's in business. At least that will boost her spirits for now."

"I hate to give her false hopes. What if your friend doesn't come up with the cash? Why don't you tell her yourself?"

"I'm sure he will. I just talked to him and told him what I had gleaned from the audit. He says if those figures can be verified, he would work out a deal. The reason I don't want to tell her myself is that, well, if on the outside chance it doesn't work out, I don't want to be the one who lets her down. With you handling it, it would be just a financier who didn't come through. With me, she might take it more personally."

"Okay, I'll call in an hour."

Before Neville called back, I woke her with the excuse that it would soon be time for dinner. She probably would want to freshen up. She really didn't seem to care about anything until Neville called.

"Oh, Neville, that's wonderful! How long will he keep the offer available? Well, yes, I understand he will need to study the reports. I'm sure they are all in order. Good. Well, I'll talk to Bates and Taylor and get back to you. Yes, later this week, or at latest Monday."

She was absolutely radiant when she replaced the receiver. She had a new excitement about her. It was different, it was the excitement of ambition—no sexuality. She was still beautiful, but in a way that showed determination.

She had set her heart on keeping the company more than ever. I had to be careful; if she couldn't keep Bates and Taylor, accepting defeat was going to be doubly hard now.

When she hung up, I asked with a smile, "Good news?"

"Fabulous news. Neville has contacted someone, an investor who says he's interested in loaning up to five hundred thousand to help me keep the company."

"That's terrific," I said with enthusiasm. "Now all you have to do is persuade Bates and Taylor to stay, and you have everything you want."

"I *will* have everything. This business…and you." She said it with a sudden tenderness.

I felt a sense of relief. Had I any doubts? Obviously, I had. For the first time I was seeing Sheila with a sense of purpose that seemed to transcend her need for me. I felt that the business had become a rival. God, how childish of me. She was merely showing the same kind of determination I felt when I was committed to something. But I wasn't sure I was comfortable with it. It was new, and I supposed I'd get used to it. I would have to get used to it.

As I was thinking, her fingers were on the dial.

"Mr. Bates, Sheila Clegg. Fine, thank you. Yes, I'd like to talk to Mr. Taylor and yourself about the future of the company. Could we meet at my house this evening? Yes, I understand. About eight o'clock? Fine, I'll see both of you then."

She turned again and leaned back against the doctor's old desk with a look of satisfaction.

"They are coming tonight at eight. Can't make it earlier. Taylor is coming back on the shuttle this evening. He just signed the documents with the Pentagon for that contract they've been working on."

"How are you going to persuade them to stay?"

"I don't think that they could just quit. They have just negotiated this big contract. That should be enough work to keep everybody busy for a while. I'll tell them that if they want to leave, fine. At the salaries they've been drawing from the company, plus all the perks, I will be able to hire someone to replace them." She lifted herself by her palms and sat easily upon the desk. "I take the *Wall Street Journal*. Every day you see advertisements for top executives. Well, I'll advertise in there, the *Globe*, the *New York Times*. I'm sure lots of qualified people would jump at the opportunity to have a relatively free rein."

This sweet, innocent young lady had just been transformed from a miserable, moping, despairing wreck into a dynamic businesswoman. Naive, yes, but with a will to win. I suddenly felt she could do it.

"Sometimes he talks to me as though he expects me to take over some day…," Sheila said on our first date. What had I said?

"If that's what you want to do, you probably will." I hadn't dreamed, then I would be a party to it.

# Chapter 16

I drove her home in the Fiat and told her I would call later.

"I'm going to visit with my mother and father this evening, Sheila, so be sure to answer the phone before your mother. I don't want to upset her by having to hang up without speaking."

"I will, I will. Talk to you later, darling," she said as she kissed me goodbye at the end of the street.

I didn't know how "David Bernstein" would feel about it. Would a prudent investor really take a flyer with half a million? I didn't care. It was probably her money by rights anyway, all the money that the firm had paid out in blackmail over the years. She could have it all if she wanted it. All that was left, that is.

The original plan of getting Fuller's to incriminate themselves had backfired. I had their money, but I'd never had any intention originally of using it for personal gain. However, I realized that once the line had been crossed, there was no turning back. The death of Mr. Dirkson had been an accident, but killing the two thugs was deliberate. It had been self-defense, but it would be hard to convince a jury that my motives were as noble as they seemed to me at the time.

I felt a deep sense of sadness about Barry and also Mr. Clegg, but no remorse for what I felt I had to do. Threatening Fuller caused me some guilt feelings. Using his children to scare him had been too much; it had put me on their level. Yet one way to beat his kind was to be willing when necessary to be even worse than they were, to threaten the things in their lives they treasured most.

I had made myself judge and jury. I decided I had to make them pay; that was the end of it. Using the money to help Sheila seemed the proper way to close the whole affair. We could start our lives together the way we'd always dreamed.

As promised, I called her at about nine o'clock.

"Sheila, this is John."

"I'm so glad you called, Gerry." She used Gerry Dirkson's name, Chief Inspector Dirkson's son. It was like a knife through the heart.

"This is John, darling."

"Yes, I know. I'm fine, how are you? Please, Gerry, I know this is a lot to ask, but could you please call the police? You would know who to ask for. There are two gentlemen here that have been requested to leave and refuse. They have been threatening me, and I want them out of the house."

"I'm on my way," I said, hanging up the phone.

I broke every speed limit, missed every stop sign, and arrived at the house in less than five minutes. I couldn't find a parking spot until I rounded the corner.

As I left the car, I heard Sheila shouting, "And don't you dare come back here! From now on, you talk to my attorney!" The door crashed shut with a resounding bang.

Bates and Taylor were just closing the gate with the same kind of energy as I stepped into the gateway next door. There were no lights close by, and I stood in the shadows as they walked to the car parked only a few yards away.

Most of what they said was unintelligible, but they were furious.

"Goddamn little bitch, who does she think she is?"

"She'll ruin everything we've worked for."

"Fuck her. Let her have it. We'll start our own company and put her out of business."

"Don't be stupid, Harry. We've got too much invested, too many things coming to a head right now. No! We're staying. She's as good as dead." He said the words in the same kind of flat tone that I used talking to Flynn.

I held my breath so they wouldn't hear me, and I broke into a sweat that belied the coolness of the evening. I could feel my anger rising as I listened to them. I almost confronted them but decided on a different course.

The car pulled away, and Sheila, who must have been watching them out of the window, suddenly opened the door. I could hear her mother crying helplessly.

"I'm going for a walk, Mother. I'll be back in an hour or so. Go to bed. Don't worry about it. I know what I'm doing. I'm the boss now, and they will either do as I say or get out."

She closed the gate more carefully than the previous departees, as I stepped out of the shadows.

"Oh John, you startled me. I got rid of them. Did you see the nuns beat it? They were mad as hell. They were yelling and shouting, 'You can't do this, we'll sue,' all that kind of nonsense, but they knew they couldn't win, so I told them straight out. 'Think about it overnight and let me now in the morning. Either you stay with a contract for five years and a noncompete clause for another five, or you leave right now with a month's severance pay."

No wonder they were ready to kill her. She had backed them into a corner and given them an impossible deadline to make a decision—with little way of saving face.

"I saw them leave. They seemed very upset—couldn't you have given them until next Monday to think about it?"

"No, sir. I have already composed the advertisement for both positions, and I showed them. They will go to the paper at ten o'clock tomorrow unless they agree to sign the five-year contract. I need to know if they are with me or not."

We walked to the car and drove around. I tried to reason with her.

"Look, you're not even sure if you can get the money if they leave. This investor, he might get cold feet if he knows you've fired the two top people."

"That doesn't matter. I'll find someone else. You know, if Neville could find an investor so quickly, well, there has to be others. When investors see the size of the contract we just landed and the résumés of the candidates that respond to the advertisement, well, I have no doubt I can pull it off."

"Sheila, please don't get too carried away. Give Bates and Taylor a chance. They are the ones that landed that contract. You don't know if there is a cancellation loophole in it. What if that happens and Bates and Taylor form their own company, renegotiate the contract, and steal it away from you?"

"They'd better not even think about that. I'd sue them for every penny I am paying them, plus everything they own. There was an article last year about how some executives had done something similar. They lost everything. The court ruled that their previous firm had to be awarded the contract. Plus, additional damages had to be paid by the firm who awarded the contract, and there were significant personal damages awarded as well. Whoever their contact is in Washington had better watch out for himself. I could probably find the article if I went back to the *Wall Street Journal*. I think it was around February last year. I think Neville would love a case like that. He looks like someone who would be great in a tough legal battle."

I had created a monster, a lovely monster. She was so confident. The fright I heard on the phone less than half an hour ago, that must have been for effect. She wasn't scared of anything. However, she wasn't aware that the game could get awfully rough and dirty.

"Still, you agree. If they come around and decide to stay, they are your best bet for getting the money and making a success of the whole thing?"

"Absolutely. If they decide to stay, I will treat them with every respect. I will listen to their advice. There will be no hard feelings. I can understand them being mad tonight. They thought they had the whole thing sewn up, and I turned the tables on them." She almost grinned. "Well, we'll see. I told them to call Neville's office before ten tomorrow. He will let me know their decision. If it's yes, they are staying. I will go to the office, and we will have a meeting. If it's no, they are leaving and then I plan to go down there still. But I will have Neville obtain a court order for them to leave. They will turn over the keys and leave the premises with only their personal effects. Come to think of it, I probably should have a locksmith change all the locks."

"Call me tomorrow and let me know what happens, and I'll see you Sunday," I said.

I sounded more confident than I felt.

She kissed me with feeling, but I wasn't sure the adrenal in pulsing through her was entirely for me.

# *Chapter 17*

The plan of Fuller's was becoming clearer. It wasn't just a case of blackmail all these years. He had been trying to weaken Clegg's, to cripple it financially so that he could take it over. Fuller's and Clegg, Bates and Taylor were the two major construction companies in the northeast. Combined, they would rival some of the biggest in the country. I didn't know what Bates and Taylor were planning, but whatever their scheme, they weren't going to harm Sheila.

It was almost midnight when I called Harold Bates.

"Mr. Bates?" I hadn't woken him up.

"Yes."

I continued in the flat whisper I used when I called Flynn.

"Mr. Bates, you don't know me, but it has come to my attention that you and Mr. Taylor have some plans that I do not approve of."

"Who is this?"

"This is someone who has the power to ruin you financially and personally, and I will definitely see to it that you hang—either legally or by my hand—if one hair on Miss Clegg's head is even pushed out of shape."

"What are you talking about? I have no idea—"

"Shut up and listen. I have in my possession the ledger that details the payoffs you made. If you want proof, I can provide you with names of some of the recipients. Not those that were speculated about in the newspapers. Others whose names have never been mentioned before. The case was never closed, and even if there is a statute of limitations on the crime, there is no statute that would protect you and the people in the ledger from the IRS. They will want their pound of flesh from everybody. Not only back income tax but jail terms." I paused, but he didn't respond. "I also know that this evening you personally announced to your partner that you intended Miss Clegg to die rather suddenly. That will not happen."

"I never meant it. I was mad, just an expression…a figure of speech." He was flustered and scared.

"You will call your partner immediately and tell him of this conversation. You will also advise Miss Clegg that you have reconsidered her offer of staying with the company, that you are both prepared to stay on and sign the contracts she offered you. You will say that direct to Miss Clegg before nine o'clock tomorrow morning. You will apologize for your behavior this evening and then you will call her solicitor and advise him to draw up the documents. You will not mention this conversation to either Miss Clegg or her solicitor. Is that clear?"

"Who are you? What's your interest in this?" He couldn't disguise his nervousness.

"I'm the one who put a stop to the blackmail you were paying for years. That's all you need to know. If you do as I say, you will never be blackmailed again. You will enjoy a happy and prosperous life. If you ignore me, you are dead—yes, you heard me, dead." I paused slightly for effect. "I will not ask you for money. I will simply kill both of you. You will take the repayment of the loan with interest. You will enjoy the same salary and benefits you have been enjoying. Or take out some hefty life insurance quickly. Your families might need it."

At nine fifteen the next morning the phone rang; it was Sheila.

"I told you they would cave in!" she shouted triumphantly. "They both called this morning, and Mummy answered the phone. At first I refused to speak to them. After they had apologized to Mummy, they pleaded to speak to me. They admitted I was right. They had underestimated my resourcefulness because of my youth. Realizing after talking about it that if I could raise that kind of money, I ought to be treated with respect, and they would be happy to work for me. They said they were going to call Neville and ask him to draw up the contracts."

"Congratulations. I hope you didn't gloat."

"No, I was very civilized, just the way a president ought to act."

"So you are going in to have a meeting with them this morning."

"Yes, and every morning until I understand what's going on. Then I'll see where I can make the best contribution. I really want to participate. The trouble is, I'm only trained in accounting. The sales and operations are completely foreign to me, and all I can use there is common sense. We'll have to see. I wish you hadn't started that business of yours. You could make a great career here, but I know you're excited about your new thing."

"I don't think I could work for a boss as tough as you anyway."

"I wouldn't be the boss then. We'd be fifty-fifty, and you would always have the ability to persuade me to your way."

"I love you, and I'm happy for you. I'll see you Sunday. Then we tell your mother that other things are going to change," she countered coyly. "The last major hurdle. I almost told her last night, but I think that would have been too much. She kept going around all evening, shaking her head, saying she didn't know what had gotten into me. But I won't spoil her special evening Saturday. After that, it's my life and I am in charge. I'll miss you. I love you," she finished softly, and we hung up.

The next day was full of excitement at the shop. Peter reported that the truck had done a round trip to Burlington, Vermont. The fuel consumption was 27 percent lower. In his own car he hadn't done enough driving to say for sure, but by filling up the tank, driving fifty-seven miles and topping it up again, he felt there was a marked improvement in the consumption.

Fred strutted like a peacock, singing at the top of his voice, "We're in the money, we're in the money."

"Let's not start spending it before we've got it, Fred." I countered. "That Jag of yours still has only twenty-seven thousand miles on it."

"I can fantasize, can't I? Trouble is, with some people, they don't know what to do with it when they get it. I will have mine all planned." He was making motions of driving his Ferrari and the Porsche and probably every other sports car.

"This is just the start. We have others, you know," he said to Ben, who was enjoying the show. "This son of a bitch can make them all work, and we'll be in clover."

"Give Ben and Peter some credit. They helped a bit, you know."

"Yes, I'm sorry—a team effort. Lord, I haven't felt this good in years. All those times my relatives called me the crazy inventor. This will show them."

I shook hands with Ben. "I really appreciate the help you and Peter gave us. I hope you kept a note of the hours you both put in on the project because we need to pay you."

"Just like Peter keeps a log of his trucks and car, I keep a log of machining and assembly work. Don't worry, we won't let you get away with anything." He moved a little closer and spoke in a lower voice. "John, I've wanted to talk to you. When we first discussed my staying on for a few months until you got settled in, well, frankly, I wasn't too enthusiastic, but now your fellas have breathed new life into the game. I've been thinking that if you were interested, I'd stay on indefinitely. Not working round the clock, mind you, but just on these special jobs. What do you say, could you use me?"

"Ben, you would be welcome to work whatever hours you wanted. You tell me what you think is fair as far as wages, and you've got a deal."

He glowed all over.

"Would a coffee break every two hours be too much?" Ben was a happy man.

"Okay. Now we have to market the son of a bitch," Fred interrupted. "I'm going to start with the big three. Let me think. Who was the fellow I talked to last time?"

"Frankly, Fred. I don't think that's a good idea. I mean to take another run at CM and Chrysler."

"Why ever not?"

"Well, not now at least. Look, the last time you approached them, they reviewed your design and rejected it. They probably still have it on record. They'll pull the file, compare the new with the old, and toss it back again. It's not that substantially different, and we don't have the data yet to justify them looking at it seriously."

"I don't agree," Fred protested.

"Fred," Ben interjected softly. "John's correct. I've had some experience with the big corporations. If you are a proven entity, if you've got something already on the market, they listen intently. But they are plagued with thousands of products every day. Most of them they can never use."

"Hey, selling is something I can do. I've gotten in to see people where others have failed," Fred said pointedly.

"You certainly have, Fred," I agreed. "You got into Lands and sold me. But what if we hadn't made your tracer work? Do you think you'd have met with the same enthusiasm if you'd presented it again?"

Fred didn't have a response, and Ben broke the awkward silence.

"I think your best approach is to contact one of the larger OEM, original equipment manufacturers. Someone who has the entre to the marketplace. You need to start to network yourselves, contact old friends who might know someone in the right place. People you've worked with, went to school with, done previous business with. Call them up, tell them you've got a hot product, and ask for their suggestions on who to contact."

Fred grudgingly nodded his agreement.

"Look, partner." I smiled. "I think you are a creative genius. So far, I've only worked on two of your designs. Both appear to be potentially million-dollar ideas. You certainly have the flair for selling. It's just, sometimes, your enthusiasm gets you going to soon." I paused to give him time to digest the compliment. "We need to do some market research and develop additional statistics. In the meantime, however, a phone call or two wouldn't hurt."

Fred smiled at last. "I know you're both right. What I probably need most of all is friends like you. Friends who don't patronize me but shake me up and make me take another look at things."

"Okay. Let's both start making a list of people we will contact over the next week or two and start calling them," I said as I slapped him on the back.

It only took two calls, one to my old alma mater, Greg Stevenson, one of my former professors who reminded me of who I should contact. The second call produced an appointment for Friday.

The activity was frenetic for the next couple of days. On Friday morning at seven o'clock I faced Ben and Fred. Ben had done a costing on the manufacture of the fuel injection system and had broken down the schedule of prices for various quantities: fifty, five hundred, two thousand, and ten thousand.

Fred, super-salesman, had prepared a set of statistics that was impressive, to say the least. With the minimal data he'd had to work with. I looked with suspicion at some of his conclusions. Close scrutiny showed that every fact was correct and every hypothesis was identified as such—a masterpiece of illusion. At first glance, one would think that we had tested dozens of vehicles. I wasn't sure that we that we weren't being a little premature and voiced my misgivings.

"Holy shit, John," Fred said excitedly. "You've challenged every comma and decimal point in the whole goddamn report." He stood up and hitched up his pants. "Show me one negative"—his finger stabbed at the neatly typed pages—"and I'll back off right now."

I stared coolly at him as he glowered back.

"You can't, can you? Okay, go for it," he challenged.

I turned my head to Ben, who sat smiling at Fred's emotional display.

"What's your vote, Ben?"

"It's a winner. I can feel it." He nodded his affirmation.

Eric Dickinson was a dynamic individual. His son and I had been classmates at MIT, and he was the VP of Research and Development at Standard Automotive. Standard Automotive were the largest supplier of mechanical parts to the OEM automobile market in the world. Eric introduced me to his top assistant, who quickly involved himself in studying the fuel-injection device. I showed them Fred's report. They asked if they could strip it and play with it for a couple of hours while I toured the facilities.

I was impressed with the assembly line, modeled after the latest Japanese plants with some innovations of their own. Lunch in the executives' dining room was very pleasant, and I couldn't help but notice the absence of Eric's assistant.

By two thirty Eric had been called into a short meeting and asked if I would make myself comfortable for a few minutes. It was a little like my first job interview. Just before three Eric appeared with four other men.

"Well, John, your invention appears to have great possibilities. We do think that the statistics need to be done in a more controlled way. But as an indicator, they certainly give us a lot of confidence. It's a gamble, of course, but we are prepared to buy the patents from you."

He named a price that literally took my breath away. Fred would have jumped at it; it would have been the pot of gold at the end of the rainbow for him."

"Eric, I appreciate the comments, and I understand the risks. After all, I have been responsible for evaluation of product development. Perhaps we have a misunderstanding. We don't want to sell the patents. We want to sell you the product. We want to manufacture it and sell direct to you and incidentally to the other auto manufacturers."

"John, I know how you feel, but you are too small to handle the volume we would need if this proves out. Even the initial order for testing would involve several thousand pieces."

He was right, but I wasn't going to let him intimidate me. The discussion progressed until we agreed that DB Manufacturing Ltd. would receive an initial order for ten thousand. The patents would remain the property of our company. When the testing period was complete and satisfactory, Standard Automotive would pay a lump-sum price for the exclusive world manufacturing and distribution rights, together with a royalty fee for each part. The royalty was a very small percentage, but when it was multiplied by the hundreds of thousands—perhaps millions—of cars, the numbers were astronomical. I also had them agree that the arrangement was only for new cars. All existing models would need a modification, and manufacturing and selling the parts for these models would be the exclusive rights of DB Manufacturing Ltd. We shook hands on the deal.

Making the first ten thousand was going to be the critical part. I wanted to control the quality. After that, success was assured.

# Chapter 18

God only knows what possessed me to go to the dance at the Hilton.

Sheila and I had seen each other immediately. I angled myself so that I could talk with the two friends I had entered with, Neil and Bruce, and still look at her. She was wearing in a simple white dress that understated her tremendous figure. She was, by far, the most beautiful girl in the room.

She caught my eye and gave me a subtle but unmistakable shake of the head. Charlie and she were talking to two other couples. I had to admit the group looked like they were special. The two men certainly looked very elegant. I could understand why Mr. Clegg had been happy at the prospect of Charlie as a son-in-law.

The trumpet player doubling as the MC announced the next dance, and the band started to play. Bruce and Neil had already identified their intended prey and moved to lay immediate claim. I smiled as I watched the girl Bruce had been eyeing. She demurely told someone who beat him to her that she didn't dance then swiftly turned into a rival of Ginger Rogers when Bruce asked her.

I talked to several girls I had dated over the years and renewed our friendships. Most of them danced rather well, and I found that the gracefulness of the ballroom was still one of my favorite pastimes. I swept within a foot or two of Sheila on several dances and caught my breath.

Mrs. Clegg had received the tribute to Mr. Clegg earlier and left with Charlie's mother and father shortly after we arrived. *Everybody will know tomorrow*, I thought. What harm would it do to have a dance tonight? I looked at Sheila and felt the craving. The dance would be over in half an hour. I thought about leaving and mentioned it to Neil and Bruce, but they both protested.

"There is nothing here that we're interested in. Let's finish the dance and then go down Chinatown and have some food," Neil suggested.

"One more dance then," I said.

"Three," they bargained.

"Two," I compromised.

They started to play a slow melody. I looked across at Sheila. She was standing aimlessly, listening to Charlie and his friend, Tony, talk. I raised my eyebrows in a questioning way. She gave me a little shake of the head and turned. She spoke to Charlie, who briefly acknowledged her and then returned to his conversation.

She looked across and gave a little nod. I was already halfway there. The look Charlie gave me was sheer hatred. He couldn't object; he already indicated he didn't want to dance.

"This is our last surreptitious dance, my darling. I'm leaving in a few minutes, and I will give you up to your keeper for the rest of the evening."

"I'm glad to hear that. This evening has been a nightmare."

She moved in closer, and our bodies molded together until we finished the dance close to Bruce and Neil.

"There's Neil and Bruce. I must thank them for the flowers and cards they sent for daddy." She walked ahead of me to reach them first.

I felt a tap on my shoulder. Turning to see who it was, I was blinded by a flash of pain and stars jumped before my eyes. I could feel myself stagger slightly. Someone had just hit me snack on the nose. I could feel the blood trickling down the inside of my nostril. My vision started to clear, and I could see Charlie and Tony standing in front of me.

"That's my fiancée you were pawing on the floor. Keep your dirty hands to yourself in the future."

"Who do you think you are anyway?" added Tony. Then turning to Charlie, "He's just a dirty mick. He thinks that because he buys a ticket, he can come and rub shoulders with decent people."

I started to turn away. Tony got braver and stepped up close.

"Do you hear what I'm saying, you streak of yellow piss?"

He put a shoe on my instep. At the same time he had taken hold of my silly tie and began tightening it. To the casual onlooker, it probably looked like one friend making an adjustment for another, but it was painful.

"You stay away from her, or I'll show you a thing or two," Tony threatened.

I shifted my weight and pushed him slightly off-balance. As I withdrew my foot from underneath his, I raised it about six inches and flicked the edge of my shoe hard against his shinbone. He gasped at the pain and bent forward to catch hold of his leg. As his head came forward, I chopped him at the back of the neck and at the same time continued the upward motion of my knee.

Tony went down as though he had been pole-axed. The girls around screamed. Sheila turned with a look of horror on her face.

Charlie started yelling.

"Look what he did. He's an animal. Not fit to be here with decent people. He's vicious." I stepped forward and he ducked behind Sheila. "Look at him. How could you stand to be near him, to let him even touch you?"

I took Sheila by both shoulders and moved her aside. I hit Charlie with one straight punch in the face. He had been moving backward, and the punch caused him to almost catapult. He slid for several feet before he came to rest.

The moment of silence that followed was suddenly broken by Sheila screaming hysterically, "I don't ever want to see you again, John Dunne! I can never forgive you for this." She was recoiling from me in a fit of rage and disgust.

I wanted to move to her and explain. She hadn't seen what provoked me. Neil and Bruce had me in a shoulder grip that I couldn't break, not without starting a fight with them.

"Come on, let's get the hell out of here before the cops come. We don't need that." They hustled me away and out the rear exit.

"Let's get down to Chinatown. I'm hungry," Neil said.

She'd listen to me tomorrow. I'd explain everything. I wish I'd never gone to the stupid dance.

Sunday morning, as I approached the Clegg house, Sheila appeared at the door.

"Don't even touch the gate," she commanded. She then took a step forward. "I saw last night the kind of person you really are, John Dunne—not my kind—and you scare me. I called the police when I saw your car drawing up, and the patrol car is on its way. If you leave now, I will tell them it was a mistake. But if you are still here when they arrive, I will tell them you are the one that assaulted Charlie and Tony last night, and they will prefer charges."

"Sheila, you must let me explain. Let me just come in and talk to you and your mother. I can clear everything up."

"Talk to my mother?" Her face twisted with contempt. "You must be joking. She'd never talk to you. She told me this morning what you have done, what you did to Daddy. Go. Get out of my life." She slammed the door as the patrol car turned the corner.

I went back to the car and wept as I drove away.

# Chapter 19

# THE BOGEEN

Monday morning's paper carried an article saying that Charles Laughton and Sheila Clegg, who had announced their engagement some months ago, confirmed their intentions to be married in a small, private ceremony this coming Saturday, July 10. The article went on to explain how her father's illness had delayed the couple's plans, etc.

DB Ltd. didn't take over officially until August 1, and I already had Ben and his men busy with the prototypes we had made. I had nothing to occupy my mind. I had gone from years of constant work and study to sudden idleness and nothing to fill my mind but Sheila. I had to get away. I decided that I wanted to go home. I wanted to go back to Galway.

The flight from Logan to Shannon was full of fellow Irish making the pilgrimage. They were either going back home or seeking their roots. I had a seat in first class, but I found myself wandering back to the rear of the plane to rub shoulders with lads of my own kind. We drank beer and sang songs, which got sadder and sadder as the evening light slipped into darkness. At last we had to stop. All the youngsters were asleep, and the young mother of one of them threatened to beat the bejabus out of the man that woke hers up.

I returned to the luxury of first class to the quizzical eye of the pretty stewardess. She seemed to be asking if there was anything I needed. I shook my head and lapsed into a state of melancholia.

"Mr. Dunne!" she was wakening me gently. "We'll be landing in about an hour. I thought you might want to freshen up a little and have some breakfast." She was holding a small hot towel for me.

"Thank you kindly." I smiled, taking the towel and wiping my hands. They still felt sticky from last night's spilled drinks.

"Would you like another for your face?"

"No, I'll use the restroom. Thank you anyway."

I stood up and walked the few paces to the lavatory. Once inside I looked at my face. The eyes were bloodshot, and my cheeks were streaked with tears. I licked my lips and tasted the dried salt. God, I looked like death.

Soap and water could perform miracles. In a few minutes I emerged reasonably fresh. Even my eyes had started to lose the red streaks as the natural lubrication washed across them. I looked better than I felt. Was coming home such a good idea?

The second cup of coffee tasted good as the hostess stood ready to refill my cup again.

"You're a lifesaver, so you are," I said cheerfully.

"And isn't it the least a coleen can do for a poor soul trying t' find his way home."

"Does it show that much?" I grimaced.

"Not now, it doesn't. But last night you nearly broke my heart. I have never heard such a crying out for love when you were singing hack there."

"That's what the devils brew does to a man. I promise t' take the pledge right now."

"And so y' should. Where are you headin' when you leave us at the airport?"

"Galway is my home. Well, that's not quite true. Boston is my home, but I was born in Galway."

"Goin' back t' see the family then, are y'?"

"Not really. Most of the immediate family is in Boston now. No, I just felt after more than twelve years I ought to come back and take a look. Sure, and I never kissed the blarney stone. I've promised myself I'll do that before I go back."

"I hope you have a wonderful time, Mr. Dunne."

"Thank you. You have me at a serious disadvantage. I don't know your name."

"Cecelia Sweeney at your service."

"And where do the Sweeneys come from?"

"Well, like you, I don't live in my birthplace. I was born in Sligo. A town called Bunduran. Now I live in Dublin, and my folks live in Gort, County Clare. Excuse me, I have to check some of the other passengers."

She floated away without hearing my apology for monopolizing her time. She was very pretty, and the tailored uniform accentuated her figure. I admired the ankles as she reached into the overhead rack to retrieve something for a lady passenger. Very nice indeed.

The landing was gentle, hardly a bump; had I not been looking out the window, I would only have known we were on the ground by the sound of the reverse thrust of the engine.

The luggage seemed to take a while, and I waved to Cecelia and the rest of the crew as they sailed through customs.

It was a good ten minutes before my bag arrived and then I headed for the "nothing to declare" sign.

"Just one moment, sir." I had been singled out. "Would you mind if we took a look at your luggage."

He was scrutinizing the landing card, which had my name and address on it and nothing else.

"Sorry for the inconvenience, sir. Have you brought any presents with you?"

"No, nothing."

"Any Duty Free purchases?"

"No, nothing." He was making me feel nervous, and I really had nothing.

"Would you mind opening it, sir?"

"Certainly." I unsnapped the locks and undid the safety belts.

He casually lifted up the two layer of clothes and felt down the sides. Replacing everything perfectly, he closed the lid.

"Sorry again for the inconvenience. Have a nice holiday."

It was stupid to feel relief, knowing I had nothing to hide, but I did. Thanking him, I hurried out into the terminal. The rental car agency was against the far wall.

"You have a car reserved for Dunne?"

"We certainly have, Mr. Dunne. A Ford Cortina."

I presented my credit card and lit a cigarette as I waited for her to finish the paperwork.

"Do you ever pick up hitchhikers?" came the melodic voice from behind me.

"Cecelia!" I turned in surprise. "Hello again."

"Your luggage did take a long time, didn't it?"

"The luggage took long enough, but then the customs stopped me. I must look suspicious."

"I was serious when I asked you about hitchhikers. I was supposed to get a ride to Gort, but apparently the car broke down on the way here. It's on your way to Galway." She raised her eyebrows, asking for help.

"Of course, glad to help a fair maiden in distress."

She was what I needed, good company. She kept me talking all the way to Gort, asking me questions about my childhood and schooldays in the US. She punctuated our dialogue with a commentary on the passing sights of the magnificently rugged countryside.

"How long are you staying with your parents?" I asked.

"Oh, I don't know. I have ten days coming, but I don't know if I can handle them that long. I've told them that I have a few days, and if I get fed up, I'll have my girlfriend send me a telegram to report for special duty."

"You're a decisive one, so you are, Cecelia Sweeney."

"Please call me Cissy."

"If you'll call me John."

"Okay, John. We're here now. Turn left down Dunroamin, and it's the third house on the right. Will y' be cumin' in for a cuppa tea?"

I hesitated for only a second.

"That would be nice. I'd love to."

Cissy's folks acted as though I was an old friend. They fussed and served the tea and soda bread on their best china. Although I stayed for less than two hours, I felt sorry to leave.

Cissy walked me to the car and said, "Thanks for the ride, John." She leaned close to kiss me on the cheek. "You know the address. If you get bored in Galway, send me an urgent telegram."

"Thank you for the tea. You were great company, Cissy. I'll be seeing you."

"Dear God, I hope so," she sighed and blushed a little as she drew back and waved as I pulled away.

Mam had given me plenty of names to look up when I arrived in Calway, but as I drove past the humble homes, I knew in my heart that I could never stay with them. I wasn't a snob, but I was used to creature comforts, the likes of which these old family friends had never known. I drove out to Salt Hill and peered for a few minutes at the sea. The all-too-familiar threatening rain clouds stopped me from getting out of the car.

I didn't consciously go, but the blue Cortina seemed to know the way as I headed west and turned down the old unpaved cart track. I could see the monument almost from the main road. It was no more than a few inches taller than the others, but I knew it was his. It hadn't been finished when we'd left, so this was the first time I'd seen it, but I knew it was his.

The only place to park was on the gravel past the entrance. The wind tore at my lightweight coat as I slammed the door and hurried back to the ancient wrought-iron gate. There had been a recent burial and a small grave over to the left was covered in flowers. I should have brought sane myself.

The grass was slippery, and my Bally shoes were not right for wandering around this rough terrain. I approached the crest of the hill; the wind seemed to be fighting me, warning me not to come. There it was, a beautiful cross and an inscription in Gaelic which, simply translated, said, "A soldier and a man for peace."

Standing in the same spot granddad had stood in, I said a silent prayer. Closing my eyes and oblivious to the elements, I mentally reenacted that last Christmas night together, Sean Donavan holding my hand and Granddad smiling proudly at us both. I was crying as Granddad had, but it felt good somehow. I'd been there long enough; looking around at the other graves, I felt sorry that I didn't have some flowers to place on Sean. There were some wild daffodils growing on the side of the path. As I pulled at the bunch, the roots and soil came with them. *That might be better*, I thought. I'll plant them, and maybe they'll continue to grow.

Using my fingers, I started to claw away some of the soil at the base of the cross. As damp as it was, it tore easily. Scooping out the loose dirt, I was about to place the roots in the hole when I felt something move. There was a basic fear of anything associated with graveyards in most everyone. I was no exception. I leapt back, slipped, and fell. It all happened so fast. I scrambled to my feet and glanced around to see if there was anyone who had witnessed my indignity. Not a soul. The occasional car winging down the main road about half a mile away. No one was looking and laughing at me. I felt a little foolish, but only for a moment. What the hell was that thing that moved? Cautiously I bent down to investigate and grinned to myself as I saw it was only a piece of wood, a plank that must have been used when they dug the hole to set the monument. It was mostly rotted away on the side that had been against the dirt, but the side which had abutted the stone was still smooth.

There were sane letters burned into it. I had to trace the letters to understand what they said, "Here lies a traitor to the cause."

I couldn't feel the wind anymore. It had started to rain, but I didn't care.

"I'll kill the bastard," I screamed. "I'll kill you. You lying son of a bitch. Sean Donavan was a greater man for the cause than anyone in the whole world, and you murdered him." The gale that was blowing tore the words from my lips as I started to beat the rotten plank of wood against the headstone. "You're a dead man, Richard Fuller. I'm going to get you for this."

It took forever to break the plank into splinters, but I wouldn't leave until it was done. The physical fury I felt exhausted me. Staggering down the path to the old gate to leave, I was soaked to the skin with sweat and rain. I had only enough strength left to open the heavy wrought iron latch and stumble to the car. Goddamn, why did I lock it? Boston habits.

Sitting in the car I recovered my strength and felt the discomfort of my wet clothes. Starting the car, I lurched forward as my trembling foot tried to control the accelerator.

Margaret Walsh, the landlady at the first bed-and-breakfast sign I stopped at, looked at me suspiciously.

"I had to change a flat tire in the rain," I offered.

"Come on in then," she said and showed me into a room with its own shower and toilet.

Bidding her a quick thanks, I closed the door and stripped.

"So, Mr. Dunne. You're all the way from Boston, are you? A lovely place, so it is. My sister and her family lived there for three years and then moved to Minneapolis. My Frank and I lived in Chicago for ten years."

"Your glad y' moved back then."

"Not really. I liked it there, but he was always saying how he missed it here. Then he got laid off, and that was the best excuse we needed. Sold up and came back, bought this place, and here we'll be until they bury us. My daughter misses Chicago though. She was thirteen when we left. Graduates next year, and she's off back to the US of A she says."

"That will be hard for both of you."

"It will, but no worse than it is for most families here abouts. Almost everyone has family over there. Anyway, you'll not want to be listenin' to me all night. What kind of entertainment would y' be lookin' for tonight? One of the tourist spots where they have lots o' singin' or one of the local's places."

She gave me the names of several pubs, and after a quiet meal at the restaurant on the square, I started making the rounds. The first place was small and filled with older men. At first they eyed me suspiciously and then smiled. They talked in Gaelic, and I had some difficulty controlling myself as they said unkind things about my soft hands and fancy clothes. One drink, and I moved on to another pub and then another.

To my eternal disappointment, I found that I enjoyed the tourist places the best: the organized communal singing; the parading of the schoolgirls to dance the reels; the volunteers who got up to give their amateur renditions. It was because everyone was there to have a good time.

I slept fitfully and was ready for the fine breakfast Mrs. Walsh served the next morning. Leaving immediately after breakfast, I drove slowly to Ballyconnelly Bay. By the time I got there, I knew that I'd had enough of loneliness and wanted to get the first plane home. The drive back was longer than I remembered, and it was midafternoon before I got to the post office in Galway.

Mrs. Walsh was full of questions about my day. I answered them as patiently as I could while I kept glancing at my watch. It was four thirty when the phone rang. It was for me.

"What kind of message is this?" Cissy's voice laughed. "An urgent assignment, should you choose to accept it. Call. It sounds like the beginning for *Mission Impossible*."

"It might be an impossible mission. I'm going crazy here. I'm lonely and—"

"Say no more, Mr. Phelps. How soon can you pick me up?

"Six o'clock."

"I'll be ready by five thirty if you happen to be a little early."

"I'm on my way."

# Chapter 20

I paid Margaret Walsh for the two nights anyway even though she protested. The traffic was light and almost free from cattle as I sped south on the N18, arriving shortly after six. Cissy was out on the sidewalk with her bags before I had the emergency brake on.

"Thank God you made it, John. Sorry you won't be able to visit with Mom and Pop, but we have to get going." She turned and kissed her father and mother quickly as I loaded the bags in the trunk.

"I'll try to get over next week if I can. If not, I'll drop you a card. Bye, I love you." She waved as she whispered, "Get rolling."

We had reached the intersection, and I suddenly realized I had no idea where we were going. She noticed my indecisiveness.

"South, head south."

"Thank you."

"Where would you like to go?"

"Hey, you accepted this mission. You call the shots."

"How's your energy level? Are you ready for a long drive?"

"How long a drive can it be? The whole country isn't that big."

"Killarney. We wouldn't get there until after nine."

"I can make it. What's in Killarney?"

"Happiness, I hope."

I drove silently for the best part of half an hour before I spoke again.

"Look, I'm sorry. I shouldn't have contacted you. I don't know what made me do it. I'll take you back if you want."

"If that's what you want, fine. let's go back."

"It's just that—"

"Stop the car. Please."

I pulled off the road on the only part that I could in front of a gate of a meadow. She got out, stepped over to the gate, leaned on it, and stared at the watery sunset. Now I was feeling terrible. I had sent her a telegram, picked her up, messed up whatever plans she had, and now I didn't know what I wanted. I opened the door and rounded the car.

"Cissy, I'm sorry. I just don't know what I want."

"Fine, you think about it. When you've decided, let me know."

"I'm confused and miserable."

"I know that."

"This whole trip was a big mistake. I just thought… Well, you were the only bright spot in the whole picture and—"

"You thought you'd get laid tonight."

"No!" I was truly shocked. "No, I just wanted to be with someone I could talk to. Someone I could share a meal with and maybe enjoy myself."

She had seen my reaction, and her face changed from scorn to concern.

"You really didn't expect that did you?"

"What? To be with someone to talk to—"

"No, I meant, you didn't just think you'd get laid."

"No, as a matter of fact I didn't."

"I don't know whether that's a compliment or not."

"I don't know either. It's just the honest truth. I never even thought about it."

"What are you running away from, John?"

As the sun settled, the hills became black in silhouette. I told her about Sheila and her marrying Charles; the visit to Uncle Sean's grave; the fact that I felt like a foreigner in my own hometown. She was cold, and we got back in the car.

"Well, you have three choices. You can take me home and explain to my mom and pop why you can't take me to the airport. You can take me to the airport and abandon me. Or you can take me to Killarney and let me see if I can successfully accomplish this impossible mission. Which is it to be?"

"An American landed on Erin's green isle," I started the song, and she joined in as I started the car again, heading south.

She guided the conversation and amused me with stories of her childhood and travels. Cissy had been with PanWorld Airways for three years ever since they had started their Boston-Shannon service. Before that, she had been with British Overseas Airways.

"We're nearly there," she said. "There was a sign back always that said, 'three miles to Aghadoe.' Mary, my sister, has a home at Aghadoe Heights. It's beautiful there. You'll see in the morning. The mountains in the background and Lake Killarney with the mist on it. Even with all the money in Boston, y' couldn't buy it, John Dunne."

"I'm beginning to look forward to it. It sounds marvelous."

"There's the sign for the hotel. Turn right and head up the hill."

Eventually my high beams lit up a cottage as I turned the bend. Cissy almost yelped with excitement. There were no lights on, inside or out.

"There is nobody home by the looks of things."

"Well, I'll be damned. Thank God I know where she leaves the key. Leave the cases until I get a light switched on. Don't want any of the little people to be grabbing me alone."

She soon had the door open, lights on, and helped me with the luggage. She lit a gas fire in the parlor, turned on the central heating, and retreated to the kitchen.

"We have pork pie and chips or leftover stew. What'll it he?" she demanded.

"We could go into town."

"There's only pub grub at this time of night. But if you're afraid of being alone with me, that's fine."

"No, I just thought—"

"Pork pie or Stew?"

"Stew."

The stew was delicious. We sat by candlelight and dipped our bread into the rich gravy, and she gazed into my eyes as I told her about my new company and invention. The more I talked, the more she seemed desirable. I could feel my inhibitions ebbing away. At last she stifled a yawn.

"I'm sorry," I apologized.

"No, I'm not bored. I'm fascinated. Go on, tell me more."

"Enough already. If you're still interested, I'll tell you in the morning. Now, which is my room?"

She stood silently and led the way to the guest room with a luxurious double bed. The down comforter looked immediately inviting. I put my suitcase down and turned to her.

"I'll help you with those dishes."

"We'll get them in the morning. Sleep well, John Dunne. The bathroom is across the hall, and I've placed clean towels out for you."

"Good night, Cissy, and God bless."

"Good night and God bless."

I heard her go downstairs and stack the dishes as I undressed and used the bathroom. I slipped into the crisp Irish linen sheets, pulled the down comforter up, and turned out the light. I felt happier than I'd felt for at least the last seventy-two hours, if not the last few weeks.

At first I thought I was going to slip quickly off to sleep, but then my mind started to turn over the thoughts of Fuller, his influence on my life and his probable unawareness of my existence. I could see his face again, smiling as he had done at Granddad's wake, silently laughing at his success and the failure of everyone else; the final insult—calling Uncle Sean a traitor; his blackmail of Harold Clegg. I was sweating and pushed back the comforter just as the door opened.

Cissy stood there, barely visible in the dark.

"This girl is going to self-destruct in five seconds unless she gets some loving."

Without a word I invited her into my arms. Her left arm encircled my neck, and her right arm went around my chest. The kiss was pure electricity, most erotic. Her tongue was like a dart. It flicked in and out of my mouth, around my cheeks and in my ears.

She was a demon's body left untouched. This was the kind of sexual experience that fantasies were made of. I was thankful it wasn't my first experience.

She brought me to the threshold of climax several times and then gently caused me to subside. I followed her every move as she directed me with tender touches and soft whispers. When eventually she decided it was time, she moved like a butterfly—softly, but with such rapid movement the moment of climax seemed to be suspended in space. It lasted so long I had a moment of panic; it had never gone on so long before. I thought my whole insides were going to be expelled. Then it was over, and we lay exhausted alongside one another.

She silently kissed me on the ear and traced her finger along my ribs. My whole body shook from the nervous reaction to her touch. I took hold of her hand to stop her.

"I think I may die," I said.

"We will die together then. I am exhausted too."

She staggered into the bathroom. When she returned, I went to the bathroom myself. I found it amazing how the human body can be so utterly exhausted and in only a few minutes recover, except for one part, that is, that might never recover from this experience. I tried to reconstruct some of the things she and I had done. It was a blur. My mind couldn't create the normal pictures. It was one continuous flow of action, like a river with a million currents that ran through many courses, but the final destination was inevitable.

I returned to the bed and laid down beside her. She wrapped the sheets over the two of us and nestled into my shoulder. We stroked one another, and I sensed she was going to sleep.

"Shouldn't you be getting back to your room before Mary gets home?"

"She's in London for a week. Her brother-in-law's wedding."

"You knew that before we left."

"Of course."

"And you just thought, 'I'll get myself laid tonight.'"

"I'd banked on it. Now, Mr. Phelps or whatever your name is, go to sleep."

Her breathing was already taking her into sleep.

# Chapter 21

I usually awoke rapidly with a strict routine: bathroom, shave, shower, and dress immediately, ready to start the day.

This was no usual morning. I awoke gradually, lying facedown, feeling her soft but firm fingers gently massaging my neck and shoulders, slowly working down to the small of my back and around my buttocks. I felt a mixture of pleasure and pain. I wanted to go to the bathroom to relieve myself, but I didn't want to tear myself away from this ecstatic experience.

She had straddled my legs. The tips of her fingernails were making feathery tattoos on the outside of my thighs.

"Good morning, my darling. Did you sleep well?"

"Wonderfully well. You were fantastic," I responded.

"You are so sweet."

She leaned forward, and I felt the soft bristle of her pubic hair touch my buttocks. She kissed me between the shoulder blades. At the same time, she leaned slightly to one side and placed her knee between my legs, causing me to spread them. Her hand slid underneath and took hold of my testicles. I couldn't wait any more. I rolled her over with my back and jumped out of bed as she let out a cry of dismay.

"What have I done?"

"Nothing is wrong, except I have to go to the bathroom."

I stood there in front of the toilet bowl, unable to do anything. She had followed me in and stood there, grinning coyly. My erection was so hard I couldn't urinate. The frustration must have shown in my face, and she giggled as she turned on the cold water tap. The sound of running water only made it tougher. She soaked a face towel with cold water and placed it on my erection. The shock was horrific. My whole body was still warm from sleeping, but the application had its effect, and at last I was able to pass water. She tormented me from behind, stroking my buttocks, reaching around and squeezing my nipples, running her fingers down my belly, trying to take it in her tiny hands, as I stood trying to control the direction of the stream. At last I was through.

"You must have been trained by someone who was a torturer," I said. "I should spank you hard."

She stopped immediately. She was very afraid. Never taking her eyes off me, she started to back away.

"Wait a minute, missy," I said softly. "I was only kidding. It was just a joke. I wouldn't do anything to hurt you for the world." I pulled her trembling body to me and held her. It took some time before I could feel her relax.

"I went too far, John. I made you angry. I am so sorry. Please forgive me."

"You didn't make me angry. It was just a little more than I could stand at the moment, but I wasn't angry. It was very exciting, actually. You are very exciting." She looked up at me. "You are the most exciting, erotic, exotic woman I have ever known. I could never be mad with you, Cissy."

She reached up with both arms and kissed me the way she had kissed me last night. Her arms cascaded down my back, and as we stood, she took hold of me with both hands. She started to stroke it as though it was the most delicate thing in the world. I don't remember reaching the bed, but there we were. She was on top of me, massaging me with her whole body. Her tiny nipples traced across my chest and along my belly. Again I was no longer in control. She could sense when I was almost at La Moment Critique, and she brought me down again. I would never know how long it lasted—a few minutes, or it could have been hours.

It seemed like my whole being was in a state of numbed consciousness, totally pleasurable. A hummingbird would have envied her ability to maintain intimate contact and yet to be totally separate except for the penetration. When I climaxed, I really thought my head would burst. She was riding wildly as though it was a last desperate attempt to finish herself.

"My God!" she cried over and over again, arching her back in relief as she tried to extract every last ounce of pleasure from the orgasm. Finally, she stopped and smiled. As she gazed down at me, I could feel her gently contracting and relaxing her muscles. She scowled as her actions caused my spent penis to be squeezed out. "You are a spoilsport."

"A spoilsport." I grinned. "Sorry, one of the laws of biology. I would have to be Superman to satisfy you."

She collapsed on top of me, and we kissed. Her kisses were different now. Before they were stimulating; now they were reassuring. They were telling me she was happy and satisfied.

I must have fallen asleep again because she called me from downstairs to announce breakfast would be served in thirty seconds, with or without me.

"Did you look out the window?" she greeted me.

"When did I have time?" I grinned back quickly and turned to see the panorama of one of the most gorgeous sights in the world.

The mountains were higher than I'd expected, and the lake was breathtaking. A light mist hung over the water, but even now the sun was causing it to shimmer slightly, a carpet of blue and gold ringed by the greenest grass I'd ever seen. No picture postcard could ever have done it justice.

I turned back to Cissy who had joined me at the window. I put my arm around her and kissed her firmly on the mouth.

"Thank you for last night, thank you for this morning, and thank you for this." I swept my hand toward the spectacular vista.

"Come on, eat y' breakfast," she dismissed the comment.

As usual, I enjoyed the bacon more than anything. Why couldn't American butchers produce that flavor? Everything was perfect.

"Cissy," she raised her eyebrows in that peculiar way. "Mission accomplished. You deserve a medal."

"A medal is it yid be givin' me. Well, that's a fine thing. Now I know they have y' in their grip."

"Who has me in their grip?"

"The Bogeen. The spirits that inhabit Galway. Sneaky little buggers, they are too. They get a fella all upset, then they let him get lucky a couple of times just to lull him into a false sense of security mind. Then they pounce on him again and drag him back. No, Mr. Phelps. My mission is far from done. We will have to fight those little devils together for a little while longer, so we do."

"How long does this cure take?"

"You'll have to be tellin' me. When you know you no longer need me, you'll simply say, 'The Bogeen have buggered off, so you bugger off to."

"What if you bugger off before the Bogeen have left me?"

"Ah, but they won't. Y' see, the Bogeen have me also. They only attack in pairs, and they'll only leave together."

"When did they attack us?"

"On the flight coming over."

"It's a good job we met each other again, isn't it?"

"It sure is, I would hate to have had to give that customs fellow a bottle of scotch for nothing."

"You mean…"

"I told him to hold you up just long enough to get rid of the rest of the crew. I knew it was a matter of life and death for both of us."

The next few days were heaven. We toured the mountains and streams around Killarney and drove down to the little seaside village of Killsale. I realized I'd never had a carefree holiday before. Always with my parents or other friends from school, but never like this. I almost proposed, but I think she anticipated it and changed the subject quickly. Every night we made an earnest attempt to rid ourselves of the dreaded Bogeen.

"Your big moment has arrived. Today we both kiss the Blarney Stone."

The ruins of the centuries old Blarney Castle stood above us. It had been drizzling all day, and although I wanted to go through the fabled tradition, I also wanted to get on the road back to Killarney.

The spiral staircase of stone steps was slippery from the dozens of other foolish folklore lovers who had made the trip before us. As we emerged at the top, a rotund gentleman greeted us.

"You ought to have an elevator installed," I wheezed, more than a little out of breath.

"Sure, and if y' come back next week. Aren't they startin' the work on Monday?" I half believed his baby face.

"So where is it?"

"What, the Blarney Stone, or the gents?"

"The Blarney Stone," I laughed.

"Over there." He pointed to the far wall in the center. "The gents are downstairs where I'm headed now. I'm afraid y'll have t' wait until I get back if y' plan t' kiss it. I have to hold y'." He disappeared down the steps.

Holding the handrail, Cissy and I cautiously made our way to the point he had indicated.

"Oh, I see now," Cissy exclaimed. "So many people have told me how you have to lay on your back. Look, see, the stone is down there. You have to lay on your back while you hold onto these metal straps and lower yourself backwards then kiss it upside down. No wonder he has to hold you while you do it."

"Cissy, it's too cold and miserable to hang around for him. If he has to go all the way to the bottom and then back up, we'll die of exposure."

"John Dunne, I didn't come all this way to miss this opportunity. Let's go back down one flight and see if we can fight of the Bogeen a little."

"You must be some kind of a pervert to want to do it in one of those miserable roans."

"All in a good cause." She shrugged.

"Look, you want to kiss it. I'll hold you. Come on, lay down." I unfolded the blanket that he obviously used for the ceremony and draped it in position.

Cissy protested mildly but cooperated. Positioning her safely with her center of gravity well over the solid surface, I gently lowered her backward. Her tiny hands grasped the straps, and I lowered her to kiss the stone. Pulling her back to a sitting position, her face was flushed from the blood rushing to her face. The wind caught her hair, and my heart leapt. I kissed her quickly, then more firmly.

"Do that again. Please. I don't quite know which tasted the best, you or the stone." I obliged.

"Okay, let's be off. I'm not waiting for him."

"Oh, John. Please. Don't leave now. It'll be bad luck I'm sure. The Bogeen, remember."

"Cissy…"

"I knew it. I knew they'd win." She turned away and started to move back along the slippery walkway.

"Okay" I said, throwing myself on my back and grasping the straps, pulling myself backward toward the opening.

"Jesus Christ!" I heard her scream as my hands started to slip on the wet metal straps. I could feel my buttocks sliding on the blanket. Oh my God, I'm going to fall.

I felt her hand grab my belt, and my back almost snapped in two. I couldn't see anything but the stone wall and, in the upper quadrant of my peripheral vision, the long drop down to the ground.

"Can you get a better grip?" she yelled hoarsely.

"I don't think so," I croaked.

"Try, God Almighty in heaven. Try. I can't just hold you like this. I have to brace myself better."

I felt the tension ease on my belt, and I gripped as tight as I could; but my hand still slid, and my buttocks followed. It was only an inch, but it seemed like a foot.

"John, you're going to have to give me one of your hands." Her voice sounded frantic, and it scared me to death. "*John. You're going to have to trust me.*"

I quickly contemplated how long I could lay like this, cissy desperately holding my belt and my hands gripping the wet metal straps; how long before the blood rushing to my head totally disoriented me, and I couldn't grip any longer.

"*John.* For Christ's sake, give me your hand."

As I released my right hand, I felt the left one slip with the added weight, and my buttocks slide a little more. I reached out and felt Cissy grab my wrist, and I grabbed hers. At first I felt as though I was locked, as though my rear end was acting like a pivot and ramming my face into the wall. Then I felt it slide a fraction in the right direction.

"Did you kiss it?" I couldn't believe my ears. "What?"

"Did you kiss the goddamn thing? The Blarney Stone."

"You must be—"

"I'm not kidding, kiss it now, you bastard, or I'll let you drop, so help me."

I kissed the Blarney Stone.

Steadily she pulled. I felt her hand let go of my belt and apply both arms to the task of raising me. Suddenly she paused.

"Now listen, Superman. We're almost there. When I raise you these last few inches and you can get your head out of that hole, I don't want you suddenly catapulting forward, or I'll go sailing backward over the goddamn railing. Do you copy?"

"I copy. Get me out of here, please."

The last few inches were the easiest. As my face became horizontal, I was looking into the crotch of Cissy's jeans, and I could see the cause for her concern. Her whole body was straining upward and outward; the only thing stopping her from flying backward was the resistance of my weight.

Slowly we adjusted our relative positions and finally embraced each other.

"You goddamn idiot, you ever pull a stupid stunt like that, and I'll let you go."

"Was that perhaps the Bogeen trying to get you to bugger off?"

"If it was, they nearly succeeded. Can we go home please?"

"I mentioned that a few minutes, or was it years ago?"

The drive home was quiet. Neither of us was deliberately not talking. We just felt comfortable together.

The routine of the evening followed its normal course, and as we were about to drift off to sleep, I said, "You saved my life today, Cissy."

"I hope it was worth it."

"Will that help fight the Bogeen?"

"Maybe yes, maybe no."
"What happens if we never beat the Bogeen?"
"I can't tell you that."
"Why?"
"You're not ready to handle it."
"When will I be ready?"
"Soon. Good night and God bless."
She didn't hear my response.

# Chapter 22

The telephone was ringing downstairs. Cissy was already halfway there before I knew what was happening. She was sitting cross-legged on a settee as I made my entrance.

"The Bogeen is really testing us now."

"How's that?"

"That was a call from my supervisor. They need me on a flight from Paris to Rome tomorrow."

"You don't think I'm ready to be left alone?"

"I think you should be locked up after yesterday." I shrugged helplessly. What did she want me to say? "I have to fly from Dublin to Paris tonight, then tomorrow morning I fly to Rome and back the same evening."

"Then what?"

"Then I have three more days to try to complete your—our mission."

"What do you want to do?"

"I don't want to go. But… Look, I don't think it would be good for you to be left alone here. How about…" She raised her eyebrows, telegraphing the thought. "How about you come with me. I think you'll be safe from the Bogeen in Paris during the daytime. It would mean we could have two nights in Paris together."

"When do we leave?"

"As soon as we've made this place respectable again. One hour."

Cissy had no duties on the flight to Paris, so we sat together in the first class and acted like newlyweds. Two of the girls knew her and gave her appreciative looks.

"Where would you stay in Paris?"

"Usually at the Hilton, but I'd rather not with you."

"If money was no object." I almost said, "If you were on your honeymoon," but I caught myself in time.

"I would pamper myself and stay at Le George Cinq. Some claim that it has lost its place as the premier hotel, but that is because it refuses to compromise on its commitment to personal service in favor of catering to the fast-moving businessman. Frankly, I believe gracious living is a tradition that should be preserved."

"Gracious living at Le George Cinq it is. It's only for a couple of nights." Cissy snuggled up close and purred.

She'd been to Paris several times before and gave me a whirlwind tour of the nightlife, finishing the night with a bateau ride down the Seine and then a visit to a jazz club called Le Chat Qui Peche. It was almost three when she reminded me that we had to fight the Bogeen before we went to sleep because she would be gone by seven in the morning.

I was nine o'clock in the evening when the phone woke me. I had spent the day aimlessly missing Cissy. I tried to read a book but had fallen asleep. I never did that normally.

"John, darling." It was Cissy, a long way away. "I'm still in Rome. An incoming flight from Bombay has been delayed, and we have to wait to make the connection for it. It will be two, maybe three, before I get in."

"I'll wait up for you. The Bogeen has been working overtime." She laughed pleasantly.

"I love you."

It was the first time either of us had said it.

"I love you too," I responded immediately.

"Wait up for me."

"I will." The line clicked dead.

I washed my face, changed clothes, and went downstairs. Maybe I would eat at the hotel and then go to Le Chat. The dining room was full, and I really wasn't in the mood for a graceful dining experience. I would pick up something at a cafe.

I had walked only two blocks when I was stunned by the sight across the street. Coming out of the Hotel Le Clair were Sheila and Charles with two other couples. A taxi was being called for them by the doorman. I blinked. My eyes weren't fooling me; it was her. I didn't feel any heartache. It was as though I had pre-resigned myself to the surprise.

As I was considering the odds of this sort of thing happening, I noticed that two men standing in the hotel's entrance drive were obviously watching the group also. One of them was a very athletic-looking type; the other was dressed rather shabbily for this neighborhood. The shabby one was pointing the group out to the athletic one, and then they split up. The athlete ran to a white Citreon parked at the curb and started the engine.

I instinctively flagged down a cab that was about to pull into the hotel entrance. As Sheila's taxi pulled out, the white Citreon followed.

"*Excusez-moi, parlez vous Anglais?*"

"*Non, monsieur.*"

I pointed at the white car. "Follow that Citreon," I said, praying that he understood. "*Le Citreon Blanc, allez, allez.*" I motioned with my hands.

"*Ah, mais oui.*" He pulled out into traffic and quickly caught up with the car.

The taxi stopped at one of the nightclubs Cissy and I had been to the night before in the Place Pigalle. As the group entered the club, the white Citreon found a parking place on the crowded square. I paid off the taxi, tipping the driver generously, and took a seat at a table across the street.

I remembered the show lasted for approximately one hour. I ordered some food and a drink and asked to use the telephone. It was inside. I called the club across the street.

"Bonsoir, Club Pigalle."

"What time does the next show start?" I asked, knowing that they all spoke English.

"The show is starting in just a moment, and the next one will be at eleven thirty, monsieur. Would you like to make a reservation?" I hung up without responding and returned to my seat.

The white Citreon was still parked, and the driver was casually smoking a cigarette. I made a note of the license plate number on a paper napkin.

The hour passed slowly. My mind was working overtime. I couldn't imagine why they were being followed, but they certainly were, and I intended to find out what was happening. I considered confronting the fellow in the white Citreon but decided against it. He might not speak English, and why would he tell me anyway?

The crowd had started to leave, and the taxis appeared as if on cue. They knew precisely when the affluent tourists would be coming out. One of the other men in Sheila's group had secured a cab. I wasn't so lucky; not a taxi on my side of the street, and more people wanting them than there were taxis. Their taxi circled the square, and the white Citreon was only two cars behind.

I started to run after the cars. It wasn't difficult because the traffic was so heavy. At the bottom of one of the side streets, I noticed someone had left a bicycle leaning against the wall. I tucked my trousers into my socks as I had done thousands of times before and pushed the bike down the Boulevard de Clichy, jumping on as I ran.

The traffic nicked up speed and then the taxi stooped outside Cyrano's, the restaurant next door to La Moulin Rouge. The two other couples got out, and after some delay, Charles got out also. He leaned back into the cab and spoke to Sheila several times before he shrugged resignedly and closed the door. He handed some money to the taxi driver and waived to Sheila as the taxi pulled away. They hesitated on the curb for a few moments. The white Citreon passed without their noticing as they turned and went into Cyrano's.

I had to pedal hard to keep up with them. I guessed that the only place Sheila would be going without the others would be the hotel. A bike can go places a four-wheel vehicle cannot. I had a vague idea of the direction of the hotel and cut away from traffic, down the back streets and alleys. It was the most uncomfortable ride of my life. The cobbled back streets of Paris were far worse than anything we had in Boston. Several times I almost wrecked, and I was sure the hike would shake itself to pieces.

I had no way of knowing whether I had actually beaten the taxi hack to the hotel, but it only took a few seconds to find out. The taxi rounded the corner, and the white Citreon was immediately behind. The taxi pulled into the wide half-circle driveway, and the Citreon followed but slowed to a stop and pulled to the side near the entrance.

I had crossed the street and was halfway up the exit portion of the drive when I heard the engine roar. I broke into a full sprint. It was a race. I had only about a third of the distance to cover, but I didn't have the horsepower that he had. His wheels were spinning because of his over revving, but he was gaining speed rapidly.

Sheila had stepped out of the taxi as the doorman opened the door. She had started to cross the driveway when she heard the screech of burning rubber. She was frozen, flatfooted, directly in front of the hurtling white Citreon.

I drove my shoulder into her from behind and lifted her off her feet, much the same way I had been lifted when I broke my collarbone. My feet were still pounding the asphalt as I tried to maintain my momentum. We crashed into the shrubbery adjacent to the hotel steps and fell in a heap.

The doorman helped me up and started attending to Sheila.

She was unconscious. She would be very sore around the back of her rib cage for several days, but I was reasonably sure nothing was broken.

"Monsieur, that was very brave. You saved the lady's life. I should call the police. It is too bad I didn't have the time to get the plate number."

"Don't bother with the police. There must be thousands of white cars in Paris. It would only upset her and her husband having to answer a lot of questions. I think it was just some crazy drunk. Lucky, I happened to be close and was able to do something. Look, I'm a friend of the family. I really think we should get Mrs. Laughton to her suite. Could you get the key from the desk for me?"

Sheila had started to come around and was very disoriented. She thought she recognized me then refused to believe it. I assured her it was me, and after a few minutes she calmed down a little.

"John, what happened? And what on earth are you doing here? I thought I was going to be run over, then I thought my mind was playing tricks when I saw you. It was exactly like a nightmare."

"Just a crazy accident, Sheila. Don't worry about it, it's all over. Let's get you to your room. You'll be fine when you have recovered your wind. Sorry I had to hit you so hard from behind."

"You saved my life. Thank God you were here, John."

The doorman had already got the key and was holding the elevator. He accompanied us to the room, and as he was leaving, I attempted to tip him, but he refused.

"Please don't say anything to Mr. Laughton when he returns. Let Mrs. Laughton tell him about it if she wants to."

"As monsieur wishes." He departed quietly.

"Let me fix you a drink," I said, crossing to the bar. "Napoleon brandy or what?"

"A little Grand Marnier please," she said weakly.

She sipped the liquor for a couple of minutes and then looked at me and started wringing her hands.

"The last time I saw you, I hated you. I never wanted to see you again. Now you turn up out of nowhere and save my life. How come you happened to be there at precisely that moment?"

I told her essentially the truth except I transposed the earlier coincidental sighting of her for the more recent moment.

"It isn't so much a coincidence as you might expect," I said to her. "After all, you are just off the Champs Elysees, which is one of the busiest tourist places in the world. Anybody and everybody who ever comes to Paris walks down the Champs. And if you think I'm following you, I want you to know I've been here for almost a week and certainly didn't know where you planned to spend your honeymoon. That wasn't in the papers, and you didn't discuss it with me. How would I have found out? Did you tell anyone you were coming to Paris?"

"No one. Charles's father made the reservations through a travel agency in Bradford."

"So there. I'm not following you. I have accepted your decision. I just wish you had given me a chance to explain myself."

"I couldn't conceive of any explanation that could justify your actions. I was so appalled and humiliated it was unforgivable."

"Sometimes, Sheila, things happen that you are unaware of, and they may be beyond your comprehension. That doesn't mean they can't be explained, given a chance. Take tonight, you may or may not be satisfied by my explanation of how I came to be where I was, but I'm damn glad that I'm not having to explain to Charles how you got run over." I started toward the door.

"John, please don't go. You're right, I should have given you a chance. I'm probably a lot like Daddy. He would never let you talk to him. Stay and tell me what happened."

"It's too late, Sheila. All it would do is compound the situation. It's better you leave it alone."

"John, fate decided you would be there this evening and bring us together again. You mentioned that I should have heard you out. I think, under the circumstances, you should tell me regardless of the consequences."

"You are sure you want to know the whole thing?"

"Yes."

The description and reenactment of the scene on the dance floor caused her expression to change from amazement to horror to despair.

"That's it," I concluded.

"What about Daddy? Mummy said Daddy told her you'd been blackmailing him."

I took a deep breath. Starting from the beginning, I told her the whole story, excluding only my deductions regarding Barry's death. That would have to remain an accident in her mind.

"Your father was being blackmailed by someone. He was under an awful lot of pressure. He'd been keeping a second set of books, and if anyone found them, he would have gone to jail. When I told him I knew about the ledger, his mind must have snapped, and he had the stroke. Later I removed the ledger from its hiding place and destroyed it. When he went down the cellar looking for it, and it was gone, he knew that I had taken it and probably fantasized I would blackmail him again. It is ridiculous when you think about it logically. I was only fifteen when he had the stroke, but he must have been paying the blackmailer for years. God, I was in short pants when it started."

The tears came in short sobs and then in great waves as her body heaved to try to shake off the agony of the discovery.

"I just wish you hadn't been in such a hurry, Sheila. Couldn't you have waited even a month? Why did you rush into getting married so fast?"

"*Because I'm pregnant.*"

The words floored me. "You're *what*? How long?"

"Two months. I tried to tell you that night at your house. You were so excited about your new business you didn't want to think about having children. Sure, later, you said, and we almost got into an argument. Then you made me agree not to discuss the subject again for the rest of the weekend. I was going to surprise you when you came to see Mummy, and I would have told her we were getting married, and that would have been that. Then after the fight and when Mummy told me what Daddy had said, I really hated you. I believed it. I had no one to turn to, and I had to get married as quickly as possible. I didn't want everybody talking about my little bastard son of John Dunne."

"He can have the marriage annulled. I am sure that Charles will agree. Surely he wouldn't want to be the father of my child."

"No, I've made a commitment to Charles. I love him. Not the way I loved you, but I do love him. He'll never know, and he will cherish the baby. I really did think about it a lot, and I made a decision that was a conscious one. As it turns out, I made a wrong decision, but I have to live with it."

"*You* have to live with it," I echoed, almost screaming. "What about me?"

She cowered back with a horrified look on her face. Her expression caused me to stop, and my arms fell limply to my sides.

"I have to live with it, and you have to live with it because of what I just saw in you," she said, almost in a whisper. "John, I love you with all my heart, but you terrify me. I've seen that look come into your eyes, and I fear for my life. That's why I was so easily convinced when Mummy told me the blackmail story. Inside I know that you would never hurt me or anyone you love, but there is a violence in you that scares me."

She stopped to catch her breath.

"I was so easily convinced you had done those terrible things. I was wrong. But even then, when you're around, people get hurt. Going back to Webber—he's the scum of the earth, but he'll never be right again after what you did to him. I can't be happy with that thought. Charles is kind and loving, and we will have a normal life. If I come back to you, every time I see that face when you are angry, it will remind me of Daddy. Like it or not, you frightened him to death."

She was right. If Charles were to walk into that room right now, he would be dead. I did have the capacity to kill, and she sensed it. Maybe I should get out of her life.

I turned, reached slowly for the door, and opened it. Walking out without looking around was the most difficult thing I had ever done.

Particularly as I could hear her crying. But that was the end.

# Chapter 23

Waiting for the lift and the ride down to the ground floor took an eternity. How in God's name could she do this to me? I wish I could tell her that she either marry me, or there is no deal from David Bernstein. Divorce Charles and let me be the father to my child, or there will be no loan.

*What are you talking about, you fool? What about Cissy? You just spent the most fantastic week with a lovely girl that showed you a side of life that you have always dreamed about. Sheila scarcely came into your mind.*

I loved Sheila. I will probably always love her, but she has also been a continual nightmare. Most of the time I spent with her in the last few months were stolen evenings, an occasional night. Lately she had been obsessed with the business. Could I really live with that on an everyday basis? I had spent more time talking and really getting to know Pat in the last week than I had probably spent talking with Sheila in the last four months since we got back together.

*Jesus Christ, your child is involved,* I reminded myself. But I don't have any control over that. *Forget her, get on with your own life. But it isn't that simple. I have to make the loan. I'll put the loan together from DB Ltd. and then shut everything else out of my mind, except… I had told her tonight's episode was an accident. It obviously wasn't. Who could be wanting to kill her and why?* The lift doors opened, and I stepped out with my mind racing.

"Excuse me, monsieur, could you spare a moment?"

The doorman was now dressed in street clothes and had been waiting for me near the lift in the lobby.

"Yes, what is it?"

"Could you come this way. I assure you that it will take just a few moments of your time." The quiet French-accented, flawless English was most reassuring. He led me down the hallway to a door, which opened into a small room. He motioned for me to have a seat.

"Permit me to introduce myself. I am Pierre Letour of the Deuxieme Bureau. You are surprised, no? I have been working, how do you say, undercover, as a doorman here for some time. Perhaps you would be so kind as to tell me who you are?"

"John Dunne, and I am staying at the George Cinq."

"John, you don't mind if I call you John, do you?" I nodded. "This evening you were involved in a very strange situation. Would you care to explain…"

I told him approximately the same thing I had told Sheila, that I thought it was just an accident.

"Plausible, but not convincing. For us to have a freer exchange of information, let me first tell you what I know."

He leaned back comfortably and lit a Gauloise.

"I had seen the man who drove the white Citroen earlier in the evening. I observed him in front of the hotel and saw him get into the car. He is someone we have had under observation for some time. I had not made a note of the license plate because there were many cars parked around the hotel. When he left in such a hurry, he was out of sight before I could see it."

He inhaled his cigarette smoke with a half-grimace, half-smile.

"I did make a note of the time, however. While you were upstairs with Mrs. Laughton, I took the opportunity of checking with the various taxis around the hotel, to see if any of them had observed a white Citroen. One of them had. An American gentleman answering your description had asked him to follow one. He dropped you at Le Place Pigalle. Shall we start again?"

This time I told him a slightly expurgated version of the truth. My previous relationship with Sheila, her decision to marry Charles, and the pure coincidence of seeing them in front of the hotel. The fact I had seen the shabby fellow point Sheila's party out to the athletic one was what caused me to follow. I was merely obeying my instincts.

"I do feel badly about borrowing the bike. Is there any way I could find out who the owner is and return it? I will gladly pay for damage."

Reaching for the phone, he made a quick call and returned his attention to me.

"The bicycle is taken care of. It had been reported stolen. I have given instructions to return it to the owner."

"I do have something for you—the license plate." I produced the napkin I had written it on.

"Well done, well done."

He picked up the phone again and dialed a number, which answered immediately and spoke rapidly in French. Replacing the receiver, he gazed at me.

"Tell me about yourself. What do you do for a living?"

He was a good interrogator, gently prodding for more details to get a clearer picture of his new acquaintance. Eventually we were interrupted by the telephone. He wrote down an address on the napkin I had given him. He hung up.

"Too bad the car belongs to someone who had reported it stolen earlier this morning. The owner is of a very respectable family and is above suspicion." He rose. "Well, John, I think we should escort you back to your hotel. You did say the George Cinq?"

"Yes, but there is no need. It's only a couple of blocks."

"But I insist. After all, you prevented a very serious crime this evening, and it is the least we can do. I just want to make sure our friend doesn't try to take his disappointment out on you."

He escorted me all the way to my suite. Out of politeness, I invited him in. He looked around and casually asked how a young engineer could afford such luxurious accommodations. I explained that I had been saving up for my honeymoon and decided to blow it on one unforgettable holiday.

The phone rang, and a voice asked for Pierre. I almost told then they had the wrong room when I realized it was for him.

"Forgive me, I told them I would be coming back with you." He then broke into French. With some excitement, he wrote an address on the pad on my nightstand. "They have reported the car apparently abandoned, and I have a feeling I know where our friend is."

"Can I go with you?"

"No, certainly not. It is very dangerous. We may need you for identification purposes." He handed me his card. "Please call this number before you leave Paris. I must go now." He started for the door and did an about-face, returning to the pad. He tore off several sheets.

"Someone as resourceful as you might have seen too many movies. How you can raise an address by tracing over the sheet below." He shoved the pages into his pocket.

"Bonsoir, Pierre."

"*Bonsoir, mon amis, vous etes tres brave*. Stay out of this now. Leave it to the professionals."

He left. I hurled his card on the dresser in disgust. It was almost one o'clock, and although I didn't feel sleepy, I undressed and got into bed.

Once my head was on the pillow, I fell asleep in minutes.

The phone must have rung a few times. At first I couldn't tell if it was part of the dream.

"Hello."

"John, this is Pierre. I need you. I think we are on to something. I want you to meet me at"—he gave me an address that was in the lower-working-class section of Paris—"Oh, and by the way, bring that diary with you. The one Inspector Favreau gave you yesterday." He hung up before I had a chance to speak.

He was in trouble. He had been adamant that he didn't want me involved, and I had never heard of this inspector. I retrieved his card from the dresser and dialed the number at the Deuxieme Bureau.

"Inspector Favreau, please. This is urgent."

"Inspector Favreau speaking," the voice came on almost immediately.

"My name is John Dunne. I am staying at the George Cinq, and I have a message from Pierre Letour. I believe he is in serious trouble."

"Why do you say that?"

"He was with me earlier tonight and was quite insistent that he didn't want me to be involved in a case he was investigating. He now calls me seconds ago and tells me to meet him and to bring a diary that you gave me yesterday. I've never met you, and there is no diary."

"What is the address he gave you?"

I read him the address.

"Very well, Mr. Dunne, please stay there. We may need to speak to you late."

*Not bloody likely, I'll be there before you,* I thought.

Damnit, no taxi in sight. Even in Paris this wasn't the prime time. I ran down the Champs Elysees and at last spotted one who almost ran me down. I had to wave a ridiculous amount of money in front of his face before I could convince him to take me. Once convinced, though, he spared no rubber.

We arrived at the address. The street was alive with activity. The police car beacons were flashing, and lights were on in almost every window along the street. I strode boldly past the gendarmes until I reached the door of the ground-floor apartment. The door laid open, and the inspector was inside. The gendarme on the door was not about to let me enter.

"Inspector, I'm John Dunne. Please let me come in." He motioned to allow me to enter.

The sight was ghastly. Pierre had been tied to a chair with wire and, from all appearances, had been systematically beaten. A wire garrote around his neck was attached to his legs under the chair, and the slightest movement caused it to tighten more.

They were frantically looking for some wire cutters to relieve the situation. Pierre's eyes were bulging, and his breathing was coming in short gasps. Someone elbowed past me, circled the chair, and deftly snipped the wire. The removal of the wire from his neck was more delicate.

The room was covered in blood, and there were two dead bodies lying in opposite corners: the athlete and the shabby one—no, it wasn't the same shabby one. I went to the upholstered chair beside the telephone stand.

"May I sit down, Inspector?"

He nodded his permission. I watched with admiration at the speed and efficiency of the team as they went about their tasks. At the same time I mentally noted the number on the telephone at the side of the chair, repeating it to myself over and over again.

A doctor had arrived and was giving a shot to Pierre, and the ambulance attendants prepared to take him away. He recognized me, but he couldn't talk. His eyes said all the gratitude a man could say.

Something was sticking into my hip. My hand instinctively dropped to ease the discomfort. It was a gun, wedged down the side of the cushion. I could feel the long extension of a silencer screwed into the end. Lifting my weight slightly and simultaneously checking to see if anyone was watching me, I unscrewed the silencer. I passed it around my back and slid it into my jacket pocket. The gun itself was more awkward. Slowly I was able to slide it up inside my jacket and secrete it in my inside pocket. The exercise had been difficult and had caused be to start to sweat.

"Are you feeling all right, Mr. Dunne?" He startled me. "You see now that you would have been in grave danger had we allowed you to precede us to this address. Pierre will be in hospital for a few days. It will probably take much longer for him to fully recover, but he will be all right. Now tell me some more about your relationship."

The inspector had a lot of questions. He had asked me if I knew either of the dead men, and I briefly explained my involvement. He told me that he wanted me to be available to make a statement later in the morning. Now I should return to the hotel.

I enjoyed a silent taxi ride. As soon as I was alone, I wrote down the number from the telephone in Pierre's garroting room.

# Chapter 24

Cissy was sitting in bed, crying.

"Where the hell have you been?"

"Cissy, this is going to challenge every Bogeen you've ever dreamt of." I proceeded to tell her the story.

"Holy mother of God. What are you going to do?"

"I don't think you want to know."

"I sure as hell do."

"Cissy. If I tell you, it won't stop me from doing it. Don't even consider trying to stop me."

"What are you going to do?"

"I'm going to find the bastards who did it."

"How?"

I dialed the operator.

"*Parlez vous Anglais?*"

"Yes, monsieur."

"An associate of mine made some long-distance calls from another phone in the last few hours, and I would like to reimburse the other party for the costs. Yes, I have the other number. The number that the calls were made from." I read it to her.

"Could you tell me what the costs were—anything since six this evening or yesterday evening?" I said, suddenly remembering what time it was.

It took several minutes of waiting, but eventually, "Yes sir, there were three calls to England, all person-to-person to a Mr. Dowd at London 46287. One to Germany, station-to-station, Stuttgart 559840." She gave me the costs, which weren't of real interest.

"Cissy, I'm going to London."

"I'm coming with you."

"It's dangerous."

"No more than my job these days."

"I'm glad you're coming. It isn't time for the Bogeen to bugger off yet."

"I'm not too sure about that, but I'm coming anyway."

I showered and changed as Cissy packed our bags. We'd be ready if we decided to leave and went down to the lobby. There were several private telephone booths from which I could make my overseas calls. If I could trace calls from a particular shone, so could the Deuxieme Bureau. I didn't want them traced to my suite.

"Where did you expect to pack this?"

Cissy's face was white as I turned to face her. She was standing across the room with the gun.

"I told you it was dangerous. You can still back out. Put it in my bag. I'll just have to hope—"

"You're as crazy as they are. All my goddamn life I've been surrounded by crazy men." She was on the brink of tears as she struggled with the zip on her overnighter.

"I said, put it in my case."

"I heard you. You wouldn't get past the check-in counter. Don't say another word." She sniffled and cursed under her breath as she completed the repacking.

The hotel operator slaked a station-to-station call to the London number. It rang and rang, but no answer. It was only seven fifteen in the morning. The calls had been made person-to-person; maybe it was a business number. I'd try later.

I called Neville's home number.

"God, where are you, John? I tried to reach you last week, and nobody knew a damn thing." I apologized, telling him I'd made a quick trip to Ireland.

"Well, everything looks good as far as the Clegg, Bates and Taylor deal. Bates and Taylor have agreed to everything, much to my surprise. So if your investor friend is still agreeable, we can put the whole thing to bed." He hesitated. "The situation with you and Sheila, does that change anything?"

"No, not at all. He makes business decisions. Look, I'll talk to him later in the day. Either I will call you, or he will have his attorney call you to set up the loan papers. He may ask you to prepare them. Would you mind?"

"Not at all. As long as there is no conflict of interest. Sheila is my client first. As long as the terms are equitable, I have no problem."

"You will hear from one of us in a couple of days." We said our goodbyes and broke the connection.

Cissy was waiting in the coffee shop. We ordered some breakfast. Cissy hardly touched hers. I leaned over to whisper to her, but she raised her London number every twenty minutes until nine o'clock then, lines started to get busy. It was nine thirteen when the answer came.

"Continental Travel."

"Sorry, wrong number," I said.

A travel agency. Where were they located? I tried to get a London phonebook, but there were so many areas in London it was difficult to know which one. I placed the call again.

"Continental Travel."

"Yes, I'm interested in going abroad. I don't know where to go. Whether I should take a tour package or what? If I came in, could someone give me some help?"

"Certainly, sir, one of our consultants would be delighted to assist you."

"Where are you located? I just got your number from a friend."

"Number one Barking Lane, just off Tottenham Court Road. We're on the corner actually, but the address is Barking Lane. Shame really, everybody knows where Tottenham Court Road is, nobody knows Barking Lane." She continued to prattle on with detailed instructions on how to get there from any location in the greater London area. I thanked her and said I would try to stop in later in the day.

There was an early afternoon flight to Heathrow that we could catch.

Inspector Favreau was not available when I called his office. We took a taxi to the hospital in the hope of seeing Pierre and found Favreau visiting with him. I introduced Cissy, who shook hands with both of them quietly.

"Pierre has difficulty talking as you can imagine, but he has confirmed your account of how you became involved and vouches for you. Perhaps if we could step outside for a few moments, we could quickly finalize my report."

Favreau and I left Pierre with Cissy with a promise to return in a few moments. The inspector's questions were formalities: what was my home address, etc. As the individuals involved were both dead, there would be no trial, so I was free to leave Paris. I told him that I would be leaving on the early afternoon plane.

"Ah!" he exclaimed. "I am glad you said something. I must call my assistant at Le George Cinq and inform him it is all right for them to return your passport." He started to leave as a doctor approached Pierre's room.

"One moment, Doctor Claudet. May I introduce Monsieur Dunne, a good friend of your patient's. Perhaps while I make a quick telephone call, you could reassure him regarding the prognosis for Letour." He hastily departed.

I hadn't considered that—my passport. I could have been tied up indefinitely.

Dr Claudet was very positive regarding Pierre's anticipated recovery. Fortunately, his English was good, and he could explain the extent of the injuries. No broken bones, but several torn muscles and ligaments. The majority of the suffering he had undergone was from cigarette burns when he had been tortured and, of course, the wires around his neck that had been strangling him.

He delivered his report quickly and then began speaking informally, "Other than this unfortunate incident, how have you enjoyed Paris?"

"Marvelous. I will certainly come back for a longer trip next time."

"Where are you staying?"

"L' George Cinq. I think the place is magnificent."

"One of the finest hotels."

He entered a discourse, comparing the cuisine at the George Cinq with several Parisian restaurants. He became quite animated and seemed very knowledgeable. I got the impression the greater passion in Claudet was fine food, not medicine.

Inspector Favreau returned as the Dr Claudet was writing the names of two restaurants I must visit.

Favreau asked a few more questions and then explained that one of the two dead men was Colonel St. Clair, a St. Cyr graduate who had been a rising star in the army. He had been a major figure in the Organization Algerie Societe, less affectionately known as the OAS, an organization which had terrorized France in the late fifties and early sixties. When DeGaulle had granted Algeria independence and the OAS had been officially disbanded, St. Clair had stayed in the forces only a few months before retiring as one of the youngest colonels ever. He had dropped out of sight for several years and then reemerged in the late sixties as an advisor to Ghaddaffi in Lybia.

I remembered vaguely the major points about the Algerian uprising, the fight for Algeria to become independent. Many of the most influential families in Algeria considered themselves as French as any Parisian, even though many of than had never set foot on the French mainland.

It was all reminiscent of the Irish problem. Many of the people in the northern six counties of Ireland felt they were just as British and were as opposed to Ireland being totally independent. Having been raised in an Irish Catholic family and on the fringe of the IRA, I had received basic training in hatred of the Brits until I'd had a chance to find out for myself that the people we were hating were fundamentally no different from us.

I said to the inspector, "Politically motivated as Col. St. Clair was, why would he be involved in an attempt on the life of an American lady? I can assure you I have known Mrs. Laughton since she was sixteen, and she doesn't have a political thought in her head."

"That is a mystery that will go unsolved, I am afraid. We have already run a check on Mrs. Laughton and her husband. We find nothing in our files nor do Interpol. It is obvious someone wants her killed, but we have no motive. Nor can we say with certainty that it was an assassination attempt…or rather, we do know, but anyone else would call it speculation. The reason we know is that Pierre has been working underground for some months. Terrorism is his special assignment.

"He's had St. Clair under observation as best he could, but up to now we have had nothing to arrest him for. We had hoped that if he made a false step, we could bring him in and gain some solid intelligence on the movement."

"I'm sorry you couldn't take him alive. I can see how he might have been an invaluable source of information."

"We made the decision before we stormed the house that we had to shoot to kill. Pierre's life was at stake. He alone is more valuable than fifty St. Clairs. He is a unique and talented individual. He works mainly alone and has refused several opportunities for promotion in order to pursue this Algerian problem. He could have been a department head long ago, possibly even my boss, but he has a misguided idea that the promotions were undeserved. He felt that things had been made easy for him because of family connections."

It was close to eleven o'clock, and I wanted to spend a few minutes with Pierre before we left. I thanked the inspector for his understanding and courtesy, said goodbye, and went into the room to see Pierre.

He was in fine spirits, considering the nightmarish ordeal he'd been through. He'd also not had much sleep. He insisted on trying to talk and started to explain what happened before he called me.

"Ah, *mon amis*. You saved my life. I will be eternally grateful. I knew that you would interpret my phone call as a cry for help. St. Clair was convinced he could make me reveal who helped me find his location. He suspected a paid informer, perhaps someone within his organization. At first I considered giving him one of our safe numbers at the Deuxieme Bureau. That would have been risky. Instead I told him my contact was at the George Cinch and that the fictitious diary was there. Of course, he suspected a trap. I insisted he could get it. I gave him a room number different to yours, of course.

Then he forced me to call and have my accomplice bring the diary to the apartment—"

I interrupted him, "Pierre, I know it is difficult for you to talk, but if you must, try to clear up a mystery for me. Why would Colonel St. Clair want to kill Sheila Clegg? I mean Sheila Laughton."

"We don't know," he said. His voice unfortunately gurgled. "I can only speculate that either he was hired to do it. I'm not even sure who he was associated with recently. I knew him years ago after he left the military. He had been linked with Baader-Meinhoff and the Red Brigade. These terrorists always need funds for arms and propaganda, or it was an exchange."

"What do you mean, an exchange?"

"Many of the insurgent groups in different countries have…an affiliation. They do each other favors. Almost like having credit in a bank, you see. An Israeli terrorist may kill some Englishman for an Irish purpose, a German kills a Frenchman for the OAS, a French assassin kills an Israeli, and so it goes on. Many of the problems of the world right now are being ordered and paid for by Moscow. It serves their purpose to stir up chaos in the free world."

"This all seems so unlikely," I said, "that a pretty little girl from Boston could matter to the players in international espionage."

"It would seem so to you. But believe me, there is a link. Regrettably we receive little or no cooperation from our friends in Britain. I have tried to make them to share with us what they know. They see their Irish problem as completely separate from our internal crisis. If I could only find some conclusive proof of a connection, some documented evidence that the IRA and the other groups work together, perhaps it would make a difference. I'm sorry to burden you, John. I know you are not involved in this kind of work, but you were so resourceful in stopping the attempt on Mrs. Laughton's life and also helping to save me. Well, as you can see, it is very difficult dealing with something like this."

He was tiring from his efforts to talk. Cissy helped him take a swallow of the drink that had been left on his tray. I was already formulating the potential outcome of my suspicions. I felt I could help Pierre collect the proof he needed to draw some cooperation from the British. Whatever I found in London at the travel agency, it wouldn't precipitate any action on the part of the British law-enforcement authorities. No crime had been committed on British soil. The attempted assassination had taken place in France. But if I could provide Pierre with the evidence, he could certainly bring the information to the attention of the British authorities and perhaps argue his case more persuasively.

My watch said eleven forty.

"My God, we have to get to the airport."

Pierre spoke to an attendant who had entered, and a gendarme appeared to provide transportation, first back to the hotel and then to the airport.

Cissy called ahead to the hotel, and our bags were waiting at the door, and the bill was ready. As soon as I stepped back in the car, the gendarme switched on his colored beacon light and took the most efficient route to the airport. Thanks to Pierre, we would have no difficulty making our flight.

I realized I was leaving Paris with a very special feeling for him. He had a quiet courage that I liked. I also liked his sincerity, his selflessness. He must have felt something about me too, to entrust me after all to do the right thing to save him. I had a few minutes to think about his international-terrorism theories. What connection, then, did this St. Clair fellow have with a Mr. Dowd at a travel agency in London? Surely, they wouldn't call there for travel information, not the same people who tried to kill Sheila Clegg—ah—Laughton. It was too much of a coincidence. Perhaps we would find out at the corner of Tottenham Court Road and Barking Lane.

# Chapter 25

Cissy and I separated at the terminal. She pulled her overnighter past the security checkpoint, chatting easily with the other flight crews. I joined her in first class. Her hand reached out for mine and gripped it tightly.

"Are you all right?" I said as I kissed her cheek.

"I'll never be all right again. Poor Pierre. I've never seen anything like that before. I've never heard anything like that before. Jesus Christ, these people live in a different world."

"I'm afraid they don't. They live right next door to you and I." She shuddered.

"How long have you been involved in this sort of thing?"

"In one way never. In another way, all my life. It's too complicated to talk about now. Wait until we're alone."

On the way out to Tottenham Court Road I told Cissy the details of Uncle Sean, how he'd been murdered by Fuller, the rage I'd felt when I'd found the message about him being called a traitor to the cause, how Fuller's company had operated their blackmail scheme, and how I had innocently become involved.

Her face was grim as she shared with me a similar story of how her brother, Francis, had been swept up in the romantic ideology of the IRA. He'd been killed by the Provos in Belfast. She told of other friends, both men and women, who had met untimely deaths in the pursuit of a united Ireland.

"The trouble is, you can understand how they feel, almost. But when they're gone, it seems like such a waste. I've felt the heartache before of losing someone, but I've never witnessed what they do to one another. That picture of Pierre and the sound of that gurgling voice will stay with me forever."

We were sitting at the intersection looking across to the corner at Continental Travel. I started out of the car.

"Jesus, Mary, and Joseph, and all the saints in heaven pray for us, and what in God's name do you plan to do?"

"I'm not sure yet. I just want to get a look at this fellow, Dowd. The chap the person-to-person calls were made to."

"Wait a minute. I'll go. I'll ask for Mr. Dowd. I'll say that a friend had recommended him and ask for some brochures on the Creek islands.

"Which friend?" I asked.

"For God's sake, John. It doesn't matter. He won't recognize the name anyway. Farrel Butler. Farrel told me to see Dowd." She was gone before I could object.

It took only a minute for Cissy to return, saying, "The fellow with the bald head and snorts coat. They're closing up shop now."

We watched Dowd leave and walk to his car down the street. Now we had to stay close. The traffic was so slow we kept him in sight.

"What are we going to do? Why are we following him? What if we lose him?" I could tell these questions were screaming inside Cissy, but she was silent as we pursued the Austin with the bald head.

Eventually we reached a nondescript working-class residential neighborhood, typical of hundreds in the greater London area. It was much quieter here than the hectic business area we had left on Tottenham Court Road, rows upon rows of red-brick two-story houses, the front doors opening directly on to the street, and the paved backyards having enough room to house the outside lav and a dust bin.

Dowd parked his Austin about three houses from the end of the street and walked in the door of number 5 Coldbrook Terrace. I went down to the tiny back street that separated the backyards of the parallel rows of soot-covered homes. Doing a neat three-point turn, I parked, positioning the car so that I could see the door, but no one looking out of the window could see us.

"Stay here, Cissy. I'm on my own now."

"You'll get knocked down, crossing the bloody street without me." She was already out of the car and striding purposely toward the house.

The door had was answered promptly.

"Could I speak to Mr. Dowd?"

"And who's askin'—Oh, fuck." I let him see the gun trained on his midsection.

"Sure, and we're old friends from way back," I said in my strongest Irish brogue, then whispering, "back up, or I'll blow you in two."

The shabbily dressed one from Paris was struck dumb. I pushed him in the door and closed it with my heel. Simultaneously Dowd entered the room, drying his hands on a grimy towel. He recognized Cissy immediately from his conversation at the shop less than an hour ago.

He dropped to the floor behind the settee and scrambled back into the kitchen. Pushing both Cissy and our newfound friend out of the way, I rounded the settee to see Dowd at the back door about to open it and flee. I shot him in the left rump. The gun made a soft "hut" sound, but Dowd screamed. I crossed quickly to him and hit him on the head with the gun butt, and he fell to the floor.

Returning to the living room, I found Cissy standing there with the shabby one behind her. A gun had appeared, and it was held at Cissy's head.

"Drop it, drop it now, or I'll blow her goddamn head off. Who the fuck is you anyway?"

The living room was small, only about twelve feet from wall to wall. Less than five feet separated us. If I dropped the gun, we were both dead. He left me no choice. The top quarter of the shabby man's head disappeared as soon as I pulled the trigger. He fell on top of Cissy, who collapsed under his weight. I pulled the bodies apart.

The sight of the brain hanging out of its skull was one of the most curious sights I had ever seen. I must have hit him just below the eye, on the upper cheekbone, and the bullet had traveled upward and torn the back of his skull clean away. There was blood on the wall and the drapes.

Although blood was still oozing out of his head, none appeared to have got on Cissy. I lifted her on to the settee and returned to the kitchen. Dowd was still lying facedown where I had left him. Taking a dish rag to avoid leaving fingerprints, I quickly checked the contents of the drawers and cupboards, finally settling on the cord from a couple of the lamps in the living room.

Using a sharp kitchen knife, I split the insulation and had enough to tie Dowd's arms and legs to four anchor points, leaving him spread-eagled on the floor faceup. I stuffed the dish rag in his mouth and secured it with the tie from around his neck. When I was confident he was immobilized, I took a sauce pan, filled it with water, and doused him with it. It took several pansful to bring him round.

I had seated myself on a hardbacked chair, facing him with the gun hanging loosely in full view.

"Welcome back, Mr. Dowd. I know there must be a lot of questions on your mind right now, so I'll answer some of them. One, Mrs. Laughton is still alive and well. Two, Colonel St. Clair is dead, along with your other accomplice in Paris. Three, your friend who answered the door, who was also in Paris last night, is dead in the living room." I let that penetrate his startled brain.

"You are bleeding from your arse quite profusely, and if we don't get you to a doctor quick, you might be dead pretty soon yourself. You are probably saying to yourself, 'Is this man going to kill me?' The answer is most assuredly yes…unless you give me enough information to convince me you are telling me the absolute truth. Do you understand?" I removed the tie and dish rag.

"Go fuck yourself."

"Not my style."

He struggled helplessly as I replaced the dish rag and tie. Sitting down again, I pointed the gun at his testicles, lowered it slightly, and pulled the trigger.

"Mr. Dowd, you don't have a lot of time. I will show you no mercy. That is the last shot I will waste." The stench was horrendous. He had voided his bowels in one uncontrollable movement. "The next one will remove a kneecap then your entire plumbing. After that, I don't think you will be able to answer any questions because of the pain, so I will blow your head off." He was starting to cry.

"If you tell me what I want to know, I will leave and call an ambulance. Within a few minutes they can be here. Hopefully, they may save you. Now what's it going to be? Nod if you are willing to answer my questions, and don't play games, or I will become impatient. Understand, this is not a negotiable situation for you."

His head nodded feverishly. I removed the gag.

"Who are you?" he shrieked desperately.

"Your life depends upon you not knowing that. I would seriously advise you not to try to find out. Take your retirement from this game after tonight. Now I'll ask the questions." I sat in the chair again. "Let's start with who ordered Mrs. Laughton to be killed?"

"I got my orders by phone. The fella that told me to do it is called Fuller."

"Why do you take orders from Fuller?"

"He's my boss. He owns the travel agency."

"Unusual work for a travel agency, isn't it?"

"Yes."

"The travel agency is a front then. Who for?"

"Fuller. He's an American. I think he's in with the Mafia. He launders his illegal money through it."

"Dowd, I'm losing patience." I leveled the gun at his crotch.

"No, wait, it's part of—oh my God, they'll kill me if I tell you."

"I'll kill you if you don't. Tell me, and you have a chance to run for it." I smiled inwardly at the thought of him running in his present condition.

"It's the IRA. They use us to be able to move around freely and as a post office."

"What kinds of things do you do for them?"

"Phony passports, traveler's checks. We have contacts in the duty-free shops so they can get weapons through customs in all kinds of packages."

"How did you know what Mrs. Laughton looked like? How did you know where she was staying?"

"I suppose another one of the travel agencies made the reservations, and they sent us a photo of her."

"How many travel agencies are there? How many does Fuller own?"

"About thirty-five, I think."

"I'm going to turn this place upside down, so save me some time. You need it more than I do. Where is the photo, and where is a list of the other agencies?"

"The photo is in the sideboard drawer, and the list of agencies is back at the office."

"You realize I'm going to have to go back to your office to get it. Do you have that much time to lie here like that?" He started to cry again.

"There might be one on the top shelf in the living room behind some other books."

He was getting weak; he had lost a lot of blood, and the wire I had used to tie him with had cut off his circulation. His fingertips were already blue. I wasn't going to get much more out of him. In fact, I didn't know what else to ask him.

I replaced the gag and went to the bookshelves. Cissy had not said a word but joined me in the search. The list was there, and the photo was in the sideboard along with a letter, typewritten. No letterhead on the stationary, but it had gone through a postage meter in Boston. I could guess whose.

I returned to the kitchen to Dowd, who was undergoing extreme main. His eyes were pleading for me to loosen the wires. I was tempted to let him free.

"Stand back," Cissy said quietly.

She shot him through the head. There was nothing left of his face, simply a hole where those appealing eyes had looked at me only a fraction of a second before.

"That's for Pierre," she wept.

It was almost seven o'clock. The street was deserted, except for some teenagers playing touch rugby further down the street. I took the precaution of dragging the shabby one into the kitchen.

"Let's get out of here, Cissy. Are you ready?"

"I think so. Give me your arm to steady me."

"When we go out, keep your head down. We are going to walk calmly to the car. All right?"

"Yes." She trembled.

We reached the car without passing anyone. In seconds we were back on the road into London.

"Hail Mary, full of grace, the Lord is with thee. Blessed art thou amongst women, and blessed is the fruit of thy womb Jesus. Holy Mary, mother of God, pray for us sinners now and at the hour of our death. Amen." Cissy repeated and repeated the litany.

We spent the night at the airport hotel at Gatwick. The only flight we could catch the next day left at two o'clock. Neither of us had slept for forty-eight hours, so we drifted off in each other's arms. Neither of us were interested in sex.

# Chapter 26

It was ten thirty the next morning when I walked into a travel agency just down the street from Harrods. It was one of the seven agencies in the greater London area that had been on Dowd's list.

"I'd like same brochures on Italy and Greece, if I may?"

"Certainly, sir. Are you interested in tours, or do you just want to stay at a nice hotel on the beach?"

"Well, I haven't suite made up my mind. Perhaps I could take something on both types of holidays?" I tolerated the sales pitch and acquired several brochures. "Could I have an envelope to put these in?"

They were most obliging. No one doing business with them would think they were in the terrorist business.

In the car I replaced the brochures with the list of travel agencies I had received from Dowd and inserted an unsigned, neatly printed four-page report of the extent of their activities as best I knew them, stressing the tie-in with Fuller's. I also enclosed the copy of the letter that had been with the photograph of Sheila, telling where she and Charles would be staying in Paris, and the telephone bills from Dowd's agency. I made the suggestion "they" should check the telephone bills from St. Clair's apartment in Paris to verify the link. I gave the opinion it might be more beneficial to interested parties not to close them down but to infiltrate them. I mailed the package to Pierre. He might guess who would send the package to him but, I felt confident he wouldn't betray me—he needed the information to open up lines of communication with the British. Even so, I was sure that no one could prove my connection with the killings.

Cissy was already seated as I entered the plane.

"So how was your holiday?" Neville inquired.

"Oh, nice and quiet. Paris is beautiful, found a great jazz club there." I continued to tell him some of the highlights. "Look, I know you're busy," I said changing to the subject of my call. "David Bernstein is quite willing to loan the money to Sheila on a couple of conditions. The note will be a personal one to Sheila, secured by 20 percent of the company stock. The other condition is that David wants to have the right of first refusal on the sale of any stock of Clegg, Bates and Taylor. That is to say, if for any reason Sheila should wish to dispose of any of her shares, even give then to family members, he would have the right to purchase those shares."

"This would only be for the period of the loan, correct?" Neville asked. "When she has paid the loan off, she would have no further obligation regarding the transfer of stock." I hadn't thought about that. "John, are you there?"

"Yes, I'm here. Let me ask you to hold a second. Better still, I'll call you back." I hung up the phone and reconsidered my plan. It was obvious that Fuller had tried to have Sheila eliminated so he could purchase her stock. With her out of the way, there would be no other family member to inherit who would be interested in running the business. Either Charles or her mother would be easy to convince to sell. However, if someone had the right of first refusal on the purchase of any or all of the stock, it would make it pointless for anyone to do her any harm. But if she paid off the loan, that would leave her vulnerable again. Several minutes passed as I sat in remorseful contemplation. Cissy entered the room silently and sat opposite.

We stared appreciatively at one another for a long time. She had recovered her composure, but she would always look different to me now.

I called Neville again.

"Sorry that took so long. Had to give David a call."

"Yes," he said, "I understand."

"Well, David says no. He wants the right of first refusal on the transfer of any shares, or there is no deal. He did say, however, that on the transfer of stock to any children, he would not be unreasonable. He would transfer the sane rights to their stock. Should the children wish to dispose of the shares, he would again have the right of first refusal. That only really guarantees that Sheila or her children would get the best price for the shares."

"What about the terms of the loan?" Neville queried without comment. "We never did discuss interest and length."

"One quarter of a percent over whatever the rate of the savings certificates are paying at Shawmut Bank. Interest-only payments to be made quarterly to DB Ltd. The principal may be paid in full or in part whenever she wants. Frankly, I feel that is fair, don't you?" I didn't want any interest, but it would be outrageous to say that. It had to appear as though it was a business loan.

"Fair? I think it's marvelous. She couldn't have got that kind of deal anywhere. Does this fellow have other money to invest or loan? I have some land on the Cape that we could develop into a holiday camp for wayward girls."

"Good, he'll use the same attorney he used with my lease. You will he hearing from him within the next day or so," I said, ignoring his levity.

"Great, well, the only thing she might squawk about might be the stock option. But I think I can persuade her that it is a form of protection for her. By the way, we had to settle something while you were gone. That name for your company, Fred said to go with DB Designers and Manufacturing. I hope you agree because I've got a lot of work to do over if you don't."

"That will be fine. Look, are we all set to close the deal and start up August first?"

"We will be. Everything is okay on my end. I'll get the papers over to you and Fred by the end of this week."

I replaced the receiver and looked again at Cissy.

"What are you going to do about Fuller?" she asked.

"I don't know."

"You're going to kill the bastard, aren't you?"

"Probably."

"How?"

"I don't know."

"You won't be able to just follow him home like Dowd."

"I know."

"You'll have to find out about his movements. Plan the thing properly."

"Cissy, I know all that."

"No, you don't, you horses ass. You made one screwup after another." She had raised her voice not to a shout but to a level of intensity that hurt my ears.

"You should have gone to the police with the evidence on Clegg. You trusted your schoolboy buddy, Barry, and he got himself killed. You almost got yourself killed with that cop and again with your cousin Sean at the Y."

My mouth gaped in protest as she recounted the tragic comedy of errors I'd told her about.

"Don't be stupid," Cissy continued. "You mustn't have anything to connect you with this Fuller business. I saved your life at Blarney Castle. I don't want you to throw it away doing some macho-hotdog stunt."

"Who suddenly made you an expert?"

"I'm not, neither am I am personally involved in this as you are. I can make inquiries without raising any suspicions that you might. I want you to promise you'll do nothing for at least a week. I have some contacts here who might be able to get me some information. I have to go back to work tomorrow, but I can get away next Thursday. Swear to me you'll not make a move until we meet again."

I had no lead. She was right. I swore I would wait.

"Are we going to fight the Bogeen tonight?" I said softly.

"We can try." She smiled wryly.

# Chapter 27

I met Cissy the following Thursday at Logan Airport as she came through customs. She looked marvelous, laughing and talking with her fellow crew members and distractedly looking for me. We hugged each other with great intensity.

I led her to the new Porsche I had picked up only the day before and told her of the exciting happenings with the company.

"God, that's so great. Everything is working out. The American dream come true. I'm glad for you, John."

"So what did you learn about Fuller?"

"Very little yet. I have a meeting this evening with someone who says they may have what we need."

"Where are we meeting?"

"I'm meeting my source alone. I don't want you to know who it is nor them know you. I'll be at your apartment as soon as I can. Now drop me at the Howard Johnson's please."

She was determined, and I couldn't persuade her differently.

It was after midnight when she arrived at my place.

"How did it go?"

"Terrible. What was that nickname your cousin Sean used for you?"

"Danny Boy."

She opened a briefcase and tossed a glossy photo, which had obviously been blown up, onto the coffee table.

"Five hundred thousand dollars for the elimination of the person known as 'Danny Boy.'"

There were other photographs of Sean in various locations. Always with other people around. None with me, thank God.

"They will find you, John. If you continue to see Sean, they'll get you. They have run down almost all of these other people in these pictures, and some of them have just disappeared. Sean is about as healthy for you as the Bubonic plague."

"The only virus is to cut off the head of the snake."

"That won't stop them. Killing Fuller won't stop that. He's got to leave immediately. Disappear."

She was right again.

"I'll take care of it. I'll send him away. Set him up in business. What have you learned about Fuller's movements?"

"There we have a break. He and Flynn are into the entertainment business. The kinky kind. He has a retreat in a place called Chicopee, Massachusetts. It's about ninety miles from here. He and Flynn have frequent 'business' meetings there. They also use it for 'recreation.' This coming weekend they are having three girls over for fun and games. All of the girls are users, heavy into heroin. Neither Fuller nor Flynn use drugs to my source's knowledge, but they enjoy the exploits of the girls that do. It should appear as though they have killed each other. A fight perhaps. When it is over, one could be mortally wounded but kills the other before he dies. That's why I say it is dangerous. And we must not invite any long-involved investigation by the police."

"What about witnesses?" I asked. "The girls, are they to die also?"

"That's where I come in. I'm going to be one of the girls."

"No way."

"It'll be all right. I know two of them. They used to work with me on the airline until they got hooked. Now they work in the Combat Zone here in Boston. I persuaded them to let me take the place of the third girl. I told them I needed the money. I can make sure they are so high they'll believe any story I tell them of what happens."

"Cissy, I can't let you do this."

"You don't have much choice. I'll be there on tomorrow night. You either come in and rescue me, or God only knows what will happen to me."

We argued for ages, but she wouldn't relent. I finally accepted the plan.

"How do I gain entrance?"

"This is a key to the side door." She produced a standard Yale key.

We spent the next couple of hours going over the details of the project. We both fell asleep fully dressed in the living room.

It was difficult to hold below the speed limit on the turnpike. My foot wanted to get me there as quickly as possible, but it would have been stupid to be stopped for speeding. Finally, I was at the "Fuller Retreat." The gun and silencer in the glove compartment were the same ones I had used before. Cissy had smuggled them over on our return trip. The key let me in through the kitchen entrance. The downstairs rooms were deserted, but there was plenty of noise coming from the upstairs. Someone was crying, and there were screams of pain. My heart was pounding with fear as I climbed the steps and approached the roan cautiously. I needn't have bothered. The concentration of the group was on a subject so sickening I wanted to vomit.

Fuller and Flynn were jointly being serviced by one girl. Flynn was standing at the side of the bed screwing the girl from the rear as she was performing orally with Fuller. The two of them were transfixed by the sight of a second girl with a whip. She was beating another couple who were tied up in the most fiendish fashion. Both of them had their wrists bound and strung from the ceiling. They had chokers around their throats, and the man was performing anal copulation with the girl. He was blindfolded. The girl had alligator clips attached to her nipples, and the clips were strung to the ceiling by thin leather strings. It was Cissy.

Every crack of the whip created screams. The lash drew blood from the buttocks of the blindfolded man and caused him to thrust deep into the rear of Cissy. She helplessly lurched from the thrust and pain, only to scream again when the alligator clips attached to her nipples bit even deeper.

I tried to control my revulsion. These people deserved to die. Flynn was first. His eyes rolled in disbelief as I put a bullet through his heart. Fuller tried to stand up, but the hole in his forehead slowed him down. He fell backward and knocked over the home-movie camera that had been recording the entertainment.

I turned my attention to the girls. Cissy had passed out. She was totally suspended by the choker and the alligator clips, which seemed to be slowly tearing away the nipples from her body. The man had slumped and was hanging from his wrist holds.

The whip snaked around my hand, and the pull almost wrenched my shoulder out of the socket. I charged the girl has hard as I could, crashing her against the beautiful ornamental fireplace. The mantle broke her neck. The girl on the bed was lying with her eyes wide open, staring right at me.

"What's your name?" I hissed at her.

"Thelma," she said in a dreamy voice. "They said this was going to be a 'snuff film,' but this is top shit." She was higher than a kite.

"You got any more stuff?" I demanded.

"Sure, honey. Poppa always has plenty for his friends." She almost collapsed as she staggered to the dressing table where the drug paraphernalia was scattered.

"Fix me a good one, Thelma," I said soothingly. I almost lost my patience, waiting for her to make the fix, but I realized that the movie was still rolling. I checked it. The lens was now facing a radiator, but I couldn't be sure that it had not caught an image of me when I entered the room. I turned it off and returned to Thelma.

"Come over to the bed, and I'll make you feel good all over."

Finding the vein was easy. I only had to plunge it into the general area of all the other marks. She died in a few seconds.

The twosome in the chokers, the performers, now had my full attention. Cissy looked as though she was close to death. The choker had probably killed her. I pulled with all my strength at the rope that held the choker, and the hook gave way. The weight of her body was now taken by the bench that she was handing, bent over during the anal intercourse. Her legs were covered in blood. Much of it was from her partner, but there was a steady flow from between her legs. I tried to detect a pulse but felt nothing.

I turned my attention to the man. He had passed out but was now recovering. He was crying and asking Cod's forgiveness for everything. He had a familiar look about him, but the silly mask hid his face. I removed the blindfold and almost wished I hadn't.

"Please let me go. Don't whip me again."

His face was ugly and twisted in pain. He didn't recognize me at first, and then the realization of who I was hit him. He had been my boss at Lands, Guy Williams. He looked around the room and saw the carnage and started to weep.

"Betty sent you, didn't she? She found out and sent you to save me from these beasts. Thank you, thank you, I'll never leave her alone again. I promise I'll be a model husband and father. I'll be celibate. I won't even touch her. Whatever she wants, I'll do it. A divorce—yes, a divorce, I'll never see the kids. You tell her, whatever she wants, I'll do it."

He rambled on as I untied the bondage straps. I led him down stairs to the study where there was a desk and writing materials.

I sat him at the desk, placed paper and pen in front of him, and said, "Write this: My Darling Betty, I am so ashamed. How can I ask you to forgive me? You knew that I was weak, and I ignored your pleas. Now I've gone too far. These men have made a film of me, and I cannot bear the thought of the disgrace it will bring to you and our son. Try to forgive me."

He wrote in a shaky hand as I spoke the words.

"Now, I don't want you ever to see her again, is that clear?" He nodded.

"Okay, sign it."

His quivering hand signed the letter, all the more in character for what he was about to do. He laid the pen down, and I took his hair in my left hand, jerked back his head, put the gun in his mouth and pulled the trigger.

Fuller's papers revealed only one file that was significant to me. It was labeled "Danny Boy." The only paper that disturbed me was a note from Staincliffe, Sheila's old solicitor:

> *In response to your recent memo on the subject of the person known as Danny Boy. During my initial, and only, discussion with Miss Clegg shortly after her father's death, she was accompanied by a young man who I had presumed to be her fiancé. When I subsequently saw the photographs in the newspaper of the bride and groom, I was surprised but not alarmed.*
>
> *Upon reflection, however, I feel that this individual, whoever he was, could be a violent and vicious person. He did, in fact, threaten me and terrified me. Perhaps casual inquiries of Miss Clegg might reveal who was with her that day at my office.*

I returned to the bloody scene upstairs. I unloaded the film from the camera and exposed the whole thing, making it look as though it had burst open during the fight. I decided not to take any chances with Thelma. I shot her through the heart.

I took Cissy in my arms and laid her gently on the floor. She was still breathing. I took some towels from the bathroom and tried to clean up the blood that was drying on her legs. The alligator clips came away easily, and I glared through tear-filled eyes at the desecration.

"You took your old sweet time, Danny Boy." Her voice was weak but controlled. "Get me out of here, will you?"

"You need a hospital."

"I need two thousand aspirins and several days in bed. Let me out of here." Her voice was stronger.

Using the towels to diaper her, I found a snare blanket to wrap her in and carried her downstairs to the car. Before we left, I returned to the study. Removing the silencer, I placed the gun in William's hand and left.

It was seventy-two hours since the nightmare return to Roston. She had insisted on me telling her everything that happened. I told her the details, how I had left William's and that it would appear that he had killed them and then committed suicide; how I'd killed both the other girls, and she nodded silently. I showed her the letter from Staincliffe and explained how it was related.

"What about Sean?" she asked.

"He leaves tonight. He'd already decided himself that he'd need to disappear. He'll have plenty of money to do whatever he wants to do."

She nodded with satisfaction. Although she'd never met Sean, she cared immensely about his well-being.

"What's happening with the loan to Clegg's?"

"Everything is complete. She's out of my life for good now."

# Chapter 28

Cissy was regaining her strength rapidly. It was almost a week since her ordeal. Twice she had been out of the apartment alone to do some shopping, and her spirits were high.

When I arrived home from work that evening, she had made a candlelight dinner for us. We talked about Ireland, particularly Killarney, the wonderful times we had had there. I desperately wanted to ask her to marry me, but she never gave me a chance.

"I'd like to fight the Bogeen tonight, if you feel up to it." She smiled coyly.

"If I feel up to it. God, you're the one who…"

"I'm ready."

"Let battle commence." I led her gently to the bedroom.

It was as though I was a teenager again, conscious of every move. Kissing her softly, I slowly unzipped her skirt at the back and, using both hands, stretched the soft jersey wool over her hips. She was trembling. With a repeat motion, the half-slip cooperated and fell to the floor. As she felt me unloosening her blouse buttons at the back, her intensity grew. She was nervous yet certain she wanted to go through with it. I could tell she was almost desperate, and her anxiety was transferred to me. I unclipped her bra and gently eased her away from me. Hooking my fingers under the straps, I pulled the bra and blouse toward me and let them drop to the floor. As her arms slid free from her blouse, her natural instinct was to cover her still-bruised breasts. Catching her hands, I held them for a fraction of a second to see her naked beauty. She was uncomfortable, the scars still showed, both physical and mental. Her eyes downcast, not knowing what to do. I drew her close to me again.

Every male lover should wear loose shoes. Standing on one leg like a crane, trying to untie laces while kissing, is the most inelegant task. We moved to the bed. With one hand, I dragged the covers off and sat her on the crisp white linen. As I tore off my shoes and clothes, she removed the rest of her undergarments. There was a look pleasure on her face as she looked at my nakedness.

We laid there, holding one another. I traced my fingers along her shoulders and breasts. She was overstimulated, impatient, and scared.

"Cissy, I love you so much. You are so beautiful and soft. I want you to be happy and to let me take care of you forever."

"I love you," she breathed as she wrapped her arms around me again.

I moved my head down and began kissing her breasts softly as my fingers entered her. She gave a start, and the handful of hair she'd been holding was almost torn from my scalp as she viciously pulled my face back to hers.

It was painful for us both as I penetrated, and the cry of agony and relief brought perspiration to my whole body. She was at a fever pitch, and I knew that I couldn't contain myself for more than a few more moments.

"Holy mother of God," she cried, "help me, please, don't fail me now. Please, *please*," she cried as we both exploded simultaneously.

She held me tightly as though she thought I was going to leave. I couldn't have moved at that moment if the biggest earthquake of all time had struck.

"I want you to marry me," I gasped

"I do believe the Bogeen has won," she sighed.

The combination of fatigue and sexual satisfaction were too much for me. I drifted off to sleep in the middle of the sentence.

I awoke alone in bed. Where was she? I called out, but there was no answer. Her bags were gone. Throwing on my clothes, I dashed out of the house. The Porsche growled and zig-zagged its impatient way along the express way, infuriating dozens of commuters who gave me the traditional early morning blessing with their middle finger.

Ignoring the protesting traffic cop, I ran into the terminal and saw her standing with a group of uniformed friends.

"Cissy!" I thought I'd whispered it, but I could sense a thousand eyes turn toward me.

She walked toward me and embraced me. Leading me silently to a quiet corner grouping of chairs, placing her shoulder bag and newspaper on the chair behind her, she turned and took both my hands in hers.

"Last night I asked you to marry me. I thought you said yes," I pleaded.

"I wanted to. I truly did. But what I said was, the Bogeen have won. They've buggered off, John. They left us."

"What the hell are you talking about?" It had been fun using this Bogeen as an excuse, but I was past all that.

"I told you once you weren't ready to know what happened if we couldn't get rid of the Bogeen. Now you're ready. If you can't get rid of the Bogeen, you get married. We got rid of them, or at least you did."

"You're crazy. Stop it."

"John, darling. As long as there is Sheila Clegg in your life, the Bogeen will always win. You don't beat the Bogeen. By fighting them, you keep them around. When you quit fighting them, they bugger off. Isn't that just like the Irish, though, never happy unless they're fighting?"

I watched her stand and smooth her skirt. I wanted to grab her with all my strength and drag her out to the waiting car. Our eyes were locked with mutual longing as she leaned slightly to pick up her shoulder bag. She turned and walked away through the security checkpoint and out of my life.

Lowering my head to stifle the rush of sadness, I could feel the tears ready to burst forth. As I brushed my eyes with the back of my hand, I focused on the newspaper Cissy had abandoned.

Prominent Attorney's Body Found

Robert Staincliffe, well-known local attorney, was found dead last evening in his garage. The cause of death appeared to be carbon-monoxide poisoning. Local police refuse to comment on whether his death was suicide or if they suspect foul play. A coroner's report was not available as this newspaper went to press.

# About the Author

John Marron was born in England and migrated to the US in 1964 with his wife Shirley, and children Alison and Tony. He was an engineer by trade but soon gravitated to public speaking and teaching others. After his untimely death in 2018, his daughter found his manuscripts and was so taken by the work she decided they had to be published for others to enjoy and to preserve his legacy. *A.k.a. Danny Boy* is his debut novel.

Lightning Source UK Ltd.
Milton Keynes UK
UKHW012226300520
364101UK00001B/104

9 781646 285099